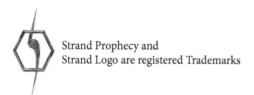

Strand Prophecy and
Strand Logo are registered Trademarks

Illustrations, chapter, and sequential art by
Daniel Gerardo Apango Goiz

Cover Art by Rob Prior.

eBook ISBN: 0-9790548-5-0
Visit us on the web
www.WinnerTwins.com
www.twitter.com/winnertwins
www.facebook.com/winnertwins
www.instagram.com/winntertwins

Dedicated to our
dad and mom
for their unconditional
love and support.

Acknowledgements

Daniel Gerardo Apango Goiz
for this incredible interior art
and
Rob Prior for
his brilliant cover art.

In loving memory
of Raphael Weiner and Cheryl Weiner.

CONTENTS

The Reluctant Harbinger

The hooded figure stood motionless on
Pennsylvania Avenue facing the
White House. His dark cloak billowed in the
evening wind as he waited.
"Soon they will be here," he thought.
"And then it will start.
All I have wanted to keep secret will be exposed."

CHAPTER 1: The Reluctant Harbinger

A throng of summer tourists streamed past the dark figure standing at the gates of the White House. Suddenly a large man in a Hawaiian shirt, his face buried in a map, collided with the cloaked figure. The map flew in the air as the man lost his balance and landed in the lap of an elderly woman resting on a nearby bench.

"Excuse me!" called out the tourist. But the cloaked figure did not respond. Indeed, he appeared unaffected, with any reaction covered by the shadow of the cloth. Just then a gust of wind exposed the figure's face as the old woman glanced upward into the bright glow of his electric blue luminous eyes. She held up her hands, looked away, and cried out, "El Diablo, El Diablo!" before fainting and crumpling slowly to the ground.

Inside a White House security building, dozens of surveillance cameras were now trained on the cloaked figure. A supervisor with a headset barked orders to Secret Service agents on the scene, then sank back into his chair and turned to the monitor as several agents approached to assess the situation.

What the White House security cameras couldn't see was the man behind the hood, black chrome exoskeleton and luminous eyes. They could not know the pain, guilt, and torment of a man consumed by his work at the expense of all else. Nor could they realize that the man was performing an act of utter selflessness. Perhaps seeking repentance, or perhaps to prove to himself that his work has meaning and that the death of his brother, Jack, had not been in vain.

But soon the entire world would know "Strand."

A host of Secret Service agents and White House security guards approached, wearing beige trench coats, wired earpieces, and dark sunglasses. They stopped a few feet behind Strand.

"Sir, you must move along, please," the lead agent, Carlisle, said.

Strand remained motionless.

"Sir, can you hear me? Do you speak English? Sir, you have to move along. Hello! Can you hear me?" He was shouting now.

Quickly, the agents began evacuating tourists from the scene before setting up a perimeter around Strand.

"Sir, you must move along," Carlisle repeated, obviously following the strict protocol for handling uncooperative tourists.

Without looking back at them, Strand suddenly spoke. "I have a message for the president."

Carlisle nodded to his colleagues. As innocuous as Strand's sentence was, it constituted a threat. The men lunged at Strand and tried to forcibly move him. They struggled valiantly but were unable to move Strand from his position. Soon, others ran in to collectively try to tackle Strand to the ground. But no matter how many joined the struggle, pushing and shoving with all their might, Strand remained motionless.

The situation had escalated, and Strand was now considered a hostile threat. A horde of agents surrounded him.

"There's metal under the cloak!" someone called out. "It must be some kind of armor!"

Carlisle held his hand to his earpiece. "Yes, sir. I understand," he replied.

He drew his pistol and pointed it at Strand. Other Secret Service men and White House guards followed suit, slowly backing away to avoid being caught in the crossfire.

Carlisle shouted, "Get on the ground and put your hands behind your head. DO IT NOW!"

Strand remained motionless. "I have a message for the president," he repeated in a low monotone.

Several police vehicles skidded into position, officers jumping out and taking cover behind the open doors. Showing cracks in his by-the-book demeanor, Carlisle shouted, "THIS IS YOUR LAST CHANCE. GET ON THE GROUND AND PUT YOUR HANDS BEHIND YOUR HEAD OR WE WILL OPEN FIRE."

A blast of wind unexpectedly blew Strand's cloak to the side, momentarily exposing his black chrome exoskeleton. Bright blue light flashed briefly from the articulated joints.

Carlisle had seen enough. This was something more than just a man. "Fire at will." It was a magnificent hailstorm of bullets, but with no effect on Strand. Officers exchanged nervous glances as they reloaded their weapons. Others dropped their guns to their sides and just stared at the spectacle.

News of a threat to the White House had traveled fast. On the rooftop of a nearby building on Jackson Place, news photographers witnessed it all. Within minutes, a CNN news crawl read: "Shootout at The White House." The major networks interrupted programming to broadcast the fierce clash.

"HOLD YOUR FIRE!" Carlisle yelled. The air was hot with smoke as the last cartridge dropped to the asphalt littered with shells.

Strand remained motionless, his back turned away from the officers. He knew that the press had picked up the story since he could intercept satellite feeds through his helmet. Things had gone far enough. It was time to break the silence.

Strand turned around slowly, giving the photographers on the nearby rooftop plenty of time to capture his movement. Most focused on the glowing blue eyes under his hood. Then he spoke.

"I am a friend and I mean no harm. I have an important message for the president."

Strand now activated equipment on his exoskeleton that broadcast his message to the media stationed nearby. Astonished television crews quickly broadcast the image of the hooded figure standing in front of the White House with a hundred officers pointing their weapons at him.

The president, sitting in his office on Air Force One five miles above Kansas, looked up as a young aide burst into the room.

"Mr. President, I think you should see this." She turned on a monitor hanging in the corner.

A CNN news anchor announced, "You are watching live coverage of the shootout at the White House... ."

Strand knew it was time. The media was listening, the world was watching and he could deliver his message directly to the president. Events had unfolded just as he had calculated.

"My name is Strand. I am a reluctant harbinger, chosen because of an accident and a debt to which I am forever bound. Mr. President, the information I am about to tell you will be available on the World Wide Web within twenty-four hours. Everything that we know is about to change. The human race and every other living creature on this planet is about to enter into an accelerated evolutionary cycle."

Strand stopped for a moment and pulled back his hood, exposing his helmet, visor, and faceplate. Traces of blue energy raced across his helmet and his gleaming blue eyes shined all the way to the photographers on the adjacent building.

"We have always believed that evolution was a slow process," Strand continued, "but it is not. Evolution happens quickly and on a grand scale. We will experience a great burst of life in a very condensed period of time, where environmental diversity and adaptation are the catalysts for new species. Those who master their environments will thrive and those who do not will become fossils."

Strand pulled a large envelope from inside his cloak and held it up.

"Here is the scientific evidence." He placed the manila envelope on the sidewalk.

"I am the harbinger, and our world is about to change. I will leave this research here for you, Mr. President."

Strand looked around slowly, taking in every detail of this moment. Then he suddenly crouched and leaped backwards high into the air, far from the cameras and the sharpshooters and over the White House lawn.

He landed directly on the roof of the White House and continued to speak calmly, as if he had just taken a step backwards.

"The future is unknown, but the facts are not. I am the messenger, I am a man and something more. My name is Strand."

He leaped from the White House roof across Pennsylvania Avenue to the middle of Lafayette Park, before a throng of satellite news trucks and reporters. Some reporters stared in shock, a few turned and ran down the street. The more seasoned reporters just keep on talking.

Reporters, Strand thought, they're a different species already.

He vaulted over the Department of Commerce and then disappeared into the haze of the capital city.

Twelve hours later in the Oval Office, the president was meeting with his cabinet and experts with the highest levels of security clearance.

"Gentlemen, can anyone offer me an explanation as to how a man survives a thousand rounds of ammunition point blank, then hops from Pennsylvania Avenue to the White House roof in one effortless leap?"

The president knew his question was rhetorical, yet he looked around at the assembled team of experts to make his point. The whole world had just witnessed something that up to that point was never thought humanly possible. The silence of the room was stifling.

Dr. Ned Vitimani, a veteran intelligence officer with tufts of white hair spilling from his balding head, spoke slowly, without looking directly at anyone. "Mr. President?" He cleared his throat uncomfortably. "This man was using an exoskeleton. That much we can ascertain from the surveillance. And this exoskeleton must have been designed to propel him a great distance, and also absorb the impact of landing.

"Yet while we think we have identified the technology we saw so graphically demonstrated today, our military currently does not possess anything even remotely similar. The closest we have are conceptual exoskeleton designs to assist foot soldiers in carrying heavy backpacks and equipment. But even these are still very much in the conceptual stage of development."

Vitimani let out a heavy sigh. Visibly shaken, face red and hands clenched, he slowly looked up at the president. Vitimani was an honored and respected scientist, but at that moment, he was just as confused as everyone else in the room. The only thing making him feel worse than letting the president down was his own ego. He was utterly disappointed in himself.

"Doctor," the president asked, "if I had asked you yesterday if it was possible for a man to jump from Pennsylvania Avenue to the White House in one leap, what would you have said?"

Vitimani squirmed in his seat. "I would have said it was impossible," he replied. He already knew what the next question was going to be.

"Doctor, is it possible that we are entering into an accelerated evolutionary cycle?"

Vitimani was trying to avoid answering directly. "I'll need some time to analyze the data. It could take a while before   we … ."

"Doctor, is it possible?" the president interrupted. He was losing his patience.

For a moment, there was silence, a silence that spoke volumes.

"I don't know. I cannot prove it one way or the other right now, which means that … that it is possible."

"Thank you, Doctor. I am glad you came to that conclusion, because the rest of the planet already believes it's possible. And when someone demonstrates the impossible on national television, it tends to add a great deal of credibility to the claim. It is imperative that we, that you, find out."

The president paused to gather his thoughts. Vitimani shifted uneasily in his chair.

"Doctor, I need you to calculate the probability of its reality in the immediate future. For now, I have to proceed with the perception that it's already real."

He then stood up, signaling to Secret Service agents stationed at the door of the Oval Office that he was ready to leave for the White House briefing room.

The president was greeted with flashes, clicks, and a flurry of questions from media as he walked into the briefing room. He would be careful in the words he chose, knowing full well that America, and the world, depended on it.

The White House spokesman walked to the podium. "The president has a statement to make. Please be seated."

The loud murmur of reporters quickly subsided. Anyone still wandering around sat down or found a place to stand and listen.

"Today we have witnessed an incredible feat of technology … and heard an incredible claim. While we can be sure of what we saw, we cannot be sure of what we were told. Our top experts are evaluating the information as we speak. However, let me be clear, this review process will continue until the scientific community has come to a reasonable conclusion. Any conjecture before that time is simply irresponsible.

"We have all heard those who profess to know when the end of the world is coming, doomsayers forever predicting the imminent demise of the human race. While these types of claims may not have been delivered in such a dramatic fashion before, that does not mean the claim is credible or true." The president paused for a moment.

"Let me assure the American people, we will determine the truth of this, and find out the identity of this man who refers to himself as Strand."

Strand sat back in his giant desk chair in the dimly lit den and flicked off the television. He folded his hands in his lap and stared at the blank screen silently.

A voice behind him snapped him out of his reverie. "Uncle Steve, what are you doing?" It was Anna, standing in the doorway looking confused.

Anna was sixteen years old; a beautiful young woman with dark brown hair. She was the only child of his dead brother, Jack.

The man who Anna knew only as her uncle, Steve Cutter, was an anthropologist before he became a technologist. He studied Darwin and evolution of species before moving on to explore the evolution of the human brain, from the emergence of cognitive thinking to the beginning of self-awareness.

In his youth and for years into adulthood, until Jack's death, Steve Cutter was a man consumed with his own objectives, his own agenda.

To Steve, nothing was more important than his research. He asked for nothing from anyone, and expected nothing in return. He rationalized that expecting nothing absolved him from any obligation. Only after the tragic accident did it become clear that no action is in and of itself an action ... and this knowledge changed his life forever.

How ironic, Steve thought. I couldn't love her any more if she were my own daughter. And if it wasn't for her, I may never have even understood love ... or felt responsibility for another ... let alone the entire human race.

"You didn't pick me up, Uncle Steve. I had to get a ride home with Carol."

"I know, princess. I'm sorry … very sorry."

"Hello? You know you're not the only one in this house who has things to do and places to be."

Anna turned and started to leave the room. As she was leaving she said, "I bet you didn't even know some terrorist got into the White House and threatened the president today."

"A terrorist? I really don't think it was a terrorist, Anna." Steve stood up, adjusted his baseball cap, and brushed by Anna on the way out of the den. Anna sighed and walked down the hall.

Two hours outside of Los Angeles in the Northern Mojave Desert, Steve's house was nothing special, a single-floor ranch built in the late 1940s. It had clapboard siding and a faded wooden shingle roof. It wasn't in particularly good shape, but it was by no means dilapidated. It looked pretty much as it should, an unassuming older Southern California home, the same that might be found in just about any suburban neighborhood in the United States.

Steve liked living there. It gave him enough isolation to work in anonymity, and enough civilization for Anna to have friends and things to do. Although if you asked Anna, she would wholeheartedly disagree.

Before her father's death, Anna lived in Pasadena, California. Their home was just around the corner from the Jet Propulsion Laboratory, where Steve often consulted on projects. For the first ten years of her life, Steve only saw Anna at the occasional family function, with no idea that he would one day become her guardian.

Family wasn't important to Steve then: his obsession was with the human brain, and why so much of it was left unused. He was fascinated by the idea that nature had wired together living tissue in such a manner as to create self-awareness, but never allowed it to reach its fullest potential.

In his research, Steve postulated that the human brain could be "rewired." He studied savants who have incredible mental capabilities, from powers of recollection to powers of computation. These people demonstrated how the brain is capable of far more than it's commonly used for over a lifetime.

Steve discovered that many of these savants had suffered a severe trauma to the head. Resulting X-rays proved that, as their brains healed, certain parts were connecting to different areas than where they were normally connected. In healing itself, the brain rewired itself, in a manner of speaking. Small pieces of brain tissue that grew to connect one part of the brain with another were now delivering electrical signals between living tissue. This resulted in an increase in capabilities regarding math and science.

In his scientific quest, Steve developed materials that were stronger than any that existed before, yet were still as thin as a strand of human hair. He built a delivery system for inserting these fiber strands through the skull. The strands would act like extension cords between parts of the brain.

Steve's testing reached a point where he had to take it to the next level. He had found a way to pierce a human skull with minimum trauma, but he couldn't complete the tests with cadavers. He needed to try it on living tissue if he was ever going to observe and improve the process.

If he was right, the strands would interconnect parts of the brain, in turn increasing cognitive ability exponentially.

The primary obstacle was that in order to test cognitive ability, there must be a modicum of cognitive ability already existing, at least enough at the beginning to judge the effects of the strands after their insertion.

Steve walked to the sliding door and stood staring out over the desert, illuminated only by moonlight. He escaped into his thoughts and obsessions, at least for a little while. There were some tough days ahead, but Steve knew there was no other way to proceed.

Thousands of miles east, Vitimani too stared out his window, an office window overlooking the Washington Monument, searching for something to inspire him or provide just a glimpse of insight. He prayed for divine intervention even though he was a man of science, but nothing of the sort appeared. He found no comfort in the moonlight or the birds in the trees. All Vitimani could feel was the urgency that a fuse had been lit.

Vitimani's office was reminiscent of a high school lab class, a desk at one end, lab instruments burning and spinning and dripping on long desks at the other end. All was as perfect as could be, everything neat, organized, labeled and cataloged, each result meticulously recorded.

Vitimani watched the flames under the experiments flicker and the liquids boil. Everything in his world was cause and effect, empirical data supporting scientific conclusions, not conjecture and assumptions of truth from the court of public opinion.

The moonlight cast shadows across the diplomas and photos hanging on the wall behind Vitimani's desk. He rubbed his unshaven chin, reminding himself why the president had chosen him to find the truth in these outlandish claims.

The doctor didn't know what bothered him more, the information itself, the way it was delivered, his embarrassment in the Oval Office, or the fact that if it was true, he hadn't discovered it first.

Vitimani's ego made him want to refute the claims, even if the theory of increased levels of radiation were true and their effects on DNA were verifiable. But the scientist in him was excited and full of optimism at the possibilities.

Possibility. The president was right in thinking that the possibility of a catastrophic event as foretold by this man called Strand created doubt in the public, and the manner in which it was delivered created credibility. Even if every claim Strand made was refuted, it would have to be refuted on a solid scientific basis.

Vitimani had been staring out the window since the last sliver of sun disappeared over the horizon hours earlier. His time was almost up, and soon the information Strand spoke of would be released to the entire world over the Internet.

The phone rang. He walked over to the desk, stopped for a moment, and then picked up the receiver.

"Yes, Mr. President, this is Dr. Vitimani."

The Brazilian Jungle

The Internet was ablaze with Strand's evidence, which he had posted to news groups around the world. The documents spread across the planet in a matter of minutes.

CHAPTER 2: The Brazilian Jungle

Steve sat at home in front of his computer and watched for news updates as Anna surfed on a laptop just a few feet away. A seemingly passive observer, he had in fact calculated the time it would take for the information to circle the globe. Billions of people would have access to his research before the hour was up.

Anna closed her laptop and looked over. "Uncle Steve, what do you think will happen? All my IM friends are scared. They say the end of the world is coming."

"Do they have an exact date when the fire and brimstone is expected?" He was trying to lighten the mood, but Anna wasn't biting. She just stared at Steve with a concerned look on her face.

"Listen, princess, that's not what's happening. Things are going to change, that's all. Everything and everyone evolves right now. From infant to old age, we're constantly changing. It's the natural order of things. We can't be afraid of what we'll become, no more than we can be afraid of what we wish to be when we're growing up. Does that make sense to you?"

Anna paused and thought for a minute, "I never thought of it that way, but I see your point." She laughed. "Maybe those old sci-fi movies were right and monster lizards will attack Tokyo." She paused. "What do you think we will become?"

"Maybe we'll just become more of what we are, maybe something wonderful. I don't know, Anna." He looked over her troubled face. "It's impossible to know the exact outcome. What I do know … is that I will always protect you. And I'll always be there for you whenever you need me. Now, go get ready for bed. Something tells me we're both going to need a good night's sleep."

Anna hugged her uncle and headed off to bed.

Steve sat back and closed his eyes.

There was so much Steve didn't know about the reaction of the planet to his discoveries. Could humanity overcome its own vanity and understand what the implications were?

Everything would be affected, from humans and animals to plants and insects. He wondered aloud, "Have we lost our understanding of how fragile our ecosystem is?" Even the loss of a microbe could be catastrophic.

Humans, especially the last two decades of the couch surfer generation, had all but lost their animal instincts for facing danger and conquering fear, whether through fighting or hunting.

Have we become a culture of words with a false perception of safety? Do we have what it takes to protect ourselves from new forms of predators?

Humans are by far the largest population of animal on the planet, thought Steve. And they may well serve as an abundant source of food for some newly evolved species. He found that thought most disturbing of all. His deepest fear was that the innocent would become the victims. He vowed to devote every waking minute to protecting the innocent before it was too late.

If something happened to Anna ... .

Steve shuddered at the thought.

He needed proof, undeniable proof that the coming change was real. In order to get that proof, he would first need to find the location on earth that had the highest concentration of sunlight. He would go there, measure the levels of radiation, and estimate the time until the planet was completely bathed in it.

The highest concentration of sunlight would be at the equator, but where exactly on the equator? The only way to know for sure was to monitor satellite photos. If something odd occurred, a noticeable anomaly would be visible in them. That anomaly would be the first place to investigate, measure, observe, and perhaps record. The smallest amount of hard evidence is all it would take to validate the theory.

Vitimani slowly hung up the phone. The office was dark except for the lights hanging over his lab tables. He exhaled deeply, collapsed into his chair, and buried his head in his hands. He knew the only way to verify any of the evidence Strand had released was to witness it firsthand. Even if being there to see it meant not living long enough to report the truth.

There was only one thing left to do, thought Vitimani. He had to determine where the highest concentration of radiation was on the earth, go there immediately, and find out if anything was happening out of the ordinary.

He looked up once more at the diplomas on the wall and at the pictures of his family. Vitimani knew that if such a place existed, he would find it.

The evidence Strand had given the president twenty-four hours ago was everywhere. Legions of bloggers debated the evidence. Most now referred to the information as "the Strand Prophecy." It was a technical paper, a scientific paper and nothing more. It did start with the words "Chapter One," so one would naturally assume there were more chapters to follow.

In the Strand Prophecy, a short preface explained the premise of accelerated evolution by citing historical periods in which many species emerged in a short period of time. Some species thrived, such as man; some species merely survived, such as the reptiles; others became extinct, leaving only bones to bear witness to their existence. Evolution was not always a slow process. Sometimes it was an explosion of life and diversity, leaving the ensuing passage of time to cull all but the fittest from the species. The raw truth of survival and extinction is that there is no remorse for or judgment of who survives to see the next century.

Chapter One documented the solar radiation data Strand had personally gathered over the last five years and compared it to official data compiled by NASA. The data on solar radiation was utilized in designing heat shields for the space shuttle, spacewalk suits, and protection for experimental payloads and satellites. In addition to space travelers, airplane pilots are exposed to high levels of solar radiation. The higher that pilots fly planes into the atmosphere, the more solar radiation presents a potential health risk, and so it is constantly monitored and measured.

The chapter mentioned a well-documented spike in solar radiation every eleven years. Scientists accept that this spike corresponds to any increase in solar flares, the brief and sudden eruption of high-energy hydrogen gas shooting from the surface of the sun. Strand concluded that specific solar cycles must exist that, when active, emit a significantly higher level of solar radiation, and that such a cycle has started. This solar radiation is so strong that it puts the DNA of all living things into an "active" status. This active DNA changes and reorganizes itself, trying to create physical "solutions" to environmental factors and genetic predispositions. A billion years of suppressed genetic evolution released all at once, bursting with endless combinations of life, affecting every last organism on the planet.

How long would the radiation last: a day, a week, a year, 500 years, 5,000 years? Even 50,000 years is a blink of an eye in galactic time. Strand gave no estimate for how long the phenomenon might last. He only mentioned the fact that radiation levels had been slowly elevating for the past five years.

Strand concluded that it wouldn't be long before the world would see physical manifestations that would prove his theories. And he warned that humans are the most abundant source of nutrition for any new predator at the top of the food chain.

Steve was staring out a window in his office at Cutter Technologies. Stretching before his eyes was an endless desert landscape, the sunrise just peeking over the horizon.

It had been a difficult choice to release the documents. He knew the public had the right to know, but he wondered if it would cause widespread panic, or if irrational people would use it as a justification for violence.

Ultimately, Anna became his guiding light. Children, after all, were the ultimate innocents, easy prey for any emerging predator, and every parent's job is to protect his or her young. Steve could not justify any set of

27

circumstances that would put innocence in danger. He could not and would not have the blood of children on his hands.

"The Strand Prophecy" was now the top story online and on television. Reporters and talk-show hosts voraciously interviewed every expert, almost-expert, and those who seemed to be nothing more than friends of experts. They even started to interview themselves. Steve watched the cable news channels tell and retell the same stories, hoping the ensuing hysteria would put pressure on politicians for an official congressional inquiry. That could take months, but at least it would keep the press busy.

The real evidence would present itself without any question of authenticity.

If they thought the jump from Pennsylvania Avenue to the White House was a trick, wait until they see a surfer grow gills or a politician venomous fangs, he thought.

Did his abilities make him think he had some obligation to bring this information to the world? Was he looking for redemption from the deep guilt he felt over his brother's death? He was full of doubt.

Am I seeing only what I want to see, or what I fear?

"What if I'm wrong?" Steve said quietly to himself.

Just then, the door to his office swung open. Hal Berstrom, a longtime employee, barged in, almost tripping over his own feet.

"M-M-M ... Mr. Cutter! Mr. Cutter!" Berstrom was out of breath. "Um ... something's happening in the Amazon."

Steve didn't say a word. He simply waited for Berstrom to get hold of himself. The pale, chubby scientist unfolded a printout and slapped it down on Steve's desk.

"Look. Here ... in northern Brazil. There's a twenty-five-acre hole in the middle of the forest that was definitely not there yesterday. And before you ask, it's not tree harvesting, there's no equipment, and there's no civilization anywhere near this place. It's not a fire, no evidence of smoke in the satellite pictures. It's very strange. I mean, the hole is literally in the middle of nowhere."

Steve looked carefully at the satellite photos. There was a discrepancy in the time stamps on the photos.

"Hal, this time stamp is twelve hours old. When did this photo come in?"

"What? Oh, um … just now. Not more than five minutes ago, Mr. Cutter."

Steve found this troubling. Generally, satellite images are available within minutes. Only someone inside the government could delay the release of these pictures.

As he sped home, Steve's mind raced.

A hole in the middle of the forest? What could it possibly be?

A mudslide? A giant sinkhole? Probably more like a wild goose chase. He didn't know what the hole was, but he knew the photos were delayed in being released. That was enough. There must be more to this anomaly than some random act of God.

An act of God? That could have a whole new meaning soon.

Steve jumped out of the car and bolted into the house.

As Steve ran quickly to his room, Anna was already following close on his heels.

"I'm coming with you."

"What?" Steve tried to play dumb.

"I know you too well, Uncle Steve. You only run like that when something big is happening. I want to go, too."

"No, Anna, absolutely not. You are not coming with me. This is boring scientific stuff. You won't like it." He walked down the hallway to the entrance of his bedroom.

Anna stood defiant. "I like boring scientific stuff.

Remember when we went fossil hunting? Or when we explored the underwater caves? What about the pyramids in Cambodia? I can do this. Please let me go with you. Besides, my spring break starts tomorrow, so if I'm not going with you … where am I staying?"

Steve paused and considered. Anna had proved quite capable on their many travels together and he loved being with her, but this could be a very different trip. "It's going to be hot and miserable, there's gonna be really nasty bugs … maybe even snakes."

Anna tried not to smile. She knew she had already talked him into it.

"You must stay right next to me at all times, do you hear? You cannot stray from my side. You will not wander around without me. I don't care how interested or excited you are. Do you understand?" Steve paused.

"This is a blood pact … you got it?"

Anna was trying to stifle a laugh and maintain a serious look, so she just nodded forcefully that she understood her uncle.

Steve walked back down the hallway to where Anna was standing and they both held out their palms. They drew imaginary knives from their belts and pretended to cut the palms of their right hands to draw blood.

Steve started. "Blood… ."

"Pact," Anna finished, and they shook on it.

Cutter Technologies had its own helicopter, a retired Army Black Hawk. It had undergone dramatic renovations and modifications. It was far more capable than anyone outside Cutter Technologies knew. From the exterior, it looked as close to a flying piece of junk as it could get. The exterior paint was a sun-faded greenish yellow. The word "ARMY" was painted over but still could be glimpsed in the right light.

The company property itself didn't seem like much to the casual observer, just a couple of converted airplane hangars and a runway near Mojave Airport.

The remote location gave Steve anonymity, and his business as a software licensor had given him enormous wealth.

When Steve and Anna pulled up to the runway, the Black Hawk was ready to go. The pilot was in his seat and the blades were spinning. They climbed into the rear cabin, closed the door and took off for the Amazon.

At 10,000 feet, two small jet engines emerged from the top of the helicopter just under the rotors. A pair of canard wings protruded from either side of the aircraft's nose, and a double set of delta wings slid out on each side. A small ramjet lowered into position under the Black Hawk. The jet engines fired and the ramjet whined.

They would be in the Amazon soon. Anna could barely contain her excitement.

"What do you think we're going to find, Uncle Steve?"

"I think we'll find a lot of people got there ahead of us." Steve paused. "I bet it will be a three-ring circus by the time we get there. We might not find anything but a bunch of scientists and bureaucrats. Try to get some rest. I'll wake you just before we get there."

Steve watched the radar and sensors closely as they approached Brazil. There was an awful lot of air traffic, mostly helicopters. Steve instructed the pilot to resume normal operations when they were within 250 miles of their destination, and to maintain a low altitude to avoid radar detection.

Steve stared at the screen, but none of the helicopters appeared to be landing. They would circle, hover, then leave.

The Black Hawk slowed and completed its

transformation. Steve waited until they were closer before he woke his niece.

As they approached the site, there were at least ten helicopters hovering directly inside the opening in the forest. There were even more in the surrounding area. Teams of scientists from every corner of the planet were descending on ropes with gear and supplies. There were helicopters from Germany, France, Russia, Britain, Australia, and the United States military. There were also a number of unmarked helicopters, most likely intelligence operatives from China, South Korea, or the CIA. There was also a military attachment armed with rifles.

Strand's media stunt at the White House and the release of the research had done the trick. The whole world was listening to him, even if they didn't know who he really was, and they were here in the middle of the Brazilian jungle to see if he was right.

"Anna, wake up, we're almost there."

Anna woke up with a startled look on her face.

"We're not going to land the Black Hawk. Put a backpack together. We're going to descend on ropes."

As Steve looked down from the Black Hawk, he could see people bouncing and sinking into the thick debris that used to be trees. Something had completely shredded the trees, leaving nothing but a thick mulch of bark and wood behind.

Steve turned to Anna. "There's no solid ground. That's why the helicopters can't land. There's nothing to support their weight."

He looked at the pilot and pointed out the windshield. "Stop over there and we'll descend on ropes. Then I want you to find somewhere to land and stay out of sight. Don't fly any more than two hours away, in case something comes up." The pilot nodded and Steve slid open the door to the Black Hawk. He checked Anna's rigging and smiled at her skills.

"Perfect, Anna, very impressive. Let's go."

Steve and Anna hooked their rigging to the outside of the Black Hawk, dropped their ropes and slid quickly down to the floor of the forest.

Steve text-messaged the pilot.

"I will check in every two hours. If you don't hear from me for any length of time past that, start heading back in this direction. No more than two hours away, just in case. Got it?"

"Yes, sir, I understand. No problem. Call me when you need me."

With acres of shredded trees against a dense forest backdrop, the environment was surreal, and the sound was almost deafening. In addition to the dozens of helicopter blades whirring, there was the eerie howling of monkeys. Steve and Anna stood in the soft mulch and looked around in awe, trying to take it all in.

"Steve, Steve, Steve. I knew you were going to be here." Steve turned to see Vitimani approaching with a big smile on his face.

Vitimani and Steve had done business with each other over the years. One of Vitimani's responsibilities was giving final approval to new technologies. Once he signed off on something, it could be used by any office or branch of the government.

"Vit, how are you doing? You remember Anna, don't you?"

"Of course. I saw the both of you coming down the ropes from that old beater of a helicopter. Is that thing really safe?"

"It flies great as long as we don't turn the engine off," Steve joked. Vitimani tried to respond, but it was a forced laugh.

"Vit," Steve said, "off the record, have you found anything yet? And who is here exactly?"

"This is how it seems to be slicing up, Steve. The Koreans are conferring with the French, and we have the Brits and the Aussies. The Chinese are talking to no one. We're not sharing any of our information except with the CIA. The tension is high."

Steve was getting frustrated. "Look, if there's something here, we're all going to see it. No one will be able to hide a discovery of this magnitude. What, are we going to start a fistfight over a mutated worm? I don't get it. This is a bad way to go at this, Vit. Can't you do something to calm things down?"

Dr. Vitimani shrugged. Steve was getting very concerned. The wonderment he felt initially upon arrival was now being replaced with a sense of imminent danger.

"Vit, my antennae are up. This is not good, and soon it'll be dusk." Steve was now staring intensely at his old friend.

"What happens at dusk, other than imminent darkness?"

"Vit, most of the jungle's predators hunt at night."

Just then Vitimani's walkie-talkie squawked. "Dr. Vitimani, you need to see this."

"Steve, Anna, come on. Let's see what's been discovered, and then see if we can avoid a fistfight at the same time." Vitimani winked at Anna and started to walk toward the camp set up by the United States.

Steve and Anna were following Vitimani at a distance when Steve said in a hushed voice, "Use your whip to see how deep this mulch is."

Anna's whip was four and a half feet long, with an additional two and a half feet of steel cable at the end.

It looked just like an old-fashioned buggy whip used on a horse and carriage. But this device was far from old-fashioned. The tip was actually a Taser capable of putting out 100,000 volts of electricity. The electroshock would immediately disrupt virtually all muscular control, leaving its target wiggling uncontrollably on the ground.

The whip was weighted so that with a flick of the wrist, Anna could reach anyone or anything within about eight feet of wherever she was standing. The main part of the whip was made with a flexible combination of carbon fiber and composite strands.

What made the whip particularly effective was the speed at which Anna could deploy it. She could flawlessly wield it with incredible accuracy and drop anyone to the floor with it in seconds. She had only used it on two occasions. In both cases, her would-be assailants were immobilized before they ever knew what hit them.

Anna pushed the tip deep into the shredded bark, trying to gauge its depth.

"This has to be at least four and a half feet deep. I can push the entire thing into the bark without touching solid ground." She looked up at Steve and pulled the whip out.

This hole in the forest is getting stranger by the second, Steve thought. He was getting a sinking feeling in the pit of his stomach. He wasn't sure what gave him such anxiety, but something was very wrong.

The remaining helicopters finished delivering their personnel and gear. They departed quickly into the distance, leaving only the sounds of howling monkeys and the occasional singing of birds.

Dusk was drawing near and the temperature was cooling as they walked and bounced on the mulch close behind Vitimani.

Scientists from the U.S. and European contingents

were huddled around something just ahead. Vitimani excused himself and pushed his way to the front of the gathering. Just as the people parted to allow him through, Steve caught a glimpse of what the commotion was about.

It was a toad. Except this toad was the size of a 100-pound dog. It sat on the ground with the tip of its nose about two feet in the air. The enormous toad also had an extra nostril on top of its head just above its eyes. The nostril opened forward and was perfectly round.

It was not intimidated by the large group of humans staring at it. Quite the contrary, the toad seemed to be staring at the humans. In fact, Steve wasn't really sure who was sizing up whom.

"Did you see that?" Steve whispered to Anna. Anna looked at Steve and gripped her whip a bit tighter.

"Crapaud Géant, we have named this creature. It is our discovery!" shouted one of the French scientists, as though his announcement would provide some kind of security on his claim. It did nothing more than increase the tension.

Vitimani exhaled. This was about to get complicated. "You can call it what you want and we will call it what we want. Let history decide what the name will be." He looked down at the toad. "Wow, you are one giant toad. I wonder what that is on your head." Vitimani slowly bent over to look inside the extra nostril.

Suddenly the toad let out a croak that would rival any car horn and then looked up toward the sky. Vitimani nearly jumped out of his skin, as did everyone else surrounding the beast.

"Maybe that's toad for back off," said one of the scientists. Everyone started to laugh.

A moment later came the sound of hundreds of croaking toads joining in. It was deafening.

The toad slowly looked back and forth at the scientists. They looked at each other and started to back away from the creature. It was no longer a laughing matter. Something big was about to happen. The toad looked up to the sky again and froze. It was looking for something. The scientists looked up as well, but could see nothing. The toad started raising and lowering its body rhythmically while it continued to look up at the sky. Each time it would raise its body, it would add its croak to the throng.

Several of the European team members noticed movement in a pond of black water just behind the large toad and sprinted over to investigate. The water in the pond appeared to be boiling. Something was visible in the water and in the surrounding plants. Maybe it was more toads, or maybe it was something else. Regardless, Steve didn't like what he was seeing.

Steve looked over at Anna. She had seen the boiling black water, too.

"Something bad is going to happen here, Uncle Steve. I can feel it." Anna repositioned her grip around the handle of her whip again. She was not a frightened little girl; she was a seasoned explorer with keen instincts. And she was right.

"I agree. Let's move back." They backed away from the crowd surrounding the toad.

The early evening started to creep in and the sky was a purple color. Aside from the birds singing in the trees and the croaks of the giant toads, the cries of the howler monkeys were now ominously missing. A part of the jungle orchestra had stopped playing.

Steve and Anna stood back-to-back, staring into the trees looking for a clue as to why the monkeys had stopped, and waiting for what might happen next.

Across the clearing at the edge of the forest, a large

howler monkey dropped from a tree and then stood up straight, holding what looked like a staff in his right hand.

"Uncle Steve, look over there. That monkey has some kind of necklace on, and he's holding a walking stick."

Steve looked carefully at the stick. It was perfectly straight. This was no walking stick. He grabbed the binoculars from his pack to get a better look. The howler monkey was standing erect like a human holding some kind of spear, which was straight and had two pegs on either side of it near the sharpened tip. The monkey wore a necklace made of pointed horns around its neck. He was looking around intensely, but not in a nervous manner at all. In fact, the monkey looked like a predator that had just located its prey. He held his head high, gazing across the jungle and up into the trees.

Anna had her binoculars out as well. "Look at that. He's watching the scientists with the toads."

"And he's standing on a rock, not on this mulch," Steve added. "Anna, come on. Let's move away from them."

Vitimani had noticed Anna and Steve. He had good instincts. His instincts told him to back away, too, but the scientist in him overrode his judgment. He looked away from Steve and Anna, enthralled by the toad and its moonlight dance.

Steve and Anna had separated themselves from the scientists by a few hundred feet now, and stopped. They were quite close to the monkey, and no longer needed binoculars to see him clearly.

The monkey had steadily observed them as they moved away from the scientists. When Steve and Anna stopped, it pointed the handle end of the spear at them and stared silently, without a howl or a noise of any kind. Its gaze was intense. This was a monkey and something more.

"What do you think he's trying to tell us?" Anna

whispered.

The monkey then raised the handle end of the spear, pointed it at the night sky, and looked up. Then he once again stared directly at Steve and Anna and started to howl. This was not the howl of fear or of a primate swinging through the trees. This howl had structure. There were highs and lows, pauses and facial expressions. The howl was almost like a song. And when it stopped, the monkey lowered its spear, still looking at Steve and Anna, waiting.

"I think he's trying to tell us that something is coming down from the sky." Steve paused and looked over at the toad. "The toad and the monkey are both pointing up."

Steve looked back at the horns on the monkey's necklace and then at the spear. This monkey was a hunter. The only question was whether he was hunting them.

The monkey saw their hesitation and seemed to nod with understanding. It looked away from them and took the necklace off. Holding it in its left hand high above its head, it then reared back and started howling a song that could be heard loud and clear for miles. When it stopped, it raised its right arm with the spear still clenched in its hand. When its arm reached full extension, the jungle surrounding the opening erupted with the fierce howls of thousands of monkeys.

The monkey closed its eyes and lowered its head while still holding the spear above its head. He dropped to one knee and lowered the necklace onto the rock. Slowly the monkey stood up. Once fully erect, it looked around deliberately at the surrounding trees and quickly lowered the spear. All at once, the songs of the howlers stopped. The monkey turned and looked Steve directly in the eye. Steve sighed with relief that they were not dinner. If the monkeys were hunting humans, it would be over by now.

"There sure are a lot of monkeys," Anna said as she

surveyed the surrounding trees. "I wonder who is hunting whom?"

A light breeze from the west rose and dusk descended. There was just enough light left to see shapes without the ability to see the details.

The abrupt end to the song of the howler monkeys did not go unnoticed by the scientists. It had broken their concentration long enough to notice floating objects illuminated in the darkening sky.

Anna looked up and saw them immediately. "What are those purple floating things?" Hundreds of what looked like purple jellyfish of all sizes were descending into the opening from above. They were illuminated from inside like fireflies, with long tendrils hanging from the bottom of their bodies.

Steve's heart was racing now. "I have no idea, but we are way past any doubt that things are changing here. Evolution, active DNA or whatever, this place is starting to creep me out. Anna, we need to cut this adventure short. Call the Black Hawk back and let's get out of here."

Steve knew that whatever was discovered here was only the beginning. He had been right all along, yet somewhere deep inside he had always hoped he was wrong. He had wished he could stay Steve Cutter forever and never have to become the Strand.

He slowly shook his head, rubbed his bristly chin, exhaled loudly and watched the purple fluorescent creatures descending from the night sky.

"The Black Hawk pilot says he's on his way," Anna said, "but it'll take him about thirty minutes to get back to us."

Steve knew his objective for the next half hour was to stay alive.

The purple objects stopped descending at about twenty feet and hovered. They created a fluorescent purple canopy that illuminated the mulch where the scientists were standing. The resulting glow was as bright as day, but a day in some other world. Certainly nothing like this had ever been seen before.

A few of the scientists from the European and American teams stepped closer to the black water pond for samples and a closer look.

A military attachment assigned to protect the group from China started shooting a number of the floating creatures. The soldiers popped the creatures with bullets, and their lifeless jelly bodies fell to the forest floor. Scientists gathered them in a pile for observation.

Toward the edge of the jungle, Anna jumped. "Something just moved under my feet, Uncle Steve."

Steve looked down and could vaguely see illumination through the shredded bark. He grabbed Anna by the hand and ran toward a rock outcropping next to where the monkey was standing.

The monkey looked at Steve as if to say, "I told you so." It had been trying to protect them, but they hadn't understood the real danger until now as they ran for the rocks to escape whatever might be hiding under the mulch on the jungle floor.

Hundreds of toads began to emerge from the surrounding jungle into the purple light, jumping thirty to forty feet in the air. They were heading toward the soldiers and the scientists at the pond. A great horn emerged from the head of each toad. What the scientists had thought was a nostril was actually the sheathing for the toad's deadly weapon.

The toads jumped one last time and dove toward a group of armed soldiers with horns extended. Random shots were fired at the last minute to repel the attack, but the soldiers were impaled where they stood. Terrible shrieks of death filled the air. The battle had begun.

Steve and Anna reached the adjoining rock near where the monkey was standing and turned to watch. The jungle floor erupted with a purple glow from below the mulch.

Anna was frantic. "Uncle Steve, what about Dr. Vitimani?"

Steve could hear choppers in the distance. Across the clearing, the remaining soldiers circled the scientists and started shooting the toads as they jumped into range.

More toads were emerging into the clearing and from the pond. They were now jumping high into the air, using their horns to stab the hovering purple prey, devouring them before they even returned to earth. The soldiers and scientists scattered to avoid becoming collateral damage. Most didn't make it out alive.

Steve and Anna watched with horror as the final cries of the scientists who had not escaped the toads faded away. Below them small purple animals emerged from the bark and started to float upward.

"Don't touch the tendrils," Steve warned Anna. "This is a giant nest of some kind."

As the creatures floated past them, he saw that their bellies were full of a fluorescent purple gas.

Steve looked at the monkey. The animal was kneeling down to pick up the necklace on the rock and failed to see a large toad with its horn extended jumping up from the forest floor.

An instant later, Anna leaped from the rock in the direction of the toad. The monkey looked up just as Anna's whip struck the giant toad. The amphibian's body couldn't absorb the 100,000 volts of electricity and exploded in a great gory mess, most of which landed on the monkey.

Steve grabbed Anna's hand and pulled her back onto the rock.

The monkey slowly stood up, drenched in toad, and walked over to what was left of its head. He reached in, ripped out the horn, and peeled off what remained of the muscle to reveal an oblong hole in the base of the horn.

The monkey turned around, picked up the necklace from the rock, untwisted the vine it was made of, and threaded the horn onto it. He twisted the necklace closed and held it over his head. The forest exploded again with the song of howler monkeys, only this time the wild beasts sang a song of imminent mayhem.

Anna shuddered. "Uncle Steve, something else is moving under the bark."

Steve looked down. Something big under the bark was moving in the direction of the dead scientists.

More and more of the small purple creatures rose through the forest floor and ascended to the sky. The toads were in a feeding frenzy, continuing to attack and devour the floating creatures. They would jump into the glowing ceiling, disappear for a moment, and then re-emerge as they returned to the forest floor.

"The Black Hawk is almost here," Anna whispered.

Anna and Steve now watched with disbelief as hundreds of glowing eyes emerged from the mulch. Snakes, with sharp, jagged teeth. They opened their humongous jaws directly below the toads and consumed the amphibians in one swallow. The hunters had become the hunted, as dozens of snakes exploded through the mulch and devoured toads all across the clearing.

Steve's jaw dropped with amazement. It was a trap for the toads set by the snakes. They were feeding on them. No, they were harvesting them.

The monkey lowered the necklace over its head, raised its spear and howled. Around the entire perimeter of the clearing, howler monkeys jumped onto rocks armed with spears. They stood studying the mayhem playing out in front of them.

The monkey looked at Steve and Anna, then over its shoulder at a path directly behind them, leading away from the clearing. There was a small break in the trees a few hundred yards in the distance.

The howler monkeys jumped onto the forest floor into the purple illumination and joined the battle.

"Anna," Steve shouted, "this way! The Black Hawk can pick us up at that clearing." Steve grabbed Anna's hand and they ran as fast as possible down the pathway, through the trees, and toward the clearing.

As Steve was running, he looked back and saw the flashing lights of a helicopter through the purple light. There were loud thuds as the helicopter fell sideways and exploded.

Steve stopped. Was that their Black Hawk?

Gas spewing from the helicopter exploded, setting the mulch on the forest floor on fire. Soon all of it would be ablaze.

Nothing could survive that heat, Steve thought.

If it was his Black Hawk, the pilot was dead.

"Uncle Steve, is that our Howler?"

Running from the blaze toward Steve and Anna was the monkey. Chasing him closely were a dozen enormous glowing snakes, their mouths open and jagged teeth protruding. The reptiles were a hundred feet long and five feet thick. And they were catching up quickly.

"They're chasing him, Anna! Run! Run as fast as you can!"

They turned and bolted, but the monkey was faster. It was catching up to Steve and Anna, and the snakes were right behind. As they ran under the canopy of the trees, they could hear movement in the branches above them.

Something was up there watching them as they ran by.

The glow of the blaze from the helicopter crash grew larger as more and more of the mulch caught fire, casting long shadows on the ground. Steve looked down and saw the shadow of the monkey running behind him. He could also see the snakes beginning to overtake them both.

"There's the Black Hawk," Anna yelled. "Run, Uncle Steve!"

Hovering over the clearing up ahead was their helicopter. Steve was relieved to see it, but they still had to get there in time. At least Anna would have to get there in time.

Without his exoskeleton, Steve was just a man, nothing more. But they finally made it to the opening. Steve saw the rope ladder drop for Anna from above. He slowed his pace. He had to confront the snakes to give Anna a few extra moments to escape, even if it meant that he would be killed.

Steve looked down at the shadow of the monkey overtaking him. The shadows of the snakes suddenly merged with his as the monkey passed him by. Steve jumped into the air as he reached into the side pockets of his backpack. He grabbed his revolvers and spun around in mid-air, prepared to shoot the snakes. He was expecting to see the glowing snakes, but instead saw a rain of howler monkeys riding their spears from high in the treetops. Their spears had pegs near the tips, which they held with their feet as they rode down. They skewered the snakes like icicles falling from the sky.

By the time Steve hit the ground and stopped sliding on his back with his guns drawn, all of the snakes were dead and the troops of howlers were reclaiming their spears.

Steve's jaw dropped in disbelief. The monkeys were in

the trees the whole time and had laid a trap for the glowing snakes.

Okay, Steve thought. I'm impressed. These monkeys are smarter than a lot of humans.

Anna was standing below the rope ladder dangling from the helicopter trying to process what just happened. "Uncle Steve, are you all right?"

Steve stood up, put his revolvers away, and dusted off his shirt.

"These monkeys saved our lives twice tonight."

The Black Hawk hovered above with its floodlights shining down.

Steve joined Anna at the rope ladder and turned back to take one more look before leaving. The monkeys gathered at the edge of the clearing holding their dripping spears.

Their Howler was right behind them, standing erect. He met their eyes with a piercing stare. It was a proud moment, even though he was still stained with the remnants of the toad Anna had killed with her whip. He took the necklace off and held it high above his head for the other monkeys to see and walked over to Anna.

Anna looked over at Steve.

"He's not going to hurt you, Anna. He's giving you the necklace as a gift. You saved his life, Anna."

Anna bowed down and their Howler gently lowered the necklace over her head and onto her shoulders. He dropped to one knee as the entire troop of monkeys began howling a song of victory. It was also a song of friendship and a song of thanks.

Anna bowed again to the howling troop and climbed up the rope ladder to the Black Hawk with Steve right behind her. He closed the door, gave Anna a hug, and signaled the pilot to get moving. The helicopter rose quickly and disappeared into the night.

Steve vowed that he would never be caught in that situation again. If he had his exoskeleton on, if he was Strand, Anna would never have been in danger. He had kept his identity a secret from her long enough. The days of Steve Cutter were coming to an end and the days of the Strand were just beginning.

Steve put on his headphones. "Anna, can you hear me?"

"Yes, Uncle Steve."

"Anna, I'm proud of you. Your mom and dad would be very proud of you." He sighed deeply. "There's something I need to tell you, though."

"Thank you, Uncle Steve, and please don't take this the wrong way, but we just survived monsters, fires, snakes, and giant toads. Can we just give it a rest for a few hours? I'm really, really tired. And hungry, very hungry." She reached into her backpack.

Steve laughed. He was smiling ear to ear. "Whatever you have to eat, I get half. I'm older and need more energy than you."

"Ha! Get your own. This is mine." She started wolfing down the granola bar, but relented at the last minute and gave her uncle the last bite of it. She yawned and leaned against his shoulder.

Steve let Anna fall asleep on him as the Black Hawk flew through the night. He was wondering if he would ever be able to sleep again.

Can one man make a difference?

Soon the world would know that Strand was right, that the planet had entered into a period of rapid evolution. He looked down at his hands and slowly flexed his fingers. How long could he keep his identity a secret? He stared out the window of the Black Hawk, lost in his thoughts.

The pilot spoke over the headphones and broke his concentration. "We will be at *Gaia* in about ten minutes."

Steve had been awake for hours watching video monitors of surveillance cameras back at Cutter Technologies in the Mojave.

Anna had been sleeping since they left Brazil. She was no longer a little girl, he thought. She was skilled and she was formidable. She had come so far since her parents had died. He felt a pain deep inside. Would Jack be alive if he had acted differently before the accident? Would he have experimented on himself if she hadn't been hurt?

Steve wondered about his friend Vitimani and flipped a switch on the console. He dialed a number using the keypad next to it.

"Sarah? Hi, this is Steve Cutter. Is Vit okay?"

"Steve," an older woman said, "of course he's fine. Did you two have a nice lunch? I am making dinner now and expect him home soon. You may want to see if he has left the office yet."

"Sarah, Ned and I didn't have lunch."

"Try the office. Bye now." She hung up.

Sarah was Vitimani's wife of thirty years. She was a warm and wonderful woman, and he couldn't imagine what she was talking about, let alone finishing a phone call without asking how you were doing. Vitimani hadn't been home in at least fifteen hours. Something was very wrong.

Steve turned back to the video monitors of the surveillance cameras at Cutter Technologies. He watched as three black Chevy Suburbans drove up and four men emerged from each. He toggled another switch on his console to turn on the audio coming from the surveillance cameras.

Two of the men remained outside while the others

entered and walked up to Jeanie, the receptionist. "We're here to see Steve Cutter, please," one of them said.

"Mr. Cutter is not in at this time. Did you have an appointment?"

The man doing the talking paused for a moment. Someone else was talking to him through a Bluetooth.

Several of the men started to surround Jeanie.

One of them reached into his jacket and handed papers to the receptionist.

"We'll need access to the entire building. This is a search warrant."

Jeanie looked stunned and simply sat back in her chair.

Steve was getting angry. A search warrant? A search warrant? Under what pretense? Why?

GAIA

The ship Gaia was their home away from home.
Steve looked out the window of the Black Hawk
at the magnificent vessel.
She was a converted supertanker over 1,100 feet
long and 250 feet wide. She sat ten stories above
the water line and another seven stories below.

CHAPTER 3: GAIA

The Empire State Building could fit comfortably in her hull, but at the altitude they were flying, *Gaia* looked like nothing more than a dot on the horizon.

It had taken a mere twelve months to convert her from a rusting, retired hull to a floating city, complete with parks, streams, and a small lake or two.

She was completely self-contained like an aircraft carrier, and could stay at sea almost indefinitely. This was a good thing, since very few harbors could accommodate her massive size.

There were large elevator platforms to transport the Black Hawks from the hangar to the flight deck. There were research facilities, testing facilities, employee housing, restaurants, a movie theater and, of course, great fishing.

Below deck were submarine docks.

Each side of *Gaia* had dry docks for three support vessels, each of them 150 feet long. When the ship was near a port, this fleet of six boats would be used to shuttle people, food, materials, and supplies back and forth.

An aircraft carrier of this size has a population of about 6,000, but *Gaia* had a skeleton crew of about 600. *Gaia* was a work in progress. While she had been converted in a short period of time, she was not complete. In fact, she might never be complete. Parts of the ship were an unimproved shell where specific projects were developed. When completed, that part of the ship would be demolished to make way for something new.

It was a perfect environment for Steve to accelerate his research while maintaining his autonomy. Steve invented all of the new technology. A support staff of scientists, lab technicians, writers, secretaries, and others provided test results and documentation to make the technology saleable.

There were parts of the ship that Steve alone had access to, parts that after *Gaia* launched no one would see. These were locked behind large steel doors that were rarely opened. These doors were the source of much speculation by the crew, not only because they were always locked, but there were times when movement could be heard behind them.

Anna woke up when the Black Hawk lowered its landing gear. "*Gaia*? What are we doing at *Gaia*, Uncle Steve? I thought we were going back to the Mojave."

"Just a precaution, princess. Don't worry. You'll be back to finish school in no time."

The Black Hawk landed on *Gaia* and the door slid open. The warm, salty ocean breeze welcomed Steve and Anna as they stepped on deck.

Dr. E was waiting for them when they landed. She was the chief biologist and an expert in animal life. Usually a pleasant woman in her thirties, Dr. E could be a tiger when provoked. It was clear to everyone who met her that she was able to communicate with animals better than people. But if E were happy, everyone would be happy. At least that's the way it seemed.

Steve opened his backpack and removed three small plastic baggies. "E, this stuff marked Toad, Jellyfish Worm, and Snake, you've never seen anything like this. I guarantee it."

E was bubbling with enthusiasm as she held up each baggie to get a better look.

"The glowy stuff is the jellyfish worm," Steve continued. "These creatures float, or fly, or kind of a combination of both. There's some kind of intelligence with them as a mass entity. I also think it's toxic, or at least the vapor in its gas bladder is. Anyway, you gotta get on this, like now. We need answers, especially if this truly is toxic."

E was smiling ear to ear. Steve knew her well. She wouldn't sleep until she had some answers. That's just the way she was, and it's what Steve loved about her.

One of the crewmen, Stanley, noticed a small puddle of blood on the deck near the rear wheel. He dropped to one knee and scooped some blood onto his finger to confirm that it was fresh. He took a quick sniff to make sure it wasn't paint and peered up into the wheel well.

"Mr. Cutter," the man said urgently, "there's something here you have to see."

E and Anna followed Steve as he walked over to the crewman.

"What's going on, Stanley?" Steve asked.

Stan shifted his weight, took off his baseball cap, and scratched his head. "Well, if I didn't know better, I would say there's a dead monkey in the rear wheel well."

Anna dove to the deck and looked up into the opening.

"Howler! Uncle Steve, it's Howler!"

Steve leaned over. "Anna, is he alive?"

"I can't tell, he's jammed in there … and there's a lot of blood."

Cutter Technologies had modified the Black Hawks by adding retractable landing gear to aid in supersonic flight. Howler was stuck inside the compartment, drenched in blood, and completely silent.

"I think one of the bolts pierced his shoulder," Anna said, "and one of his legs looks like hamburger." There was a moment of silence as all waited.

"He just moved an eye! He's still alive!" Anna reached to grab Howler, who was barely conscious.

"Anna," Steve intervened, "let Dr. E look at him."

"No, Uncle Steve, I got him. He trusts me. Come here, you crazy monkey."

As Anna reached up, Howler released his grip on the wheel well and dropped into her arms. He turned his head, struggled to open his eyes again, and placed his hand on the toad horn necklace around her neck. He exhaled deeply, then closed his eyes and went limp.

Anna looked up with tears welling in her eyes as E placed two fingers on Howler's neck.

"He's not dead, not yet. There's a pulse, but we don't have much time." E was very serious when it came to animals and she immediately assumed control of the situation.

"Stan, bring a stretcher. Anna, you'll ride on the stretcher. Try not to move the monkey until we can get him to my lab."

Anna and E had grown fond of each other over the years, and Steve knew the sight of Anna this upset would galvanize E. If Howler could be saved, it was E who could do it.

As the crew ran the stretcher carrying Anna and Howler off the landing deck, the Black Hawk slowly descended into the helicopter bay.

Back in the nation's capital, the president looked out over the rose garden from a window inside the White House.

Giant toads, floating jellyfish, and toxic gas are one thing, but his chief scientist comatose in the hospital? It isn't exactly what he had hoped to hear this morning. Top scientists from around the globe had rushed to Brazil, the majority now slaughtered by mutated jungle animals or burned in the ensuing fire. Vitimani had been fortunate to survive at all. The CIA still had a team in the forest monitoring the situation, but the president worried for their survival as well.

Early news reports in the worldwide media spoke only of an accident involving helicopters in the Amazon that killed some of the greatest scientific minds of the day. Coverage focused mainly on university students across the planet and their plans for candlelight vigils that evening.

The president thought, Strand did it just right. First he makes an incredible claim, and then he lures the only people who can disprove it to Brazil, where they're slaughtered, every last one of them. What kind of madman is this?

As the president sat down at his desk, he knocked a small round mirror on its side. Framed in sterling silver, it was a gift from the first lady the day he took office. She presented it to him during a rare quiet moment on Inauguration Day. It was early morning in the Oval Office, and he still remembered the exact words she said when she gave it to him.

"You are an emotional man," she told him, "and your feelings influence your decisions. You can't help it, dear. It always shows on your face, which is why I'm giving you this mirror. If you're lost in your own thoughts, look in the mirror. You will see how you are feeling, and it will help you gain perspective on your decisions. You are the president of the United States of America and the most powerful man on the planet, but if you can see yourself as others do, it will help you control your emotions."

The president picked up the mirror and looked at himself. He saw an angry man, angry that people had died, angry that Vitimani was hurt. And he had a predisposed urge to blame it on Strand. He didn't like theatrics and he didn't like getting played a fool in front of the media.

He looked out of the window again and onto the south lawn. Suddenly, a cloaked figure dropped to its knees in front of the window. It was a man, but it was something more. It was Strand.

The president jumped out of his chair and stood tall and erect at the window, not intimidated in the least. Strand's cloak covered most of his exoskeleton as he stood up. The piercing stare of his luminous eyes met the president's unwavering gaze for a long moment.

Strand reached into his cloak, pulled out an envelope, and held it up for the president to see. He turned and walked toward the French doors a few yards away.

As Strand advanced, he retracted a portion of his exoskeleton to expose a portion of unprotected arm. He wanted the president to know for sure that he was human and not a machine.

The president walked over to the French doors to meet Strand. Whatever technology Strand possessed, it was far superior to anything in the U.S. arsenal, and now he was flaunting it by circumventing all security and dropping in for uninvited visits.

The president's face was red with anger as he opened the doors forcefully.

"State your business here."

"I simply wanted to deliver this, sir." Strand held out an envelope.

The president looked at the envelope for a moment. He knew that if Strand was there to kill him, he would already be dead, so he took the envelope. Another door in the Oval Office abruptly opened and Secret Service men rushed in with guns drawn.

Strand's exoskeleton quickly closed around the exposed arm.

"I am the harbinger, nothing more. I am giving you Chapter Two. It will be released on the Internet in twenty-four hours, but I wanted you to have it first."

"Show your face, Mr. Strand."

"Sir, that wouldn't do either one of us any good. Thank you for your time."

Strand turned and walked toward the lawn.

One of the Secret Service men lunged at the president, tackling him to the ground to get him out of harm's way, while the rest of the agents took up positions and began firing at Strand. More agents emerged from all directions and added to the gunfire, but the bullets were ineffective against the exoskeleton. Strand continued to walk until he came to a spot in the middle of the lawn.

"Incoming cruise missile!" yelled one of the Secret Service men. In the distance, a dark shape flew toward the White House.

The Secret Service men stopped firing. The bullets were having no effect. They watched the missile change course and head directly for the Oval Office.

Strand turned to face the president. "Mr. President,

I am the harbinger, the missile rider, the messenger and nothing more. I bring you this information out of respect for you and your office. All I ask for in return is your respect for my evidence."

The president shook loose of the Secret Service man, stood up, and started to walk toward Strand.

"I don't like your methods, Mr. Strand. If you want respect, try using the front door. I promise no one will shoot you then."

Strand looked at the sky and back at the president. "Next time … I will come to the front door and announce myself first."

The cruise missile slowed as it approached the White House.

It was no ordinary cruise missile. This was a cruise missile and something more. Attached to the top of the missile were a metal saddle and a windshield.

The missile aligned itself directly toward Strand and turned over, flying upside down no higher than thirty feet above ground. The windscreen hinged forward toward the ground, and a handle similar to a trapeze extended from it. Strand crouched down, jumped in the air, and grabbed the handle on the missile.

The missile rolled over again. Strand swung his body around and dropped into the saddle. He was riding the missile like a flying motorcycle.

Strand fired the missile rocket and shot straight up into the sky before disappearing into cloud cover.

"What on God's green earth was that?" the president asked.

A Navy officer who was part of the team firing on Strand spoke up. "It looked like a Tomahawk cruise missile, um, motorcycle, Mr. President."

"How far can he get, Lieutenant?"

"It has a range of 550 miles, with at least a thousand pounds worth of ordnance, sir. If he replaced the bombs with a fuel tank and added a couple of rockets, at least double that."

"Can we track him on radar?"

"Well, the missile emits a very small radar signature, which makes it almost impossible to positively identify on radar. If he flies within thirty feet of the ground, we probably won't be able to track it. And if he stays in the clouds, we can't get a visual ID.

"Is there anything else? What about a heat signature?"

"Well, sir," the lieutenant said hesitantly, "it's a small object and it really doesn't have much of a heat signature."

"He's outmaneuvered us." The president was not happy. Not happy at all.

"Yes, sir. Well, good thing he's on our side. Isn't that right, Mr. President?"

On our side? The president thought to himself. He remembered the slaughter in Brazil and worried about Vitimani.

"I think he's on his own side with his own agenda and I don't trust him."

He stared at the envelope in his hand. If Strand uses the front door next time, he thought, we'll be ready for him.

Missile Rider

The Tomahawk missile cycle used a modified fuel, giving it a range of over 6,000 miles. Strand was cruising 550 miles an hour; subsonic to be sure, but still very fast, especially when riding on top of it like Slim Pickens in Dr. Strangelove.

CHAPTER 4: Missile Rider

He made it back to *Gaia* in about three hours. Once there, he quickly made the transition from Strand to Steve. After everything was packed safely away, he went below deck to check on Howler.

Anna and E were in the same place as when he had left, both hovering over Howler on an operating table. The monkey was in bad shape. Most of the damage was concentrated on the left side of his body. His shoulder was freshly bandaged where it had been impaled by a piece of metal. Howler had several other deep cuts, broken bones, and severed nerves in his spine. Every bone in his left leg was crushed except for the ones in his foot, which were relatively untouched.

"How's he doing?" Steve asked as he entered the room.

Dr. E walked over to meet him. She looked exhausted. "He is alive, but that's about it. From time to time, he opens his eyes to see if Anna's still by his side."

As if on cue, Howler slowly opened his eyes to check for Anna. She caressed his hand for a few seconds before he fell back to sleep.

She came over to join Steve and Dr. E by the door. "E has some kind of magic touch," Anna said. "Otherwise, he'd be dead."

"Good thing we didn't go supersonic," Steve said. "He never would've survived that."

"I think he's gonna make it, Uncle Steve. But he can never return to the jungle." They looked at each other silently.

Steve put his hands on Anna and E. "You two make quite a team. Keep it up."

Anna yawned audibly, and it triggered an even bigger yawn from E. "Go get some sleep, Anna," E said. "There's nothing more you can do today."

Anna nodded, yawned again, and headed out the door.

Steve watched her through the glass as she disappeared down the hallway.

If the howler survives, thought Steve, he'll become something more than a monkey. He saved our lives, and most importantly, he saved Anna's life.

And for that, I owe him a life — a good life.

It would soon be evening. Steve was going to be busy. He had to prepare.

The missile cycle was a decommissioned Tomahawk cruise missile junked by one of Steve's defense contractor clients for a new model. A metal saddle, a windshield, a small canard wing in the front, an additional fuel tank, and external rocket boosters were added. Each one provided twelve seconds of thrust, just enough to get the cycle off the ground and into the air. Cutter Technologies built several versions of the missile cycle, all of which were stored on *Gaia* except one. That one was safely hidden on the beach at Normandy, France. Other than being a great tactical location, it seemed appropriate from a poetic standpoint.

Steve went back to his office on the *Gaia* and checked the security cameras at Cutter Technologies in the Mojave. The unwelcome visitors were still there. Most employees had left for the day, but the CIA or the NSA or whoever they were remained. He switched the monitor to check the security cameras he had installed in his house. He could immediately tell the house had been searched. There were also three black sedans parked in the street with agents inside waiting for him to come home.

"We can't go home, can we?" Anna had quietly entered the room in her pajamas. She spoke in a hushed tone.

"Not today, Anna," Steve said. "That much is for sure. We'll see what happens tomorrow." Steve turned around in his chair and faced her. Anna walked over and sat in his lap, for the first time in years.

"Uncle Steve, what did you want to tell me when we were on the Black Hawk?"

Steve looked at his watch and sighed. This was an important discussion and he didn't have time for it now.

"Listen, princess, we'll talk about it later. I promise. But right now, I have something for you." Steve swung his chair around and opened his desk drawer. He pulled out what looked like a brand new cell phone.

"A cell phone, Uncle Steve?" Anna looked puzzled.

"No, it's — hold on." Steve squeezed the side of the object and a split second later it extended like a car antennae into a whip four feet long. There wasn't a steel cable attached to it. It was just the whip portion.

"It's a whip," Anna whispered.

Steve flicked his wrist and the whip responded flawlessly, snapping right and left and then retracting into the case. "Anna, I want you to keep this with you at all times. You can set the power to one third, two thirds or full with this switch on the handle where your thumb goes." He handed it to her.

"Thank you so much! This is awesome!" She gave him a big hug. "You know, you've become like a father to me."

"Anna. You have no idea how much that means to me." He gave her a big squeeze and stood up, lifting her off his lap and gently onto the floor. "Now get outta here, ya brat. I got work to do." He said it with a big smile on his face. The biggest smile Anna had ever seen from her uncle.

A few minutes after Anna left the office, Steve toggled several switches on his desk. One bolted the front door and the other opened a hidden panel behind the desk. This secret hatch appeared at first glance to be part of *Gaia's* hull until it swung open to reveal a dark hallway. Steve entered the opening and the door slowly closed behind him.

As the hatch sealed shut, the hall lights flickered on. Light blue bulbs illuminated the length of the hallway but not much more. At the end of the hallway was another door with a biometric panel. Steve walked up and placed his hand on the flat device. It took the scanner only a moment to verify Steve's identity, and with a flash of light and a clicking sound, the door opened into a large room. Inside the room and along one wall was a row of exoskeletons. Each exoskeleton hung in its own open locker facing forward, just as the jerseys of the professional athletes' do when awaiting the next game.

Each exoskeleton was different, some apparently lighter, some much heavier. Each was specifically geared to a particular type of operation.

For long missile cycle flights, the lighter exoskeleton was used. For short flights and missions where there would be large jumps and potentially heavy artillery fire, the heavier suit provided an advantage. Steve had used the heavy one both times he went to the White House. There were a variety of other exoskeletons that did not have any body armaments. One even looked like it had additional arms.

On the far wall in a glass case hung one suit noticeably different from the others. Standing eight feet tall, it was much larger. And there was no way to enter the suit, at least no way easily apparent from outside the glass case.

Across from the exoskeletons were shelves, bins, and lockers containing a multitude of devices and electronics that could be attached to any of the suits. There were heat sensors, radioactive isotope detectors and biological hazard detectors, jamming devices, radio broadcasting transmitters, satellite receivers and transmitters, and a few shoulder rockets. Any specialty gear could be added to the exoskeleton with a few clicks.

Steve's transformation into Strand was a process he loved and feared at the same time. Maybe it was the power of the exoskeleton that surged through him, maybe it was flying a cruise missile at 550 miles an hour, or maybe it was the sheer freedom that he loved. Whatever the reason, it was intoxicating. It gave him virtually limitless power and the confidence to use it. But it was exactly those thoughts that he also feared.

Steve didn't want to lose his humanity. He didn't want to become more machine than man. He had only truly been awakened to his humanity since the death of his brother and his unexpected role as Anna's provider.

Steve opened a locker, removed his wig, and placed it

on a metal globe similar to a giant ball bearing. He put on a dark blue jumpsuit made of spandex. The suit was a type of thermal underclothing that could regulate his body temperature while he was inside the exoskeleton.

He went over to where the exoskeletons were hanging. As he walked, he caught a glimpse of himself in the mirror. He walked past, then stopped and leaned back to look at himself for a moment. He started to laugh. There he was in all his glory, bald head and a skintight jumpsuit.

"You are one weird looking dude, Steve Cutter," he said to the mirror. "No wonder you don't have a girlfriend."

He walked over to the open locker containing the lighter exoskeleton. Directly in front of it were two stainless steel oval pads attached to the floor. Steve turned around and placed his feet over the pads. This was the part he loved the most.

Steve tightened his body and raised his arms so they were perpendicular to the floor, and then he held his breath. Seconds later, the suit moved forward and hugged him from behind as it attached to his arms and legs. Metal ribs reached around and attached across his chest.

The exoskeleton was black chrome, but at the joints an eerie luminous blue glow oozed outward whenever he moved his arms and legs. The nanotubes in the exoskeleton reacted like a living material, mimicking the operation of muscles. They contracted and expanded with a force one hundred times that of an average man.

Steve walked across the room and opened a box on one of the shelves. He lifted out a thin black rubber skullcap. Not meant to cover the entire head, it started at the neck before widening at the ears and narrowing once again at the top of the forehead. The front came to a point like a widow's peak and had a symbol which consisted of a hexagon with an elongated 'S' symbol drawn through it.

He placed it carefully on his head. It fit him as snug as a glove. The helmet now surged to life, with thin blue traces of light glowing like a circuit board.

Moments later, his head was flooded with information. He was aware of everything happening on *Gaia* simultaneously, from temperature to engine speed to the direction the ship was traveling. He could feel the compass and magnetic north, he was aware of exactly how many of the crew were working and how many were sleeping. He was constantly aware of the status, documentation, and testing of the new technologies. He was a man and something more.

When he opened his eyes, he was Strand. There was a different look to his face, a faraway look, a look of preoccupation, the look of a thousand things happening behind his eyes at the same time. Yet at the same time, it was a look of total control.

On a shelf adjacent to where the skullcap was stored rested a black chrome helmet. Strand put it on over the skullcap. The helmet attached itself to the exoskeleton with a few clicks and clacks. He mounted several sensors, transmitters and other devices on his chest. They were like so many vertebrae, except on the front of the exoskeleton instead of the back.

One last shelf held something similar to football shoulder pads. These were the short burst rocket thrusters he always wore when riding the missile cycle. The short-fire rockets gave him a few seconds of float time once he jumped to grab hold of the missile cycle. The timing on his jump was critical when mounting. If he was off by even a second, the missile cycle would fly by and he would fall back to earth. While Strand always wore the rockets when flying, he had never needed them.

Strand's hooded cape stood without assistance in one

corner of the room. It was made of a black fabric capable of standing on its own. It was impervious to radar and most kinds of radiation. It was an integrated part of the exoskeleton, acting as a large antenna once it was attached. Strand wrapped himself in the cape, exposing a door directly behind where it stood.

He stopped for a moment and stared at himself once again in the mirror.

"Only a man," Strand said to his reflection. Instantly, the exoskeleton extended itself around his arms and legs, covering him from head to toe like a medieval knight. He looked down at his hands and flexed his fingers, the blue energy peeking through the black chrome. He looked up at himself again.

"And something more." A visor and face plate extended to cover his face, leaving the shape of a face in black chrome, with glowing blue eyes and small luminous traces of blue running across his cheeks and chin.

On the fourth floor of *Gaia's* control tower, the missile cycle was moving into place, engines on and going through a preflight test. Strand emerged from the tower and walked toward the missile cycle. The strands in his head and helmet linked him to the systems on the missile cycle. He double-checked all onboard computers and completed an internal diagnostic as he jumped into the saddle. He leaned forward and tucked his body under the windscreen, grabbed hold of the handles, and placed his feet on metal stirrups, leaned forward and launched the missile at full throttle. It roared to life and took off, rockets thundering in the night sky.

Within minutes he was traveling 400 miles an hour. *Gaia* had disappeared into the darkness behind him. No one could hear him howling with exhilaration as the missile cycle accelerated. It was the power and freedom.

He was as happy as he had ever been, happier than he had ever thought possible.

Evolutionary Free-For-All

Strand had brought the president Chapter Two of his paper, which everyone in the media and Internet community now referred to as the Strand Prophecy.

CHAPTER 5: Evolutionary Free-For-All

It began with two stern warnings above the table of contents:

We must protect the innocent and save the human race.

We must provide a brighter future for our children, and our children's children.

Table of contents:

1. The confirmation of accelerated evolution and active DNA found in the Brazilian jungle.

2. Fabric designs for the manufacture of hooded cloaks that provide protection against mutating radiation.

3. The potential disruptions in the food chain that may occur with simpler forms of life.

4. The genetic predisposition and environmental factors that increase probability of accelerated mutation in higher life forms.

5. Dangers, symptoms of mutation and warning signs to watch for.

The president slammed the Strand document onto his desk.

"What I don't like is that we have no control. We cannot ascertain if this information is correct, and yet it will be the de facto truth in twenty-four hours. This Strand character is reckless and dangerous. And the country will be looking to its government, to me, but I have no facts and certainly no time."

The president's anger was palpable as he sat back in his chair.

The first lady was sitting on a large couch in the middle of the Oval Office. "But what if he is right?"

"He's a crackpot and he's dangerous. It doesn't matter if he's right."

The phone rang and the president picked it up. "Yes?"

His wife got up and walked over to his side.

"Hold on a second, Dwight." He covered the receiver as his wife leaned down to tell him something.

"I'm going to keep the kids indoors for the next few days," she said quietly. "They're just getting over colds." As she looked deeply into his eyes, he knew exactly what she was really saying. There was no chance she would take even the slightest risk when it came to her own children.

"I'm gonna have to get back to you on that," he said, and hung up the phone. There was no simpler truth, no stronger emotion, no truer an instinct parents have than to protect their children.

"I'll see you in a little bit. I just have to make a few more calls. What about a quiet dinner for two tonight?"

"That sounds wonderful," she said, and pecked him on the cheek before leaving the room.

The phone rang again and the president answered.

"Yes? Who is here? At the front gate now?"

A single bead of sweat trickled down the president's forehead.

"Yes, all right, send him back."

There was obvious commotion on the other end of the line.

After a few long seconds, the president continued. "I'm sorry. Did you say he's gone? Where on earth did he go?"

Suddenly he saw movement outside the window.

"Oh, never mind, I think I know."

The president hung up, walked over to the French doors, and flung them open.

"Well, I didn't say you had to walk through the building, you know. It's just kind of expected."

Strand stood silently at the door. His electric blue eyes were much more profound at night and made him look even more alien than usual.

"Please state your business here, Mr. Strand."

"Did you read the papers that I gave you, Mr. President?"

"Yes, I did, and I cannot confirm any of what you have written. You are going to scare the public with this. It's irresponsible to present this information without presenting a solution at the same time."

Strand stood motionless. He was descrambling encrypted key codes blocking access to military and Secret Service computers. He was also listening to Secret Service and police radio transmissions. He wasn't finished descrambling all of the chatter, but Strand knew there was a military "operation" under way in which he was the primary target.

Strand also knew they would never shoot at him while he was standing this close to the president. Once the president was out of harm's way, all bets were off. He had to assume they would not hesitate to use every method of lethal force available to bring him down. He would have to hurry.

"New species will emerge," Strand explained, "whether through genetic predisposition or specific environmental factors. The ultimate revelation is that these mutations can be controlled."

The president opened his mouth to contradict Strand, but Strand cut him off. "There is going to be more than one species of human on this planet, and that, sir, is a fact. The emerging changes, the dangers, and the risks must be brought to the attention of the population at large.

"Deal with this for what it is, and you will be remembered as one of the greatest leaders of modern times. Close your eyes to this ... and you will bring pain and suffering on a biblical scale. This is an evolutionary free-for-all, a shake-up in the food chain, and a potential reorganization of the dominant species on the planet. If we humans cannot adapt, we will be replaced. This is the cold, brutal reality of the situation."

The president's posture had tightened considerably as he listened to Strand. The words struck deep. He had been dealing with this matter only superficially. He had never considered this a possibility.

Strand finished deciphering the encrypted information and knew there was a large military force waiting for him just outside the White House grounds. There were attack helicopters, surface-to-air missiles, UAVs, and jets armed with air-to-air missiles.

The president finally spoke. "You are a danger and a threat to our national security, Mr. Strand. Even if you are right, you are acting irresponsibly and recklessly. Most of all, you are arrogant. I will not take further action without collaborated facts from experts, without consulting with the top minds in science to determine the probability of different scenarios unfolding. I will not take action based on one man's perception of the facts, no matter how much that one man has made our military look like amateurs."

Strand was busy launching twelve additional missile cycles from *Gaia* as he stood listening to the president. At the same time, he was hacking into Air Force aeronautic computer navigation systems and writing a virus that would disable the computers. Even this small virus would force the military to immediately shut down the computers to stop the virus from spreading through all of its systems.

"What was the purpose of giving me this information first?" the president asked, "other than using this office as a public springboard for your personal objectives? Well, I'll tell you this much. This office will not be used by you to gain credibility, nor can you use your superior technology to force this country into believing your story. You might have the technology, but that does not automatically give you credibility, or the right to exploit this office under the guise of being an ally."

Strand's countermeasures were in place. The newly arriving missile cycles would create diversions as well as provide multiple targets on the radar. Meanwhile, the virus he wrote would shut down the navigation systems on military aircraft and helicopters in the immediate area.

"But what if I'm right, Mr. President?"

The president's anger was getting the better of him. His face was red, his hands were clenched, and he practically stomped over to his desk. As he did, he caught a glimpse of his face in the small mirror. He was certainly outraged, but still in control.

"Not yet, Mr. Strand. I'm not ready to answer that question. I need more time."

"How much more time do you need?"

"What?"

"How much time do you need, Mr. President?"

"What do you mean?"

"I simply want to know how much time you need to assess the accuracy of the information, to check with experts, and to come to a decision as to whether what I'm saying is really true." Strand also needed to buy more time for his missile cycles to arrive at the White House.

The president found the question unsettling. He still felt Strand was pressuring him for his personal agenda and exploiting the office of the presidency. It had never occurred to him to simply ask for additional time to review the information.

Strand now realized the helicopters and military aircraft converging on the capital had alerted the media.

"Mr. President, how much time do you need?"

The president paused. He was a strong and willful man, not a man to be bullied, not a man to be intimidated. "Two weeks."

"Okay. I will release this in two weeks. If you need to contact me before that time, place an ad in the *Wall Street Journal* stating: Investor Wanted for Advanced Brazilian Toxin Research."

Strand turned and started to leave.

"Wait," said the president.

Strand stopped and turned to face him.

"Why are you giving me this additional time?"

"Mr. President, I may be unconventional, but I'm

certainly not your enemy, sir, all you had to do was ask. You obviously think I have some sort of agenda in which you are an unwilling pawn, but I do not. I have only a mission to protect the innocent. What I have written is true, and the risks I have taken to bring it to you first are great. Do you think I'm unaware of what awaits me outside these doors?"

Strand paused and checked the status of the military operation.

"I am not responsible for anyone who dies tonight while trying to use lethal force against me. Those deaths will be on your hands, sir. I came in peace and I plan to leave in peace. The force assembled in preparation for my departure will be defeated, and not without loss of life and damage to this historical city. The blood and destruction will have happened on your watch."

Strand turned and walked farther onto the south lawn.

"Wait, hold on a moment," called the president.

Strand stopped for a moment, but did not turn around. "They will attack unless you stop them, there is no in-between." He continued to walk away.

The president ran over and picked up his direct line to the military commanders. "Stand down! Stand down immediately! Let him pass!"

Strand stood in the middle of the south lawn and looked skyward. There were no fewer than thirty attack helicopters in a circle around the White House, hovering with guns pointed directly at him. He could hear multiple jet fighters flying high above. Behind the circle of attack helicopters were Marine Harrier jets positioned as a secondary offensive line. The sheer amount of military hardware pointing its guns at Strand was an awesome sight to behold.

Strand stood listening to helicopter blades chop

77

through the air and waited. No one was firing, yet no one was leaving.

Just then his missile cycle dropped to within thirty feet of the ground and rolled over. As it flew upside down, Strand jumped and grabbed hold of the bar on the windshield. The missile cycle rolled over and he dropped into the saddle.

Strand flew like lightning over the roof of the White House, and the attack helicopters kept him in the middle of their circle, flying sideways with guns pointed as they left the White House. This ballet of deadly machinery continued to follow Strand on the missile cycle as he flew away from Washington toward the Atlantic Ocean.

The other missile cycles from *Gaia* were now at 30,000 feet and directly above him. Strand knew the Marine Harrier jets were ordered to intercept them and that an aircraft carrier off the coast was launching additional planes as backup.

Strand throttled the missile cycle's jet engine to full and fired the rockets. The missile cycle was now completely vertical, and in under a minute it climbed to 30,000 feet to meet the other missiles at over 600 miles an hour. The helicopters could not keep up with him, while the Harriers were still accelerating. The Navy jets already in the air could see nothing but distant flames spewing from the rockets.

At 30,000 feet, Strand directed the missile cycles to regroup and fly in formation for thirty seconds, just long enough for the Navy pilots to confirm that there were more of them. The cycles fired rockets simultaneously and then went vertical. Flying at almost supersonic speed, only the rocket fire was visible to the Navy pilots.

The missile cycles broke formation at about 40,000 feet, each going its own direction. It looked like an enormous flower opening its petals. Abruptly everything went black, as the rockets stopped and the flames burned out. All that remained was dark sky for miles.

Strand directed the missiles to power down their jets to an unassisted glide until they dropped twenty to thirty feet off the ground and below radar detection. He met with them so they could all return to *Gaia* in formation at full throttle.

The president peered into the night sky at the flame from a single rocket, then twelve firing vertically at one time, until the flames disappeared as they separated and flew in different directions.

He shook his head and walked back toward the Oval Office.

Mr. Strand did it again, the president thought.

Well, at least he tried to use the front door this time.

As Strand sped back to *Gaia*, his thoughts raced. The meeting with the president had not gone as he'd hoped. Either the president didn't believe him or didn't want to believe him. The two weeks the president had requested were not unreasonable and so he had agreed to it. But someone might die somewhere as a result of the request for additional time, and that thought infuriated Strand.

He accelerated the missile cycle to just under supersonic speed. Once back on *Gaia*, he could focus on creating an antidote for the toxic gas sample he'd retrieved from the Brazilian jungle. Hopefully, he could find a way to channel his anger and frustration into something positive for mankind.

The Destruction of *Gaia*

Morning broke across the deck of Gaia
with a warm light and a slight breeze.
The magnificent ship glistened as the
sun reflected off her glass.
It was easy to forget just how big she was
during the night when looking out
from the control tower into the darkness.

CHAPTER 6: The Destruction of *Gaia*

Steve hadn't slept since returning from his meeting with the president. In fact, he couldn't remember the last time he really slept. Certainly, it must have been before the trip to Brazil, and it was starting to show on his face. His body needed rest and he knew it had better be sooner rather than later.

The cell phone on his hip buzzed. It was E calling. Every wireless phone could be reached from anywhere on the ship.

"You're up early this morning," E said.

"Look who's talking." He smiled. E was compulsive about her work, just like he was.

"This stuff from Brazil is like nothing I've ever seen. The results are still unclear, but it has some really amazing properties."

"I read your reports and research data last night, E, and I have some thoughts. Meet me up on deck. We'll have a cup of coffee and talk about it."

"The usual hangout?"

"Yep, the usual hangout. See you in twenty minutes."

Steve and E had a particular spot at the bow of the ship where they always enjoyed meeting. Steve had built a sheltered structure similar to a gazebo there. Sliding glass doors either sealed the room from the elements or could be opened wide, which was especially nice on a morning like this. There was a coffeemaker, an espresso machine and a mini-fridge inside.

When E arrived, Steve was already there, the doors were open, and the coffee was made.

"I thought you said twenty minutes," E said. "How long have you been here?" She looked closely at Steve. "You look awful. You need some rest. Doctor's orders."

"E, you're a veterinarian."

"…And if I can see it, imagine what your doctor would say."

Steve smiled. It felt good to have someone care about him, and it broke the solitude he routinely felt after shedding his Strand persona.

E poured a cup of coffee and sat down next to him.

"Steve, listen to me. There are things that happen on this ship that…." E paused to rethink her words. "There are certain locked doors behind which things are, um … happening, yet not one person from this ship who I've talked to has ever entered one of these rooms. There are rockets that fire during all hours of the night and reports of machines, robots of sorts that move in the shadows of the streets at night." E looked up at Steve and paused. She wasn't getting the reaction she had hoped to see.

Steve shifted uneasily in his chair. This isn't how he wanted to start the day.

E sensed his discomfort. "Look, Steve, I believe in you … and one day … when you're ready, you'll tell me what's really going on." She stopped and locked eyes with him. He straightened in his chair and cleared his throat.

E waited for a moment, hoping Steve would take this opportunity to level with her and explain some of the stranger things happening on *Gaia*. Unfortunately, a brief moment of optimism became a long, uncomfortable silence. It was obvious Steve wasn't ready to start talking.

"Steve, I don't care how strong you think you are, you are killing yourself slowly. Your body needs rest to heal. You have to take better care of yourself, if for no other reason than Anna."

Steve felt the buzzing in his head that comes from serious lack of sleep. He knew E was right.

"You're right. You're absolutely right, E. I'll rest tonight, I promise."

"Fine then, as long as you promise."

"Cross my heart, hope to die. No, wait." Steve chuckled. One day he would tell her everything, but that day was not today. He trusted E, but that wasn't the issue. If he confided in her, she would then have the burden of keeping his secret. And E would have enough to worry about in the coming weeks.

Steve smiled and the tiny wrinkles around his eyes grew a little deeper, but his face radiated happiness.

E got up, exited the gazebo, and stood at the ship's railing, sipping coffee and staring out at the ocean. "You know, Anna is an amazing young woman. I don't think she realizes just how special she really is. Aside from the fact that she's graduating college before most girls her age are graduating high school, she has something more. She's been working with me in the lab on Howler, and her comprehension is astounding. It's remarkable, Steve. She puts ideas and concepts together faster than anyone I've ever met. Oh, except you, of course." E laughed.

Steve joined her at the railing.

"I'm so glad to hear you say that. I think she's an amazing young lady myself. Of course, I'm not an objective observer." Steve paused. "You know, she's going back to school in a couple of days. This is her last semester, and she says she wants to be here with us on *Gaia* after graduation. Sounds like you two will have a good time working together."

"We've already talked about it at length," E said. "It's going to be a lot of fun."

"That's a load off my mind. Thanks, E." Steve turned around and leaned his back against the ship's railing. "Hey, I don't mean to change the subject, but I'm wondering, how's the research going?"

"It seems all the monkeys are immune to the toxin, and we're in the process of finding out why. When we figure that out, that will give us a head start at developing some kind of vaccination. Howler's blood samples are invaluable right now, and luckily, he cooperates with us with no hesitation. But it's going to be some time before we're ready for human testing." E paused and looked at Steve intensely.

"This Brazilian toxin is incredibly effective. The creature immobilizes its victim, then lands on and begins to eat it. It excretes an acid that breaks down the cutaneous tissue of its victim. Once the flesh is broken down to the right consistency, the creature absorbs the resulting matter directly into its body."

E continued, reluctantly. "The horrific part is that the victims are fully conscious while this process is taking place. They are literally being eaten alive and they know it. The victim feels pain and is helpless to do anything, except pray for death. It's truly horrible." E was visibly shaken by her own description of the effects of the toxin.

"Can the effects be reversed?"

"No, definitely not, the toxin immediately severs nerves at the base of the skull. The victim is virtually decapitated. A survivor would still have brain functions but no motor skills. They would be fully awake but trapped inside themselves, unable to move, unable to communicate. It's like being alive and dead at the same time. Unimaginable."

Steve had lost concentration for a moment. Pain and suffering "on a biblical scale" is what Strand had told the president. Now it was a clear and immediate danger, and Strand had committed to do nothing for two weeks. But now all Steve could think about was the friend he left dying in the jungle.

"Steve?"

"Yeah, E?"

"What's wrong? Who are you thinking about?"

"An old friend of mine, Ned Vitimani. He was in that jungle… and now I know exactly what happened to him."

"Oh, I'm so sorry, Steve."

"I know him pretty well. If he's alive, he's wishing he was dead." Steve didn't wait to change the subject. "What's your prognosis on Howler? I read your logs on his physical status last night."

"The crushed bones in his leg were nothing but splinters which had embedded themselves into the muscles around them. There aren't enough large pieces of bone left to reconstruct it. I removed most of the bone fragments and did what I could to stop his internal bleeding. And I've stopped any threat of infection.

"I can implant metal rods and a joint, but that will hardly replace what he's lost. As for the shoulder, the machine bolt pierced and crushed the entire bone and joint connecting the clavicle to just about everything else in the immediate area. Most of the nerves were severed to the arms. Even with a metal replacement shoulder, I don't think he'll have much mobility."

"What about his mental state, E?"

"The monkey's mental state? Are you serious?" E looked puzzled and amused at the same time.

"I couldn't be more serious."

"Well, frankly, I don't really know. He's still under heavy sedation to relieve the immense pain." E was back to business.

"E, this might sound cruel to you, but this is no ordinary monkey. I need to know if his spirit is broken. You have to cut back on the heavy medication and let him regain consciousness. Then I need you to call me when that happens. I want to see him as soon as he wakes up."

"Steve, from a humanitarian standpoint, it's best not to make him suffer. He might one day be able to live without pain or medication, but the monkey will never have the same quality of life he did before." E paused and touched Steve on the shoulder. "I can make his passing peaceful … with no pain."

Steve backed away from the railing abruptly and turned to face E directly. He could feel anger welling inside of him.

E immediately noticed his reaction. "Um, okay, off the meds it is then. Let me get on that. Yeah, I'll let you know. It shouldn't take long."

Steve turned to walk away before E even finished talking. He was distracted and suddenly anxious. He was beginning to feel that the two weeks he gave the president were a big mistake. Things were happening too fast.

"Thanks, E. I'll be around." Steve stopped before he went below deck and turned around.

"I heard all of your questions, E, all of them ... even the ones that you didn't ask directly." E smiled nervously. "And I cannot tell you how much it means to me that you have faith in me." Steve paused for a moment, looked her in the eyes, smiled ever so slightly, then turned and disappeared below deck.

E stood looking out at the ocean, not sure of what had just happened. She drank the last bit of coffee from her cup. "He can be so abrupt," she said to herself, "then an instant later ... so charming.

"Men."

The distance from the bow of *Gaia* to the control tower was approximately the length of three football fields. Steve was taking his time walking at a slow pace around the perimeter of the ship. Midway through his journey, he stopped and put his elbows on a railing. He closed his eyes and lowered his head into his palms.

Superhero or super freak, he thought to himself. When did the world become my responsibility?

The next thought he spoke out loud. "What am I doing?"

"You're trying to save the world, Uncle Steve, that's what you're doing."

Steve swung around to see Anna just a few feet away. His mind was racing, but he didn't say a word. What was she talking about? Had he made a mistake? Did he somehow reveal his identity? Was there something he had overlooked?

"You're trying to find a vaccine to the gas in those floating jellyfish worm things," Anna said, "while the rest of the world closes its eyes to what's happening."

Steve let out a big sigh of relief and smiled, but it only stayed on his face for a moment. "Anna, I think Ned was exposed to the gas while we were in the jungle. If it wasn't for Howler, we would have been, too."

"Oh, no." Anna suddenly noticed the fatigue in Steve's face. "But you're gonna be sick yourself if you don't get some sleep."

"Yes, I know, E was just telling me the same thing. Tonight I will get some rest." He looked at Anna and knew she would hold him to his commitment. "I just have to make a few calls, see if I can't get things cleared up so you can get back to school before spring break is over."

"No hurry. Really. By the way, I've been using the new whip and it's even better than the old one. Watch this."

Anna jumped in the air, executing a flawless, spinning back kick before landing on the ground, whip extended and at the ready. She remained in a semi-crouched position poised to lunge at any would-be attacker.

Anna stayed frozen in that position for a moment before cracking the whip safely away from Steve. Then in a single motion, she retracted the whip and slid it back in her belt holster.

"What do you think of that? Pretty good, huh?"

"Not bad for a rookie," Steve joshed. "Could use a little work, though."

Anna's jaw dropped in disbelief, but before she could respond, Steve grabbed her and gave her a big hug.

"That was awesome, princess. I'm very proud of you."

"You had me for a second there, Uncle Steve. Now go get some sleep. You promise me."

"Promise."

"I'm going to check up on you, but you already know that, don't you?"

"Yes, yes, I know you will. Maybe you should check on Howler?"

"That's a good idea, I will. See you later." Anna turned and left.

As Steve walked to his office, the warm ocean breeze

caressed his skin. He could walk with his eyes closed and the wind at his back and know where he was going to end up, even if he never saw the actual steps he took to get there.

That somehow seemed to make more sense to him than ever before.

I guess there's a little of everything in everything else, he thought as he walked.

His Zen moment passed as he opened his eyes and looked up. He was in front of the door to the control tower.

Would the strength of the human spirit be the door to the future?

Steve caught his mind wandering again and shook the cobwebs from his head. He opened the door.

In his office, Steve picked up the phone, and dialed Sarah Vitimani's number. There was no answer, so he called Dr. Vitimani's office.

"May I speak with Dr. Vitimani, please?"

"One moment, sir," a voice answered. "Can I tell him who is calling?"

"Steve Cutter."

"One moment, please."

But the time to transfer the call was taking too long, and Steve realized his call was being traced. He used his equipment to confirm it.

Why would they want me? Maybe they're afraid of the toxin being contagious, he thought.

"You cannot trace this line," Steve stated abruptly into the seeming nothingness. "Why don't you just identify yourself?"

"Dr. Vitimani was exposed to a toxic gas in Brazil," he continued saying to no one in particular, "we were not. This is not a contagious toxin and there's no threat of it spreading. You should know that by now. We are working on an antidote, and I will call this office periodically to keep you informed of our progress."

He paused for a moment. "When your people leave my home and my business, I will know and accept that as an acknowledgement. We'll come up with a solution and share it with the world. We are no threat. Thank you."

He hung up the phone and tapped the top of the handset, wondering if he was talking to nothing or if someone really was listening. He checked the security monitors. Both Cutter Technologies and his home were visible on different screens. He knew that the NSA would listen in on any phone call that it deemed a threat to national security, so it must have been listening.

He watched the men waiting outside each location. No one was moving, no one was leaving. He estimated the time it would take to get his message to someone in authority and for that person to tell the men to leave, then the time it would take for the men to get the message in the field and he shook his head.

"Don't play with me; you should have called them by now. I know I'm right, there's no way you weren't listening," he said to the screens. "I'm watching you, now get those guys out of there." As if on cue, two men at each location held their hands to their earpieces and then signaled for the others to leave.

"It's good when it works," he said to himself as he slapped the desktop and stood up.

Steve's positive feelings were short-lived, as the disturbing matter of Vitimani crept back into his thoughts. He left his office and went to his quarters a few floors up in the control tower. They were not elaborate by any stretch of the imagination. They were utilitarian, really nothing more than was absolutely necessary for sleeping quarters. He did have a bed instead of a cot, one comfortable chair, and a window.

Steve turned on the shower and waited for the water to get hot. He got in and stood motionless, leaning against the wall and letting the water wash over him. It felt good to rinse some of his stress down the drain.

Afterwards, he bundled himself in towels and sat down on the cushy chair by the window. He leaned back and sighed. The heat of the shower was still in his skin and the ocean breeze washed across him from the open portal window. He exhaled deeply. The invisible load he was carrying seemed to be a bit lighter, even if only for a little while.

The next thing he knew, he heard a dull pounding and quickly jumped up. He peered out the window and saw a series of explosions light up the deck of Gaia. He looked up and saw fighter jets speeding over the ship. One fighter off starboard dropped a torpedo in the water.

Anna, he thought. Where's Anna?

Steve grabbed his clothes and ran out the door. By the time he reached the deck, Gaia was ablaze and Anna was running toward him from the largest of many fires.

Tears were streaming down her face. "Uncle Steve!"

"STOP, ANNA, STAY THERE! DON'T COME ANY FARTHER!" But it was too late. The torpedo hit Gaia and exploded with a vengeance. The blast threw Anna into the air and slammed her onto the deck, limp.

Steve ran to her and held her in his arms. He looked up just in time to see the control tower of Gaia explode from an air-to-ground missile. Burning metal shrapnel rained on them as Steve covered Anna's body with his own.

"Uncle Steve," Anna said weakly.

Steve looked down. "Don't talk. Everything will be okay."

"Uncle Steve, I know who you are. You're the Strand."

Steve gasped.

How did she know?

Anna coughed and could barely speak. "But why didn't you tell me? Didn't you trust me? I trust you. I love…."

Anna fell limp in his arms. She was dead.

"NO!" Steve cried out in agony. 'NO! DON'T TAKE HER, TAKE ME. THIS IS MY FAULT! It's all ... my ... fault." Tears flowed from his eyes as he looked up from Anna, barely able to focus on E limping in his direction. She fell to one knee, blood oozing through her lab coat. More jets were approaching the ship.

"I would have followed you to the end of the world. I trusted you, but you wouldn't tell me the truth. Why?" E had tears in her eyes as well.

A missile hit the remaining structure holding the control tower together, exploding the metal shell of the 10-story structure. A massive portion of the second and third floor hurled across the deck.

Steve looked at E, who just shook her head and looked down, deeply regretting her misplaced trust. A second later she was gone, as a giant chunk of the second floor smashed into her and continued down the deck.

The ship was capsizing and sinking, and it started to roll and list. Steve dodged debris as it slid across the deck over the edge and into the sea. He was helpless, beaten and bloody. He had failed his brother, Anna, E, and all the innocents he was supposed to protect. Every last thing he cared about was gone. He had once again killed the only family he had.

Gaia continued to roll as she submerged, and Steve held Anna's lifeless body tightly as the main deck turned vertically. He began sliding toward the rail closest to the water, slamming into the railing within inches of the ocean, within inches of death. Several more dull thumps rang out and, as if in slow motion, *Gaia* turned upside down and disappeared beneath the surface of the ocean.

Steve hit his head on the arm of the chair and awoke lying on the floor. Someone was banging on the door to his quarters. He looked out the window at *Gaia* in all her glory, still in perfect condition.

"Uncle Steve, are you all right? UNCLE STEVE, OPEN THIS DOOR!"

Steve got to his feet still in shock and slowly opened the door.

"I told you I was going to check up on you."

There was Anna, alive. Steve looked at his hands and the towels he was wearing. It had all been a dream.

"Hey, you've been sleeping for hours. E sent me. She said you'd be mad if we didn't wake you when Howler was off the meds."

Steve grabbed Anna and held her close. He was crying and he didn't want her to know it.

"Okay, get dressed now. Uncle Steve, come on. Oh, and don't forget your wig." She gave him a wink and turned away.

Steve put his hands on his bald head. He'd forgotten that his wig was still sitting in the bathroom.

He was in a daze as he closed the door to his quarters. It was a dream, yet it was so real. The pain was real, too real.

He walked over to the sink and splashed warm water on his face. He shook his head and looked at himself in the mirror.

"I think I got the message," he announced.

Steve got dressed and put his wig back on. Anna must have known for a while about the wig since she didn't seem the least bit surprised.

What else was he thinking that was one way, but actually another?

Anna and E were smart. Was he underestimating them in his efforts to protect them? Was he really protecting them at all? He was keeping his identity a secret and he was playing a dangerous game with the president of the United States. If things didn't start going better, soon they would all be in grave danger.

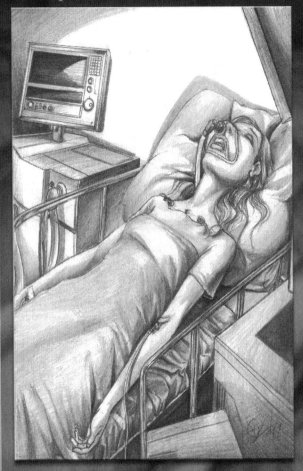

The Death of Jack Cutter

**Steve looked out from the third floor
of the control tower, still lost in deep thought.
Everything on Gaia looked new and unfamiliar
as if it was his first time seeing it.
He took the elevator down to the main deck.**

CHAPTER 7: The Death of Jack Cutter

The door opened onto a stunning vista. In front of him was the vintage town square with its park, grass, trees, and small lake. Surrounding it on three sides were authentic wood and concrete buildings, most of them two and three stories high, and a cobblestone street decorated with authentic streetlamps. Directly across the park was an old-fashioned movie theater.

Parked near the elevator doors were a group of electric scooters always available for anyone who needed to get around the ship quickly. Steve had modeled the first level of *Gaia* after small-town America during the thirties and forties. Several buildings had porches and house numbers painted on the side. The city stretched for about three square city blocks. It was surreal at first, but after a while comfortable and welcoming.

Disneyland's got nothing on us, Steve thought.

He straddled the first scooter in line and headed down the street past the town square. He made a quick right turn at the first intersection, passing in front of the theater then turned left for two blocks before coming to a stop.

E's offices were inside this brownstone. Steve took the elevator to the third floor. The doors opened onto a large room where Anna and E were waiting. Although Steve was still a little in shock from his nightmare, he walked toward them as if nothing was out of the ordinary.

They were sitting on either side of a bed in which Howler was sitting upright and alert. When the monkey saw Steve approaching, he looked him straight in the eye with the same intensity he had in the jungle. Howler's gaze never wavered as he attempted to have an entire conversation with Steve using only his eyes.

"I can't explain it," E said. "He's off all his pain meds, but he's acting like nothing hurts at all. At the same time, his wounds are all but healed. I've never seen anything like it. I was about to put him down, and now … Steve, how did you know?" E was frazzled. It was her turn for some bedrest.

Anna jumped into the conversation. "He can move his fingers and toes, but not his arms or legs. It looks pretty strange. Not much of a monkey anymore, that's for sure."

Steve sat on the edge of the bed to take a closer look at Howler's surgical incisions. "E, I didn't know what would happen when you took him off the drugs. What I can tell you is that he stopped being a typical monkey long before this."

E and Anna had been anxiously wondering what Steve's reaction would be to Howler's condition, and now they stared at Steve. Howler watched E and Anna. Howler sensed from their behavior that Steve was the leader. He also knew that this was his new troop, his new home.

Howler waited patiently while Steve examined his arm, shoulder, and leg. In his life back in the jungle, a wounded member of the troop was of no value, but it was somehow different with this troop. Howler was confused, and he looked at Steve with questioning eyes.

"Don't worry, my friend. We aren't going to let you die. Far from it."

Steve looked Howler directly in the face. There was a level of communication between them stronger than anything Steve had felt with an animal before.

"E, I want you to teach Howler to sign."

"As in sign language?"

"Yes. Choose a vocabulary that gives him the largest range of communication possible. Try to use broad movements where he won't have to use fingers. I want to be able to reproduce this language visually in the simplest terms, with only two straight lines creating each sign. I don't care if you make up some of your own signs. Just make sure it can be reproduced with simple graphics."

"Um, okay, I can do that. I think." E wasn't sure if it was a great opportunity or an impossible task.

Steve was impatient. "Now. Please start now, E." He turned to Anna.

"I have everything cleared up for you to go back to school. You may want to pack." And he was off.

Anna and E stared in silence and simultaneously shrugged. Without comment, they went off in separate directions.

Once back in his office, Steve immediately checked to make sure the government agents had kept their word. He verified on the monitors outside Cutter Technologies and his home that they had in fact left. He checked the video feeds from the last few hours and saw nothing out of the ordinary.

They could always just kidnap Anna once she got back to the States.

Steve pushed that last thought out of his head. Anna knocked on the office door.

"Uncle Steve, I'm ready to go."

"Wow, princess, that was fast."

"I always make sure I can fit everything I'll need in one duffle bag. No biggie."

"Anna, before you go, I have a few things for you." Steve had placed a couple of items on his desk and he picked up one of them. "First, take this necklace and put it on. It has a transponder built into it. If you ever think your life is in danger, press the jewel on the front and hold it for at least fifteen seconds. That will activate a sensor that will alert me no matter where I am. Wherever you are, I'll be there as fast as I can."

Anna was skeptical. "You'll be there?"

"Someone will be there as soon as possible to protect you. Hopefully, it'll be me. And as long as you have that necklace on, I can find you."

She put the necklace on tentatively. "Is someone going to hurt me, Uncle Steve?"

"Absolutely not, Anna. I'm just making sure."

He picked up the next item. "Take this cell phone. I had it enhanced with a few … special features. It never needs charging, has GPS and is a video phone. I'll be able to know where you are and track your vitals at all times."

Steve looked at a monitor on the wall showing the Black Hawk being raised and prepped for flight.

"Your ride is almost ready."

"What else you got for me? Anything with a little more style?" Anna was joking, but Steve wasn't really listening.

"Have a good time at school. I'll talk to you every day I can and I'll see you in a few weeks."

"Whatever, Uncle Steve. I'll be fine." Anna gave him a big hug and kissed his cheek before bouncing out the door.

Steve went to the observation deck on the fourth floor. The Black Hawk lifted off and he waved to Anna as it departed.

He stood watching until the Black Hawk was just a speck in the sky.

He walked quickly to his quarters and got right into bed. There was so much to do in such little time. But he needed a few more hours sleep to gear up for what came next, so he closed his eyes and drifted off.

Steve woke with a start the next morning. He jumped out of bed and ran to the window just to see if everything was all right. The nightmare from his previous nap still fresh in his mind, he was relieved to see the decks of *Gaia* glistening in the bright sunlight. It was a beautiful morning.

The message light on his phone was blinking. It was Anna calling to tell him she had arrived safely and not to worry so much.

Steve went to his office and locked the door. He toggled the switch for the secret door and went inside.

He entered the room containing the exoskeletons, donned his jumpsuit, and attached his rubber headpiece. This time he selected a much lighter exoskeleton, one that lacked the protective covering of armor. Because it was extremely lightweight, it could be worn for prolonged periods of time without fatigue.

The helmet he selected was made from a thinner version of the same black chrome used in all of the exoskeletons. The helmet visor lowered to cover his eyes, leaving the lower half of his face exposed beneath the blue glow of his eyes.

Strand stood straight and still for a moment. He was absorbing all the information flooding into his head through the strands. He took a deep breath and exhaled slowly. As he did, thin traces of blue light raced across the black chrome of the exoskeleton. He could literally feel the power of the suit and the enormous amount of knowledge he was able to process when he wore it. As the energy coursed through his body, he understood his nightmare more clearly than ever, and he knew what steps needed to be taken.

He walked over to a massive bank vault in the right corner of the room. The thick steel door was the kind usually opened by hydraulics, but this one was hanging by a single giant hinge attached to the ceiling. In that position, all 2,000 pounds of door had to be lifted by hand. Fortunately, Strand was a man and something more. With his exoskeleton, he had super strength.

He bent over, grabbed the handle of the door, and lifted it easily over his head. He entered the next room and lowered the door behind him. Small path lighting paved the way through a maze of equipment and wires. A single overhead light illuminated an elaborate high-tech chair in the middle of the room.

Strand sat on the chair and leaned against a headrest. The contacts in the back of his skullcap met with strands coming from the chair. Suddenly, light blue conduits surrounding the chair came to life. They rose like snakes from behind the chair and attached themselves to his helmet. As each did, more blue traces of light surged through the exoskeleton. Conduits connecting him to the machines ran from the chair in all directions and disappeared into the hardware surrounding it.

The path lights leading to the chair slowly dimmed.

Blue traces continued to race across Strand's skullcap and through the exoskeleton. He was now one with the machines in the room.

The strands that helped Steve Cutter become something more than a man were a fine bundle of microscopically thin but highly conductive metal nanotubes shielded with a non-conductive coating. The end of each strand contained thousands of microscopic contacts for easy connection. Once surgically implanted, they created new electrical pathways, a sort of high-tech extension cord.

The strands were designed to mimic the results of research Steve had gathered early in his career studying idiot savants. Many savants demonstrate incredible mental capabilities involving powers of recollection and computation. Each savant has a different skill, but they all share one factor. Parts of their brain have grown together in ways uncommon to a normal brain. In several cases, the different parts have been forced together as a result of severe head trauma.

When Steve first inserted the strands in his body, there was no immediate change. It took a few weeks until the brain started to fully utilize their potential. He tracked each step of strand integration as only a scientist can do by meticulously recording every insight, from moments of clarity to intense periods of introspection and withdrawal.

The end result was Strand, Steve Cutter and something more. He was now a being of superior intellect with the ability to process gigantic amounts of diverse information simultaneously. Strand could think creatively about thousands of things at the same time while also learning, inventing, problem solving, manufacturing, and analyzing. In the years since Strand became fully operational, his capacity for knowledge and aptitude with new skills continued to increase exponentially.

When Steve needed more money to continue his research, he started using his gift with technology to raise the capital. Once he began licensing his ideas, his wealth quickly grew beyond his wildest expectations and Cutter Technologies was born.

His technology was extremely advanced, far beyond anything else on the market. It was quickly adopted by large corporations and the military, and Steve amassed a vast fortune in a short period of time. He invented and created at a faster rate than could be handled by clients. But he loved it so much he couldn't stop. It was a physical manifestation of his lifelong theories as well as validation for all his research. It even helped justify his past actions to some extent.

Before the strands in his head, before Cutter Technologies, before any of the wealth, Steve Cutter was an obsessed scientist. In fact, his obsession was the excuse he used for his antisocial behavior. He refused to participate in society, preferring to hide in his work. He had made himself an outcast, the black sheep of the family, and he liked it that way.

One rainy night ten years ago changed everything.

His older brother Jack had called asking for a simple favor. His wife Sharon was buying a new car in preparation for an important trip the following day. Jack needed Steve to watch Anna for an hour while they picked up the car. But Steve didn't want to be bothered with the responsibility of a child, not even for sixty minutes. He told Jack he was buried in work and that was that.

Steve remembered looking out the window that night, mesmerized by the heavy downpour as he talked to his brother on the phone. He thought it was ridiculous that

Jack insisted on picking up a new car in this weather and at night, and he couldn't understand why Anna didn't just go along.

Within an hour, Jack and Sharon had died in an accident that left Anna in critical condition at the hospital. Anna suffered broken bones, scrapes and bruises over her face and body, and a massive concussion.

The next time Steve saw Anna, she was drowning in a sea of tubes and wires and machines and monitors. Doctors were working around the clock to keep her alive as she drifted in and out of a coma.

Steve recalled standing by her side with tears streaming down his face, convinced she wouldn't survive. Even if she did, she would learn her parents died and she was injured because of him, and she was now his responsibility.

That first day in the emergency room burned more vividly in Steve's memory than any other in his life. He remembered wiping blood from Anna's face with his shirtsleeve, as the nurses and doctors worked furiously and asked him to leave the room until they were finished with the emergency treatments.

He remembered looking at Anna's blood on his hands and thinking, what have I done? There must be a reason for this.

I am only a man, but I will become something more.

Later that night, Steve had collapsed on a waiting room sofa and wept the tears of a man lost in grief and guilt. He was searching for answers, but only found more questions.

Now as Strand sat connected to the sea of machines in his sanctuary on *Gaia*, he wondered if he was still doing all he could to protect Anna.

Was he keeping her safe with his behavior or putting her in harm's way?

That question became a realization. If he truly wanted to protect Anna at all times, he would always have to be Strand, and that meant the days of Steve Cutter were coming to an end.

When Steve finally emerged from his sanctuary, he had spent the better part of three days as Strand. He stayed absorbed in the machines, constantly researching and designing, emerging from the lab for brief periods to eat and sleep.

One creation already in use was a miniature wheelchair with skateboard wheels for Howler. The happy monkey was now scooting around the lab without assistance.

E had spent the three days teaching Howler four basic signs: one for food, one for water, one for pain, and one for appreciation. He was able to learn these quickly and easily.

It wasn't long before Howler was developing his own signs and teaching them to E. He clearly had his own language. After a while, it was unclear whether E was teaching Howler or Howler was teaching E.

E also had discovered that many acid-based compounds could neutralize the toxic gas. Virtually any type of acid would work, even in its weakest form.

As soon as Steve learned of this, he dialed Vitimani's office and asked to speak to his friend. He was put on hold again, and he spoke again to the nothingness of a call on hold. He explained the discovery, honoring the promise he had made in his previous phone call. He hung up, still not quite knowing if anyone was listening or if he was simply talking to himself. Either way, he had done what he said he would.

Steve went to the main deck and watched his employees riding scooters through the town square and strolling along sidewalks. The longer he watched, the more it became painfully clear that although *Gaia* was created as an extension of Cutter Technologies, events over the past few weeks had changed everything. The world knew of Strand, and Steve Cutter could no longer protect those that he held near and dear. His secret identity was now a dangerous liability.

He remembered the feeling of utter helplessness from his nightmare and running desperately from snakes in Brazil. He knew Anna wouldn't have been at risk in both circumstances if he was Strand instead of Steve Cutter.

Things would have to change. Mojave would remain home to Cutter Technologies and Steve Cutter, while *Gaia* would serve as the permanent home of Strand. The crew would have to leave the ship immediately, save for a select few.

Gaia steamed north at full speed and reached Miami several days later. Steve already had told the crew the staff-restructuring news, with a good number of them preparing to relocate operations to the Mojave. All six of the hovercraft were loaded, shuttling people, paper, and equipment to the Miami shoreline with the help of the Black Hawks.

There was a flurry of activity onboard as everything proceeded in an organized fashion. Massive amounts of additional supplies and crates were being delivered to the ship by a steady stream of Hercules helicopters for the few that would be remaining.

Inside the ship, construction crews were hustling to finish changes that Steve wanted complete before leaving port again. The lower decks directly under the control tower were separated from the rest of the ship with locking metal doors. The few crew members remaining on *Gaia* would only have access to the control room and engine room.

Strand lay silently in his chair in the sanctuary. He was busier than ever working and creating, but a casual observer would assume he was asleep as he remained perfectly still amid the luminous blue traces flashing along his exoskeleton and the fiber optic conduits connecting the chair with the surrounding equipment.

He continuously scanned all media outlets around the world, not only to assess what was going on but also to see what the president's next move would be. It had been ten days since Strand met with him and time was running out. The two-week commitment would be fulfilled and he would release the second chapter of the Strand Prophecy.

Strand abruptly zeroed in on a breaking news story. The Center for Disease Control was holding an emergency press conference. Dr. Jennifer Gold was making a statement concerning the incident in the Brazilian jungle. Strand patched in the audio feed.

"I have a short prepared statement to read before I take any questions," she began. The middle-aged woman looked like she had spent most of her life in the lab. She was a scientist to the core and appeared uncomfortable making the presentation.

"We regret to inform you that Dr. Ned Vitimani, a man who gave this country decades of faithful public service, has passed away. He was instrumental in forming the CDC's counter-terrorism preparedness unit. He died this morning of injuries sustained in a helicopter accident in the Brazilian rainforest several weeks ago." Gold stopped and gathered herself. She was on the verge of tears, but managed to continue.

"Our sincerest condolences go out to the entire Vitimani family. He will be sorely missed. The world has lost a great man of science."

Strand watched Gold closely. He believed that she believed the words coming out of her mouth, but he didn't buy it for a second. Strand immediately started searching government and military databases for confirmation Vitimani was really dead.

Gold continued, "We were able to recover some of the scientific data Dr. Vitimani was collecting from the crash site. We're conducting tests on the material as we speak. Although it appears to have some unusual characteristics, it poses no danger to the general public. We will be releasing the results as soon as they're complete."

Strand was seething with rage. The fiber optic conduits connecting his chair to the surrounding equipment glowed with a higher intensity and lit up the machines as they reached full capacity, clicking and humming in a strained machine melody.

Strand analyzed the government and military data faster than he'd ever been able to before. He was done playing politics; he had to find out if Vit was dead.

It was nearly midnight as Strand stood gazing out from atop the ten-story control tower. Even in the moonlight *Gaia* was a magnificent ship. A warm breeze from the east blew Strand's cloak aside, and moonlight reflected off the black chrome while traces of blue light streaked across his exoskeleton.

Strand waited for the missile cycle to finish its internal diagnostic check several decks below. He spent the time methodically reviewing every detail of what he needed to accomplish that night. He checked flight plans, weather forecasts at his destinations, and itineraries for each city once he was on the ground. He confirmed that all language translators were working.

There were two days left in his commitment to the president. He would keep his promise, but there was nothing wrong with letting the world know the next chapter was coming.

The moment the diagnostic check on the missile cycle finished, the rear wall of the fourth floor opened. It lowered into position and a launch gurney carrying the missile cycle tilted toward the night sky. He looked once more across the deck of *Gaia*.

"Forgive me," Strand told the ship, "but if something goes wrong tonight, your resting place will be at the bottom of the sea."

The engines on the cycle roared to life below him. He looked down and jumped, landing on the lowered fourth floor wall next to the missile cycle. His pulse was racing for the part he loved the most. He leaped onto the missile and an instant later the rockets fired. Strand shot off into the darkness and across the Atlantic.

The missile cycle was modified for this mission with additional fuel tanks. Strand leaned forward behind the windshield and accelerated to 775 miles per hour. After breaking the sound barrier with a sonic boom, he checked the internal operations of the missile to confirm all was functioning as designed. If the missile cycle failed at this point, he had no chance of survival. This far away from *Gaia*, the modified exoskeleton was too heavy and would sink in the ocean too quickly.

At the same time, this was the safest place to clock the top speed without any witnesses. Strand throttled the missile eastward at full speed. The engines roared louder and louder the more it accelerated.

Strand watched the speedometer gradually creep higher.

800, 900, 1,000, 1,150, 1,250, 1,350, 1,450....

At 1,525 miles per hour he broke the sound barrier again at Mach Two, and the sky exploded with another sonic boom. Strand would be in London very soon.

Europe

It was a fairly quiet Saturday evening under Big Ben.
A few tourists watched the hands of the great clock move and strike ten.
A sixteen-year-old boy named Kevin was not impressed.
It was just a clock, after all.

CHAPTER 8: Europe

A European vacation wasn't his idea of a good time in the first place, but England had proved especially boring.

While Kevin appreciated the time and money his parents spent on the family trip, he would've been just as happy to stay in America. There were just so many old buildings and historic tours he could take before he had his fill.

"Come on, let's go," Kevin said to his younger brother Paul. "We already saw this clock blow up in *V for Vendetta* anyway."

"Wait a second, one more picture," Paul said.

"It's not even gonna turn out, dork. It's too dark already."

Just as they turned to leave there was a thunderous

explosion in the distance. Passers-by ducked and covered their heads.

Paul was terrified. "What was that? A bomb?"

"I don't think so," Kevin said, and put his arm around his brother to protect him.

Air raid sirens began to whine, a sound Londoners had rarely heard since the end of World War II. The meaning was the same: something uninvited was approaching by air.

Strand reduced the speed of the missile cycle as he passed the coastline of the United Kingdom. The re-entry into local airspace resulted in a sizable sonic boom. When he reached downtown London and Big Ben, he slowed the missile cycle further before leaping off.

It happened to catch Kevin's eye. "Look, someone just jumped off Big Ben!"

Strand slapped a device halfway down the clock tower as he fell. He landed on the sidewalk directly in front of the palace. His cloak covered him completely as he remained in a crouched position for a moment. The friction of supersonic flight had heated his cloak and steam now began rising from it.

A few of the tourists ran over to Strand.

"He's over there!" Paul shouted.

"We should go help," Kevin said.

Strand rose slowly to his feet as a small crowd gathered around him in a circle. The cloak still covered the entire exoskeleton, and his glowing blue eyes under his hood were the only thing visible to bystanders.

"It's Strand!" Kevin yelled. "Paul, it's Strand!" He ran across the street toward Big Ben.

Kevin's father grabbed him by the back of the jacket. "You're not going anywhere. We're getting out of here."

"No, Dad! That's Strand and he needs help. Let go of

me."

Strand looked around at the startled faces of those gathered around him. They stared in awe, seemingly oblivious to the blaring of the air raid horns and police sirens on approaching squad cars.

"I said no, Kevin," his father said. But Kevin managed to squirm away and bolt in Strand's direction as cars raced by. "Get back here!" His father was left holding an empty jacket in his hands.

Strand saw Kevin break away from his father from his location under Big Ben. He also saw a taxi round the corner headed right for the boy.

Kevin was a smart kid, but in London cars drive on the opposite side of the street than they do in America, so he didn't think to check the other direction as he crossed the street.

At the same time, the oncoming taxi driver was busy looking over at the crowd surrounding Big Ben. He finally turned back just as Kevin ran in front of his cab. He was going too fast to stop in time, but he slammed on the brakes anyway and braced for impact.

Strand jumped with the maximum force his exoskeleton could deliver and literally flew across the street. A split second before the cab reached Kevin, Strand darted in between and grabbed him, wrapping his arms around him and then turned in mid-air.

The taxi hit Strand in the back and skidded to a stop. Strand was already airborne, flipping over the roof of the vehicle as it passed.

Strand straightened his body and fired the shoulder rockets. He lowered gently to the ground with Kevin in his arms. He put him down on the sidewalk and opened the bottom half of his facemask.

"Are you all right?"

"Yeah, I'm fine," Kevin said nervously. "Thanks … Strand."

Strand turned to the clock tower. Time was running out to complete his mission. He grabbed Kevin and leaped back to the other side of the street. When he was back where he started, he put Kevin down. Strand smiled at Kevin as the boy's family ran over to join them.

"Next time, you look both ways when you cross the street, okay?"

"Yes, sir, mister … Mr. Strand."

The crowd had grown steadily during the entire ordeal. Many were now able to see that a man was behind the mask.

Strand stood up and looked back and forth at the people who had gathered. A few police cars appeared around the corner, but they were stuck on the fringe of what was becoming a traffic jam.

"I am Strand," he began. "I am the harbinger." He turned and faced Big Ben and then pointed his right hand at the concrete sidewalk. The electric blue tubes running down his forearm surged. Seconds later, four blue lasers shot out from above his knuckles and began burning a symbol into the concrete. It consisted of a large hexagon with an elongated "S" slashed through the center.

The missile cycle was circling back to pick up Strand as a few policemen tried to make it through the mob.

Strand turned to the crowd. "You will receive a password that will open the second chapter of my paper at this very spot in exactly three days."

He looked down at the boy. "Kevin, what did I just say?"

"You said to come back here in three days to get the password for the next chapter."

Several more police cars skidded around the corner

and began to block off the area. The missile cycle had almost arrived.

Those in the crowd closest to Strand were looking at the strange symbol burned into the concrete. Everyone else kept staring at Strand as if waiting for his next amazing feat.

Strand finished. "You must all stay out of direct moonlight if you want to remain as you are now." Strand closed the bottom half of his face mask, crouched down and jumped high into the air and onto the missile cycle as it flew by. He shot quickly into the sky over Big Ben and out of town.

Dozens of policemen on the ground looked up helplessly at the dark figure flying far away into the night.

Air raid sirens were still wailing as news crews arrived on the scene, cameramen jumping out of vans to capture one last glimpse of Strand.

Kevin's mother slapped her son on the head.

"Ow!" Kevin winced and rubbed his skull.

"If you ever do that again, I'm going to kill you first."

Strand zipped across the English Channel toward the Eiffel Tower. The element of surprise would only work for so long. The missile slowed over Paris with the crack of a sonic boom.

He dropped in front of the Eiffel Tower and repeated the same sequence he performed at Big Ben. This time, things went off without incident. A crowd instantly gathered around him and grew larger and larger until Strand was surrounded on all sides. He burned the same symbol into the concrete and delivered the same message, only this time in French.

The missile circled back around and moments later Strand had left another stunned crowd of people behind staring up at the sky. He accelerated to supersonic speed and flew the missile low to the ground.

Within thirty minutes, a sonic boom announced his arrival in Rome. This time, bystanders ran to the Colosseum and onto the field where a cloaked figure was burning a symbol into the stone floor.

Strand waited for a large crowd to flock inside the ancient structure as the missile cycle circled back. He delivered his message and jumped back on the missile as it passed overhead.

As soon as Strand was at cruising speed again, he checked military channels for any activity. It was immediately clear that all of Europe was on high alert. There was no need to go to Russia or China. Strand had made his point. He was convinced no one who saw him tonight would question the authenticity of the next chapter when he released it, but he still wanted to make one more stop before the night ended.

He arrived in Madrid within minutes, and after another sonic boom headed for Puerta de Alcala, a grand monument at the entrance to the city. News travels fast, and while no one knew Strand's next destination, people all across Europe were converging on historic landmarks ready to greet him if he arrived.

The crowd at Puerta de Alcala was quite large already. Strand had definitely lost the element of surprise, so he scanned for police and military activity before deciding to land. As he had done at each stop, he placed a device high on the building above before dropping to the ground.

He landed on his feet, crouching to one knee to absorb the impact. He stood up in the center of the large crowd. Many of them had makeshift cloaks and hoods on to protect themselves from the moonlight, and they started to applaud.

As others joined in, Strand was overcome with emotion.

When the cheers and applause finally died down, a silence thick with awe took over. No air raid sirens, no police cars, no flashing lights, just the quiet support of thousands of people.

He pointed his arm at the concrete, the blue lasers went to work burning in his symbol, and soon it was complete. Strand stood with the wind giving the crowd brief glimpses of his exoskeleton. He pulled the hood back from his head, exposing his faceplate and metal helmet. He raised his arms with his palms facing up and stood for a moment without moving.

Some in the crowd looked frightened, but most were intrigued. Strand loosened his cloak and retracted the lower half of his faceplate, exposing his mouth and chin. He retracted the armor from his forearms to make sure they knew he was a man.

"Only a man," he said. "Only a man ... and something more."

Strand closed the faceplate and the armor around his forearms and slowly pulled the cloak back over his head. He was once again just a dark figure in the shadows, except for the electric blue luminous glow coming from his eyes.

The missile was closing in. The crowd turned around to watch it approaching.

A young Spanish man stepped forward. He was wearing a light brown cloak and hood. He removed his hood as he approached Strand.

"We will be here in three days," he said in fractured English and then paused. "Vaya con dios. Vaya con dios ... Strand."

Strand nodded and jumped to meet the missile. He looked back proudly as he flew away. He never counted on any support from those he was trying to protect, but there it was as plain as day. No jet fighters, no police helicopters, no aggressive threats, just love and support.

He circled back around the monument and waved to the crowd of supporters gazing up at him.

He throttled both engines to full power, fired the booster rockets and headed north. The rockets lit up the sky surrounding Puerta de Alcala. Strand quickly disappeared into the night sky leaving only a sonic boom behind.

Strand maintained a high altitude within areas tracked by military radar. This ensured that all radar stations along the coast of Europe knew exactly the direction the cycle was heading. He wanted it to appear he was going due north toward Great Britain, and let the press speculate on where his next stop would be.

But about 300 miles north of Madrid and back over the Atlantic Ocean, he dove from 30,000 feet to fifty feet from the water. Flying below the radar, he changed course, turned southwest, and accelerated to 1,550 miles per hour. Strand would be back on *Gaia* in a few hours.

He accessed the computers on *Gaia* and scanned the most recent news updates concerning any "Strand sightings." Sure enough, it was a media feeding frenzy, and the world was listening. Strand smiled behind his mask.

Kevin was at the center of the media spotlight in London. Reporters from around the world had set up satellite trucks in front of Big Ben and were broadcasting live updates. They bombarded Kevin with endless questions, and he was looking a bit haggard.

A clueless reporter from the BBC pushed his way to the front. "We understand you almost died because of Strand. Can you tell us how that makes you feel?"

"What? No. What are you talking about? He saved me from getting run over by a taxi."

"You were injured as a result of the incident. Will you be taking legal action?"

"That taxi would have killed me! What are you talking about?" Kevin made a face at the reporter.

The self-absorbed reporter continued his questioning, striking a pose. "I'm told you have a message from Strand for the people of the world. We understand Strand gave this message to you personally, isn't that correct? Can you tell us what that message is?" He was determined to present his story in the most sensational way possible.

Kevin was used to it by now and getting weary as he replied. "Strand just said to be back here in three days to get the password for the next chapter, and to protect your body from the moonlight. That's all he told me." He suddenly realized how the reporter had presented the question and a flash of anger crossed his face. "Stop twisting this around and listen! Man, you're a lousy repor...."

The reporter cut Kevin off and started to walk toward the mark in the concrete, with the cameraman trailing right behind him.

Strand chuckled. "Good for you, Kevin."

The second chapter of Strand's paper was ready to be posted globally. Strand knew it was only a matter of hours before the Internet community pushed it to every corner of the planet.

For a moment, Strand was Steve Cutter in an exoskeleton, riding a missile at 1,550 miles an hour in the middle of the Atlantic Ocean fifty feet above the water. Plumes of water erupted in the air behind the missile cycle. He looked in awe at the moonlight reflecting off the vast ocean. Steve was poised to release a document that billions of people were desperately waiting for. It seemed surreal, but at the same time quite natural, as if it was meant to be.

Strand sent the command for the computers to upload the chapter to the Internet. By the time he landed, the second chapter would be global.

Strand was done playing politics.

CHAPTER 9

Welcome to Wonderland

The next day the Wall Street Journal ran an ad: "Investor wanted for Advanced Brazilian Toxin Research." It was the president, requesting contact with Strand.

CHAPTER 9: Welcome to Wonderland

Strand was in his sanctuary on *Gaia*, reclining in his chair. He contemplated what to do next.

"Guess you're not too thrilled with me, Mr. President," Strand said out loud.

He was searching military hospital records when he found something odd. Dr. Vitimani's file was changed subsequent to him being admitted.

The on-call doctor initially reported Vitimani alive but suffering from severe paralysis. A later report listed him as dead on arrival. Fortunately, Strand found the original entries still on the backup drive. A day later, they would have been overwritten and lost forever.

Someone had also assigned a new patient number to Vitimani in the official records after his supposed time of death. Even if Vitimani was listed as officially deceased, they still needed a number to track his actual status. Finding the number was Strand's best lead yet.

He used the data to track down a "John Doe" at the American Red Cross Facility on the Naval Submarine Base in Kings Bay, Georgia. If the patient really was Vitimani and if he was still alive, he would be here.

Strand unplugged himself and went to the changing room. He needed some quality time as Steve Cutter. He yearned for a different perspective on what had just occurred. Maybe Vit was alive, maybe not, but he had to find out.

Meanwhile, the president wanted to see him. Steve changed into street clothes and unlocked the front door to his office.

A few minutes later, E popped her head through the door. "Knock, knock."

"Hey, E, come on in."

She sat down in front of Steve without saying a word. She just stared at him.

"What's going on, E? Why are you looking at me that way?"

"Nobody is left on the ship, Steve. Everyone is reassigned. Are you sending me away as well?"

"No, no, absolutely not, you're staying here with me."

"Okay … this is a big ship, Steve. Isn't it going to get lonely out here?" E paused. The long silence spoke volumes. E's eyes were welling up with tears as she continued.

"I would have followed you to the end of the world, yet you refuse to tell me the truth, Steve. Why?"

Steve looked at her in disbelief.

Those were the exact words she said to him in his dream.

E dried her eyes and looked up. "I can't do this. I can't work without trust, not with you. It will be the end of me."

Steve flashed back to his dream, E bloody and bruised and being swept away by the debris from *Gaia's* exploding control tower.

E stood up abruptly and reached into her lab coat. Steve knew the split second before it happened what she was about to do. She was going to hand him a letter of resignation. He had to act fast.

"Tonight, E. Tonight, I will show you."

A glimmer of hope and a small smile crossed her face as she kept her hand in her pocket. There was another long silence, and then tears began streaming down her cheeks again.

Steve looked deeply into her eyes. "What if I was protecting you?"

E was taken back. The look on Steve's face was a little frightening, but she leaned forward across his desk until she was two feet from his face.

"My life, my choice, do you understand me, Steve Cutter? Even if our lives are in jeopardy, it is my choice whether or not to participate.

"But if you've put me in danger without my knowledge, while I have stood by you, never demanding answers, then you have abused my trust."

Steve tried to ease her fears. "You're absolutely right, and you would have every right to be angry, but I swear there was no threat then. But now it could get dangerous."

The tension on E's face wasn't going away, even as the anger was.

"The president wants to see me, and I don't think he's happy with me. In fact, I'm pretty sure he's furious. Funny thing is ... I don't really care. I'm not a politician and I've stopped trying to be one."

"Steve, what in the world are you talking about?" She sat down again.

Steve rubbed his chin and looked at his desk as he explained. "Well, I wrote this paper about accelerated evolution … and now I've written a follow-up chapter, and he isn't too thrilled with me publishing it."

He slowly raised his head to check the look on E's face. "You wrote a paper? What in the …." And then it hit E like a ton of bricks. She involuntarily jumped to her feet with a look of shock on her face. She took a step back and fell over the chair across from Steve's desk.

It was as though all of the pieces of the puzzle had fallen into place at one time. The rockets, the long stretches of time Steve disappeared from *Gaia*, the secret technology hidden below deck, most of the crew being reassigned, all of it made sense.

E was the closest thing Steve had to a sister, and her reaction and her decision to stay or leave were crucial. Yet despite all of his technology and capabilities, there was nothing he could do to affect the outcome. It was her decision to make, and she alone had to be comfortable with it.

E's expression changed, and Steve could see the hurt in her eyes.

He stood up and started to pace the room. "I never wanted to become anything more than Steve Cutter."

E leaned back in the chair as Steve continued. "Did I ever tell you why Anna's parents were killed? It was because of me. My brother asked me to take care of her for a few hours … and I refused. And my decision put them in the wrong place at the wrong time."

Steve stopped pacing and looked at E.

"Anna was the innocent victim in all of this and she suffered the greatest loss. But she's also taught me about love and fatherhood and pride and pain and joy and fear. She is the most precious gift, E ... but her parents had to die for me to learn that lesson.

"Things are different now. I know something bad is going to happen and that the innocent will suffer. But this time ... I can do something about it."

E stood up and stepped backward, shaking her head. "Whatever you say, Steve."

"Meet me on deck at 8:00, and I promise I'll show you everything."

E left the office without saying a word.

Strand stood on the deck of *Gaia* later that night, unsure if E would even show up. He was wearing his exoskeleton under his cloak, and his hood was pulled back just enough to show his face, but not enough to expose the helmet. He was something more than a man, but more Steve Cutter than usual.

All of the armor on his exoskeleton remained in a retracted position. It now looked like a second set of metal bones had been attached to the outside of his jumpsuit.

He waited on the front side of the control tower. Behind the wall of the fourth floor, the missile cycle was running through its diagnostic routine prior to launch.

E appeared in a doorway at the base of the tower and walked toward Strand. He heard her approaching, and when she was within ten feet of him, he spoke.

"E, stop there, please." He kept his back turned to her.

"Are you staying ... or are you leaving?"

"Does Anna know?" E asked.

"No, and I trust that you will not tell her."

E paused for a moment and took a deep breath. "I'm leaving."

Steve couldn't hide the hurt in his voice. "I understand, E. Take care of yourself."

Strand started walking away from E. He knew things were about to get much more dangerous, and she had to either want to stay or leave immediately. She had made her choice and this was the end for her.

"I would like to conclude my research on the specimens from the jungle at the Mojave facility," E said. "I'm waiting to get some information back from an assistant named Rettuc in Mojave, and then I can finish. It's important work I know you're going to need."

"That work was finished last week, E."

The missile cycle's internal diagnostics were complete and the fourth floor wall started to lower.

"Completed by whom, Steve? I'm still waiting for the results from Rettuc's tests to complete the project."

"From now on, E, any question you ask me, I will answer. But you have to be ready for what the answer might be." Strand still kept his back to E.

The missile gurney was positioning for launch as the back wall finished opening.

"I am ready," E insisted. "After this afternoon, I don't think anything could surprise me." There was a dash of sarcasm in her voice.

"I completed the work, E. I am Rettuc. Rettuc is Cutter spelled backwards." Strand finally turned around to face her.

The missile cycle roared into the night sky, erupting from behind the control tower.

E flinched and looked over her shoulder. She couldn't spot the missile, but she knew it was there. "What? You are Rettuc? What have I been waiting for? Why am I here? Why do you even need me?"

The missile cycle made its turn and headed toward Strand. It rolled over and flew upside down as it approached.

E spotted the missile heading directly for them. She failed to hear the door behind her open. A wheeled robot raced by carrying a very large duffle bag before handing it to Strand. E stared in disbelief. Between the missile and the robot, she didn't know what to think anymore.

Strand looked over at E. "Maybe you should have asked that question first. Ask yourself if anything around here happens by accident, and if you know all that you think you know. Be sure of this decision, E."

He walked slowly toward her. The closer he got, the more she saw the glowing blue on his exoskeleton.

The missile had almost reached *Gaia* and E could hear the jet engine whining. Strand slung the duffle bag over his shoulder. E looked nervously at him. He was not paying any attention to the cycle that was fast approaching.

"If you're comfortable with your decision," Steve said, "then you must leave before I return." E could hear one of the huge elevators lifting a Black Hawk to the deck. "That Black Hawk doesn't need a pilot. I can fly it by remote wherever I am." He paused. "I'm hoping to bring something back, and if I'm successful, it will put you in danger. Make up your mind, but whatever your decision, there's no turning back."

E could see robots getting the Black Hawk ready for liftoff, and they moved around the aircraft with the grace of a skilled ground crew. She was overwhelmed and didn't know what to look at first: Strand, the missile cycle, the Black Hawk, or the robots.

Steve again gazed into E's eyes. "I don't want you to leave, but if you stay, you have to do so for the right reasons."

E's eyes flowed with tears again.

Steve glanced up at the approaching missile. He couldn't help but smile. "I love this part."

The armor from the exoskeleton closed around him. The visor lowered into place and the faceplate covered his mouth and chin. The only thing visible now was the eerie glow of his electric blue eyes. Steve was no longer present. He was only Strand now.

He crouched and jumped just as the missile flew overhead. In a moment, Strand disappeared into the night sky.

E stood motionless, looking over at the robots busily prepping the Black Hawk. More robots emerged carrying E's experiments and baggage toward the helicopter.

She felt like Alice in Wonderland. Nothing seemed real, but at the same time, everything seemed more real than ever. She dropped the papers she was holding in her hand, and they fluttered away in the wind.

One last robot brought Howler up on deck. The monkey was fighting the whole way with the one good arm and one good leg he still had. He managed to wiggle free, but he just fell to the deck, unable to stand or crawl. He was utterly helpless.

The robot tried to help him up, but he kicked, flailed, and howled loudly. E looked back and forth at the robot and Howler over and over again, and the fog instantly cleared in her mind.

She turned around to the robots loading the Black Hawk. "Robots?"

The robots all stopped and came to attention.

"Stop what you're doing and return everything to the lab and to my quarters immediately."

E looked up at the night sky in the direction Strand had flown. "This Cheshire cat isn't going anywhere," she said.

Traveling at 500 miles per hour a mere twenty feet off the surface of the ocean, Strand smiled widely behind his faceplate and spoke. "Welcome to Wonderland."

COTAR or Cognitive Transfer and Autonomous Rebirth

Strand flew low and took his time
reaching the submarine base.
Even though it was located fairly close to
where Gaia was currently anchored,
he had to navigate carefully
to avoid detection on military radar.

CHAPTER 10: COTAR or Cognitive Transfer and Autonomous Rebirth

He landed the missile cycle in a wooded area a mile outside the fence surrounding the base and proceeded to camouflage the missile cycle with branches.

Strand worked his way cautiously up to the fence. When he was sure no one was watching, he leapt over the fence and landed in a crouched position. He quickly bolted to a small patch of brush before squatting on one knee to examine the older buildings that were nearby inside the base.

It had not been easy to find the hospital "annex" where Strand believed Vitimani was being held. Although it was definitely a part of the Navy base, it was run by a covert agency much like the CIA, and the records were not kept in the hospital database.

After hours of painstaking scanning, Strand had found a reference to it in a supply log. It listed the delivery of a bed and other hospital equipment to the annex within the last few weeks.

Strand could not be certain if Vit was there, but everything seemed to add up. The annex at the far corner of the base was an older brick building that hadn't been used much since the 1970s. Two guards were stationed outside the small two-room structure. There was an office for nurses and the infirmary where, he guessed, Vit would be.

Strand flipped on a digital magnification system built into his helmet and spent some time observing. He monitored the movement of the guards to check for a pattern and watched the lights go on and off inside the annex to determine how often the nurses went into the infirmary. He also noted the gauge on a large propane tank one hundred feet from the annex, which indicated it was full. Then he kneeled back down in the brush and waited.

At exactly three in the morning, Strand came out of hiding and walked slowly through the darkness toward the annex. The guards were on the other side of the building, leaning against a Humvee, talking.

Strand raised his arm, aimed his lasers at the propane tank, and fired. He watched the back of the tank begin to glow as the lasers heated the metal. A moment later the tank exploded in a ball of fire.

Strand immediately went over and punched a large hole in the brick wall of the annex and then crawled inside.

The propane tank was ablaze as the night nurse ran outside toward the guards, who looked confused and a bit rattled. One of the guards listened to instructions on his radio before calling out to the nurse.

"We've been ordered to stay by our vehicle. That includes you, ma'am."

The nurse joined the guards by the Humvee. They watched the fire, mystified.

Looking around inside, Strand could tell the building had been converted several times over the years. The presence of hundreds of boxes and crates suggested it was last used as a storage facility. Most of the contents had been pushed to one side of the room so the other half could be converted into an infirmary.

In the center of the room, an overhead light illuminated a single hospital bed. It was bordered on all sides by plastic sheets hanging from the ceiling, as if whoever was in the bed was contagious.

Strand marched up and parted the plastic.

There before him, almost unrecognizable, lay Vitimani.

His relief and joy at seeing his friend alive was quickly replaced with rage over being lied to by the government. Blue traces surged in his exoskeleton.

The upper portion of Vit's face and the rest of his head were bandaged. Strand couldn't tell if it was from the helicopter accident or some kind of exploratory surgery. A life support system and an oxygen tank clicked and whirred beside the bed. Strand noticed an additional six reserve tanks of oxygen tucked beneath the bed.

He had to work fast. Reaching into his enormous duffle bag, Strand pulled out a small metal device with ten long extensions, five on each side. He lifted Vit's head and placed the device at the back of Vit's neck. It abruptly came to life and began attaching itself to Vit's skull. One by one, the metal extensions snaked over the top of his head, around his face, above his lips, and across his collar bone. The final two extended under Vit's arms and across his chest.

Strand retracted his faceplate and leaned over. "Vit, it's Steve Cutter. I know what's wrong with you, and I can't imagine what you must be feeling. There's no way of repairing the nerves, but I can offer you a new life. I have developed a cognitive mechanical interface technology that will allow you mobility and speech, not only as a man, but as something more."

He paused and let Vit process the information.

"I've just attached a device to you. Try moving your leg."

The leg didn't budge, but the device registered Vit's attempt to move it; a small green LED light blinked on and off. Strand knew this meant he would be able to communicate with Vit even though his friend was unable to speak.

"Okay, Vit, I have a question for you. It's the most important question you'll have to answer for the rest of your life. If the answer is yes, try moving your leg, and I'll know."

Strand took a deep breath and continued. "Do you want to live?"

It seemed like an eternity as Strand watched and waited for an answer. The solitude, trauma, and helplessness had obviously taken its toll onVit.

"Vit, if you live, you will be able to prevent what's happened to you from happening to anyone else. The government is hiding all of this, pretending it didn't happen, but if we do nothing, innocent civilians will be killed."

"Vit, I'm asking you this one more time ... do you want to live?"

The light flashed.

"Okay, that's all I needed to know. Now let's get you out of here, buddy."

Strand lifted him from the bed and lowered him gently into the duffle bag on the floor. He removed the IV tubes from Vitimani's arms and strapped him to a thin plastic board at the bottom.

"This is going to be a bit rough. I'm sorry, but we're on a military base, and getting out may be tougher than getting in."

Strand pulled a cord on the side of the bag. Sacks built into the sides inflated around Vit, providing insulation and padding to keep him secure during the trip.

"Vit, I'm going to close the duffle bag and carry you on my back. Hang in there, buddy. I'll see you again in no time."

Strand stood up straight and carefully hoisted the duffle bag over his back. He fastened the strap across his chest, closed his faceplate, and walked over to the reserve oxygen tanks.

He found the regulator on top of the first tank and tore it off. The oxygen hissed as it began escaping into the room. Strand repeated this with the other tanks.

Carrying Vitimani, Strand exited from the back of the building and carefully checked to make sure no surprise treats were waiting. The immediate area was deserted.

Once at a safe distance from the annex, Strand turned around and fired his lasers into the hole in the brick wall.

A split second later, the oxygen ignited and the building exploded.

Strand felt the heat from the giant fireball on his back as he leaped in the air toward the perimeter of the base. As he jumped over the fence, additional explosions of stored ammunition lit up the night sky.

Strand sprinted to his missile cycle hidden in the brush and set Vitimani down on the ground. He unzipped the bag and leaned over.

"Sorry for the rough ride, but it's gonna get worse before it gets better. Think you can handle it?"

The green light blinked twice.

"The next time I open this bag is the instant I start to make you better."

He zipped the bag shut and walked over to the missile cycle.

Strand knew he couldn't risk using the launch rockets right now. They were too bright and too loud.

He reached under the missile and lifted it over his head. The jet engine sprung to life. Strand sprinted a few steps, arched his back, and hurled it into the air. The engine swiftly took over and the missile circled back to pick him up.

Strand ran over to the doctor and slung him over his back, attaching the strap across his chest.

"Here we go, Vit. This is my favorite part. And one day … you will join me as a missile rider."

He jumped on and moments later they were riding the missile. They streaked across the landscape at 350 miles per hour, staying twenty feet off the ground to avoid radar detection.

Strand looked back at the fire burning in the distance. He saw the lights of helicopters just reaching the scene.

He accelerated the missile cycle to the edge of the

sound barrier and disappeared into the darkness of the night.

The sun was peeking over the horizon by the time Strand could see *Gaia*. He had taken the safest route back, which took a lot longer than simply flying straight back from the base in Georgia.

As he passed over the ship, he leapt off with Vit on his back, sprinted over to the control tower, and disappeared inside.

A minute later, the elevator opened and Strand walked onto the first deck. Streams of gray morning light filtered through the glass ceiling and illuminated the park.

He marched across the park and entered one of the buildings on the other side. He carried Vitimani to the second floor and opened the windows.

"We're here, Vit."

Strand rolled a hospital bed over to the window and locked the wheels. He unzipped the duffle bag and released the straps securing Vitimani to the board. He slowly lifted him onto the mattress. He angled the bed to face out the window and tilted the back up so his friend could see into the park below. Finally, he hooked a wire on the metal device up to a bulb hanging from the ceiling.

"Vit, I'm going to leave this device on for a while so we can communicate. When you try to move your leg now, this green light will illuminate above you. Does that sound like a good idea to you?"

Strand looked up and the green light came on.

"Glad to hear that. I'm gonna take your bandages off now and see what's going on, okay?"

The green light came on again.

Strand retracted his body armor and took off his cloak. He leaned over the bed and slowly removed the bandages covering Vit's head.

Blood had soaked through the material, forming a red line running diagonally from the top of his head to the left side of his face, ending just above his eyebrow.

As Strand finished removing the bandages, he saw that half of the doctor's head was shaved, revealing a surgical incision that mirrored the bloodstain on the bandages.

"Vit, were you hurt in the jungle?"

The green light flashed.

"You have a serious head injury. Did you get that from the helicopter crash?"

The light stayed dark.

"Do you know if you had surgery?"

No light.

Strand was furious. He could tell what had happened. Someone had performed exploratory surgery on Vit to determine the effects of the toxin, then reported him dead to cover up what had taken place in Brazil.

Steve shined a light at Vit's eyes. The right eye was responding, but the left eye wasn't. Steve put his hand over Vit's right eye and looked out the window.

"Can you see the park?"

The green light didn't flash.

Steve put his palm over Vit's left eye.

"Can you see the park now?"

The green light went on.

"One day, my friend, you will tell the world what they did to you, I promise."

The green light flashed twice.

"It's time for us to begin. It's time for you to become something more than you were, something more than you could ever imagine." Strand stopped for a moment as the green light flashed repeatedly.

"I have developed a cognitive machine interface; it is biomechanical and allows for the transfer of your higher cognitive functions directly to machines. You can control machines with your mind. As many machines as you want, Vit.

"The cognitive interface is accomplished by inserting strands directly into your brain. These strands are no thicker than a single human hair, yet each contains multiple pathways for conducting electrical energy. Do you understand so far?"

There were two flashes.

"Most humans commonly use between ten and fifteen percent of their brain's capacity. These strands will allow you over time to tap into the rest of it. Once they're fully connected, you'll be able to do literally thousands of things at the same time. You'll be able to solve incredibly difficult mathematical problems easily and quickly. There's more to come, stuff you won't believe, but first things first. I need your authority to insert the strands directly into your brain.

"You'll be human, but with this technology, you will be something more. It also means that you're stuck here. This is your new home…and we are your family now."

The green light started to flash and did not stop.

During the last part of his lecture to Vit, Strand sensed that E had entered the room. He was still dressed in his retracted exoskeleton, but with his secret out, it hardly mattered.

E stepped forward. "Looks like that was a yes, Strand. What can I do to assist you?"

"You can still call me Steve, all right?"

"Whatever you say. I just work here." She grinned.

"Vit, this is E. She's part of the family and I would trust her with my life. You can trust her as well."

E grew concerned when she saw Vit up close. He looked like a corpse except for the faint rising and falling of his chest.

"Um … um … nice to meet you," she said, looking to Steve for reassurance that she had done what he expected her to do.

The green light went on.

Steve smiled. "Vit, you have made the right choice. It'll take some time for your brain to integrate the strands. As it does, you will gradually acquire more capabilities, and we'll have additional equipment to help you facilitate each step. Do you see that cherry tree in the park?"

The green light went on.

"By the time that tree blooms, we'll be sitting under it having a conversation. Now it's time for you to get some rest. See you soon, buddy."

Steve injected Vitimani with a sedative and then motioned for E to follow him out into the hall.

"E, regarding your decision to stay, you know, there are no guarantees here, no security, and no pot of gold at the end of the rainbow. I don't even know if we will survive. What I do know is that this is the challenge of a lifetime. You'll be doing things no one ever dreamed possible."

Strand paused and looked deeply into her eyes.

"There is no turning back."

"You know I can't leave. What about Anna and Howler?"

Steve stared silently at E as if to tell her that wasn't a good enough answer.

E breathed deeply and continued emphatically. "I know there are no guarantees, and I don't care if the end of the world is coming. I'm not going to miss this tea party, no way, no how. I'm in."

She paused dramatically, making it clear to Steve that this discussion was over.

"So, Mr. Strand, what are you going to do about the president?"

"I'm still working on that one. In the meantime, you have to learn about biomechanical integration. You're going to be responsible for it. I'll teach you what I can, but a lot of this is going to be on-the-job training.

"First, I need you to read the file codenamed 'COTAR' on your computer. Please take a few hours and read it thoroughly. Then call me, okay?"

E nodded and smiled. She was eager to start. She disappeared down the hall and outside, returning quickly to her lab down the street.

E's mind was racing as she entered her office and immediately pulled up the COTAR file on her computer. When it asked for verification, she leaned forward and placed her eye over the retinal scanner. As soon as the scan was complete, the file popped open. It was a paper outlining the stages in which the brain assimilates the strands.

COTAR, or Cognitive Transfer and Autonomous Rebirth

STAGE ONE: INSERTION. Immediately after the strands are inserted, nothing remarkable happens.

STAGE TWO: PULSE INSIGHTS. The brain sends pulses down the strands and new cells at the opposite end become active. This is the first stage of integration. The "patient" will experience moments of extreme clarity as new masses of brain cells become active and permanent neurofibrous connections are made.

STAGE THREE: PERSONALITY REMISSION. At this stage, the moments of clarity become longer and the "patient" will feel surges in comprehension. During this time the brain is adding additional neurofibrous connections to the strands. The "patient" may feel removed and become distant due to introspection and retrospective reflection.

STAGE FOUR: EXPANDED COGNITIVE ABILITY. At this stage, the strands are integrated and unused portions of the brain become active. The "patient" will regain social skills but prefer to remain in solitude discovering the limits of their new cognitive abilities. The "patient" may exhibit compulsive behavior, particularly concerning abstract art and numbers.

STAGE FIVE: COGNITIVE CONTROL OF MECHANICAL DEVICES. The "patient" is fitted with a skullcap that connects with the strands and translates the cognitive processes into machine controls. The skullcap is hardwired into a number of mechanical arms and other robotic machines. The "patient" will learn to operate those machines, accomplishing tasks as simple as waving and as complicated as building a circuit board. The "patient" will become autonomous at this stage. All tasks related to the health and well being of said "patient" will be carried out by robots under their direct control.

STAGE SIX: EXOSKELETON INTRODUCTION. The "patient" will build macro command sets to control the individual exoskeleton servos and create a high-level language controlled via biomechanical interface. In the event the patient has complete paralysis, this software will give the patient complete physical mobility.

STAGE SEVEN: EXTENDED COGNITIVE ABILITY. The "patient" will experience an exponential increase in cognitive processing, awareness, and reasoning. A permanent location for the patient to interface with the machines is required.

STAGE EIGHT: no information available.

E realized now that the steps outlined were the exact ones Strand had experienced, and couldn't help fantasizing about having strands of her own.

She thought about it for a moment and then began to shake her head.

"Mine is a different path," she said.

After rereading and studying the COTAR paper, E walked into her lab and looked at Howler. He had been acting strange for the last several days, even before the incident on deck the night before.

Howler noticed the look on E's face and signed something with his hand.

The robotic voice spoke: "Question?"

She knew exactly what he meant. Howler had made amazing progress. They now had a language of over a hundred signs, and Howler had already grasped the concepts of future and past. E suddenly had a funny feeling in the pit of her stomach.

She signed back to Howler, asking him how he was feeling. Did he have any head pain? Howler looked puzzled and shook his head.

E turned and abruptly left the room.

Howler wheeled across the room and up the ramp to the top of the table where he could see out the window.

E ran down the street in search of Steve.

When E arrived at Vit's bedside, Steve was nowhere to be found. She examined a clipboard attached to the back of the bed. There were several sheets clipped to it. The top page said: "COTAR STAGE ONE COMPLETED."

E looked at Vit's freshly bandaged head and smiled. She knew Steve would be able to give Vit a new life, and she was proud to play a part in bringing him back from his terrible darkness.

"Are you feeling all right, Vit?"

She looked up and saw the green light blink on and off, then on for a long moment and then off again. Vit was trying to communicate something more than a simple yes or no. She turned to a robot standing idle in the room.

"Robot?"

The robot stood at attention over its wheeled axle.

"Steve? That is you, isn't it?"

The robot nodded.

"Look at the green light. He's trying to communicate something. It looks like Morse code to me. Can you whip up some kind of translator so I can understand him?"

The robot nodded and gave her a thumbs-up sign with his metal fingers.

"You know, Steve, this is very weird and very cool at the same time."

The robot rolled forward and put one arm around E's waist and picked up her hand in the other. As it started to roll forward, E stepped back. She moved forward and slowly spun around. They continued in a flowing rhythm around the room.

She was dancing with a robot, a robot controlled by Strand. She smiled and laughed as the robot raised her hand high for a final spin to end their silent roundelay.

E shook her head and looked at the robot.

"Okay, okay, thank you for the dance, that was very nice. Now, a translator if you please?"

Conversation at 30,000 Feet

The massive anchors underneath Gaia reeled inside, and she sailed east across the Atlantic Ocean.

CHAPTER 11:
Conversation at 30,000 Feet

Strand was hooked up in his sanctuary. He had yet to respond to the ad placed by the president in the *Wall Street Journal*, but there was no question about the president's true intentions.

The CDC press conference was a by-the-numbers cover-up. The more Strand thought about it, the more he realized the president had nothing left to say to defend what had transpired. His actions had already spoken volumes and the ad in the paper was nothing more than a trap.

After monitoring worldwide speculation over his surprise European tour for a few hours, Strand unplugged and went down to the first floor.

He emerged from the elevator and walked over to a bench in the park. He wasn't worried about wearing his exoskeleton and cloak outside anymore. There were only a handful of people left on the ship, and he knew exactly where each one of them was. For a moment, it was nice to sit back and enjoy what he had created, to smell the trees, and listen to the fountain bubbling nearby.

Howler was staring out a window from his tabletop vantage point. He preferred to stay in the same room as Dr. Vitimani when E was in her lab down the street. The view was better and he was never alone.

The remarkable primate had been reclusive and introspective the past few days. Signing with E was a good form of communication as long as the subjects were simple, but their system lacked emotional depth.

Howler had also adapted to using the special chair apparatus well enough to get around without limitation. But something was missing. He wasn't the carefree Howler who wheeled himself around the lab chasing after E, and definitely not the intense Howler they met in the forest. Something was markedly different.

Howler looked down at the park and spied Steve sitting on the bench. He quickly wheeled down the ramp from the table he was on and over to a small elevator in the building. He rolled in and pressed the first floor button.

A minute later, Howler emerged and wheeled across the street into the park. He stopped directly in front of Strand. They stared at each other. The stare spoke a thousand words even though neither uttered a sound.

As Strand looked at Howler, he recalled how he had planned on testing his experiments on monkeys first. That was before he decided to become the test monkey himself.

But this Howler monkey was different anyway. This monkey had saved their lives, only to be crushed in the landing gear of the Black Hawk and confined to a chair for the rest of his life.

Strand finally broke the silence. "Doesn't seem fair that you should save us only to end up like this, does it, my friend?" He met Howler's piercing stare. "But you are now more than you know, much more. And soon you'll be ready, very soon. I know waiting is hard, but be patient and the rewards will be many."

Howler seemed to respond to Strand's kind voice with recognition and a subtle nod. Strand smiled and nodded back, then his expression suddenly changed and he stood up abruptly. The look on his face went from kind and understanding to hard and stern and far away.

He looked down again at Howler. "Yes, very soon, you're almost ready."

Strand's armor enclosed around him, his visor dropped, and his faceplate extended. The time had come to deal with the president. Now he knew exactly what to do.

It was later that evening and the president was aboard Air Force One. He was in his office gazing at the mirror that his wife had given him as a newscast droned on the plasma monitor in the corner.

Suddenly the TV lost its signal and static filled the screen. There was a single loud knock on the door and a Secret Service man burst in without waiting for an answer.

"Sir," he said, "we've lost all communications and radar. We must move you to a secure area, now."

The president's eyes widened. "Are we under attack?"

"Yes, it appears a strike is imminent."

The phone rang on the desk.

"Yes?"

"You have a call, sir." It was his White House spokesman calling from the next room.

"Jack, I thought all communications were cut off."

"They are, sir, we cannot communicate with anyone outside of Air Force One. Well, except for a ... Mr. Strand?"

The president slunk into his chair again. "What is the protocol we have in place? When will the F-18's be launched?"

"The F-18's are launched within minutes of any communication link being severed. It will take them about thirteen minutes to get here. Do you want to take the call, sir?"

"Put him through," the president said through gritted teeth.

He didn't wait for an acknowledgement that Strand was on the line. "Mr. Strand, there are a number of things about you that are very troublesome. Not the least of which is your ability to navigate with such ease and recklessness around our military."

"Mr. President, I am only responding to the ad you placed in the newspaper."

"And your response is to cut off all communication on Air Force One? Are you insane?"

"Mr. President, I cannot risk going back to the White House, not after my last visit. Now, you and I both know F-18's are headed this way, and they'll be here in about ... twelve minutes. So we don't have much time to waste, do we? Is there something you wanted to see me about?"

The president stood up and signaled for the Secret Service agents to leave the room and close the door.

As he did, he bumped the mirror and knocked it off his desk. It landed on the floor and smashed to pieces. The president squeezed the phone tightly in his hand.

"Mr. Strand, you will not use me, this office, or the United States of America to substantiate your outlandish claims. Do you understand me?"

Strand wasn't swayed. "What I know is that at this very moment, you have the opportunity to lead this great nation into the future but you've chosen to just ignore what's happening ... which will bring about only death and destruction."

"That is nonsense and you know it. Listen, Strand, I don't know what your agenda really is, but I have lost my patience. What I know is that there is not enough scientific evidence to support your radical conclusions."

Strand fumed on the other end of the line. He had given the president his two weeks, but it didn't matter. The president had his own agenda, which did not include the truth.

"Are you aware, Mr. President, of the new predatory life form in Brazil that floats in the air, paralyzes its victims with a toxic gas and then eats them alive? Are you also aware that those creatures could float into any city in the U.S., bringing untold suffering? I have samples of their tissue which you could have analyzed if you still don't believe me."

"I am not interested in your claims of Armageddon. You need hard evidence. You have utilized this office for as much as I will allow, Mr. Strand. In fact, unless you release the communications on this plane now, I'm going to consider this an act of war or treason."

"I cannot release your communications and continue this conversation."

"Then this conversation is concluded, Mr. Strand."

"This choice will be your downfall, Mr. President. Innocent men, women, and children will die as a direct result of your decision. You are compromising the safety of those who elected you." Strand's voice was beginning to strain.

"History will remember you as the president who failed

his country, but I will not stand by and let the innocent be slaughtered."

The president's face was red with anger. "This conversation is concluded, and in case you have noticed the time, Mr. Strand, the F-18's will be here any moment."

"I hope your wife buys you a new mirror for your desk. You're going to need it."

The president glanced at the mirror on the floor when it dawned on him. He slowly turned to peer out the nearest window of Air Force One. A few dozen feet away flying in the blackness of the night was a lone missile rider. The president glimpsed electric blue luminous eyes and pulses of light coming from an exoskeleton as a cloak blew in the wind. It was Strand.

The president was in shock.

"Yes, sir, I've been here the whole time watching you through the window. The basic rule of jamming communications is always proximity. Good-bye, Mr. President."

Strand slowed the missile down and Air Force One hurtled past him. In a moment, he was lost again in the pitch black sky.

The president was still staring out the window. When he finally regained his composure, he stomped over to his office door and yanked it open violently.

"Where are the F-18's?" The president was yelling.

A young Air Force officer ran to the president's side, stopped, and saluted.

The president already could see in the boy's eyes that Strand had outmaneuvered them again.

"Sir, we were approximately twenty-five miles off course at the time of the incident. The F-18's were sent on the wrong trajectory. It seems, sir, that while Mr. Strand was jamming the communications and radar, he was also controlling the airplane … sir."

The young officer tried to control himself, but the nervous flicker in his eyes gave him away.

The president turned abruptly and went back into his office toward the desk. He glanced down and saw his reflection in some of the pieces of the mirror on the ground. He bent over, picked up the largest piece still intact, and examined it closely.

"Just a piece of broken glass, nothing more," he said, and threw it in the trash can next to his desk.

Strand was still fuming when he returned to *Gaia*. He had wasted weeks trying to play the political game and had failed miserably.

And if losing time wasn't bad enough, he had made a sworn enemy out of the leader of the free world. Instead of teaming up with the president to save innocent lives, he was now public enemy number one.

Strand removed his exoskeleton, put on his street clothes, and went to his quarters.

Steve Cutter stared out the window at the moonlit deck. He was so lost in thought, he never noticed the lone figure sitting on the far side of *Gaia*, quietly perched on a rail as she had done so many times before and unprotected from the moonlight.

Soon it will be morning, Steve thought.

He dove into bed and fell quickly to sleep. Today was the day he would release the password. The whole world was watching and he had to be ready for anything.

The Phantom Missile Rider

Government officials in London,
Paris, Rome,
and Madrid planned for the release
of Strand's password by setting up
large stages near the markings.

CHAPTER 12:
The Phantom Missile Rider

Each side of the stage was equipped with large-screen monitors to help the overflowing crowds see. The cities were working overtime to handle the crowds, provide sanitation services, and direct traffic.

As day gave way to night, more and more people arrived at every location. Hundreds lined up to see Strand's burn marks for themselves. Some took pictures while others merely stared, and most wore cloaks and hoods.

The media had started setting up equipment a day earlier. Satellite trucks were parked on side streets with a sea of wires and cables running to a line of reporters in front of each stage. They were prepared to broadcast live reports if Strand arrived to release the password.

By nightfall, hundreds of thousands of people were gathered at each location along with a steady stream of new arrivals. Vendors were selling food and beverages and even dark blue cloaks lined in light blue satin. There was a carnival-like atmosphere that grew with the size of the crowds.

But there were many others not at all interested in crowd control or souvenirs. They were only interested in Strand. Snipers were positioned on the rooftops of buildings surrounding the stages, helicopters circled each area, mobile radar units monitored all activity in the vicinity, and Special Forces units from various countries and interests hid in the shadows. Strand had consistently demonstrated superior technology easily outmaneuvering every military organization he encountered on every continent. And while that technology was a treat to some, it spelled opportunity to others.

In his last forays into the public eye Strand had arrived without notice and was able to depart before any military forces responded. His missions had all been surgical and effective, the one exception his last visit to the White House, where the military was prepared to strike before the president called off the attack.

This time was different. He had already published where and when he would deliver the password, forfeiting the element of surprise. Military analysts concluded Strand had become overconfident and was about to make a huge mistake. Most were convinced this time would be different and the metal menace would soon be in custody. No matter what message the second chapter held, they believed, the mystery of Strand would soon be solved.

The president was watching everything unfold on television back at the White House with his wife and daughters. He had already directed the CIA, NSA, and all military branches to remain on high alert until the arrival of Strand by land, sea, or air.

All possible flight paths between the destinations were checked and crosschecked. Agents and machines were positioned at key locations and were operating with the help of satellite surveillance. It was an inescapable web of radar and observation posts. It would be impossible for anyone or anything to go undetected.

It had become personal for the president, and he was confident Strand would not get away this time.

As darkness approached, the overall mood of the crowds began to change from festive to serious. Conversations about science, evolution, extinction, and God could be heard everywhere, in every language.

Strand had been unplugged and asleep until dusk. He awoke refreshed and alert, and immediately put on his skull cap and hooded cloak without the exoskeleton. With his skullcap, he was able to communicate with *Gaia* as well as every robot and sensor on the ship. He knew the instant anything occurred.

He caught a glimpse of himself in the mirror as he left his quarters and stopped to look at his reflection. Other than the skullcap and cloak, he was wearing only his blue thermal undergarment. His exoskeleton was still back in the office.

Strand tilted his head a bit to the side and raised an eyebrow. "I think I need a light saber," he said, chuckling as he went out the door.

He went down to the first level and across the park. He looked up to see both Vitimani and Howler gazing outside as he approached their window. Vitimani looked like a corpse that someone had propped up as a macabre prank, but Strand had something he was sure would make his friend happy.

He went upstairs and walked over to Vitimani's bed. A transparent visor swung from the back of his skullcap to cover his eyes. Strand looked carefully at Vitimani's head before pulling back his hood and reaching into his cloak. He pulled out two translucent devices that he placed on each side of Vit's head.

A blue laser beamed from the small hexagon-shaped window in Strand's skullcap just above his forehead. It scanned back and forth so fast that it appeared to be a solid blue line. The light started at the top of Vit's head and worked its way down to his chin.

Strand stood up and put the two devices back in his cloak.

"Hello, E, how are you doing?" he asked without looking at the door she had just entered.

It caught her a little off guard. "Well, um, I'm adjusting. This is all pretty weird, Steve."

Strand pulled the hood over his head and turned around. "Well, you look great to me."

Two robots suddenly emerged. One robot pulled a device and a tripod out of a box and set it up near the green light Vit used to communicate. Strand attached his device to the tripod and carefully adjusted the angle so its optical viewing window perfectly aligned with the green light above the bed.

"Vit," Steve said, "This box was made to create sentences from your Morse code. Code a sentence, then pause or say the word stop, and a voice program will speak the sentence for you."

The green light above Vitimani immediately flashed dots and dashes. Steve looked at the black box to make sure everything was in working order.

Vit completed his Morse code and a soothing

older male computer voice translated. "Thank you for everything. Stop. I owe my life to you. Stop. Is Sarah all right? Stop."

Strand pulled a stool over to Vitimani's bedside, exhaled deeply, and sat down slowly. This was going to be rough and he knew it. He didn't know how Vit would take it, but he knew he couldn't lie to his friend.

"They told Sarah you were dead, Vit, and then …," Steve said, leaning in close to his friend. He paused. "She had a massive stroke. She's alive, but she suffered severe brain damage."

Steve paused. He didn't want to continue, but he knew Vit needed to hear the truth about everything. "She thinks she just cooked you both dinner … and she's waiting for you to come home. She passes in and out of reality just long enough to ask if you're back home yet. I'm sorry, buddy. I'm so sorry."

The green light didn't flash at all. The room was quiet and still. Tears were streaming down E's cheeks.

Eventually, the light started to flash again.

"They lied to her. Stop. She was my everything … and now there's nothing left of my life. There's nothing left of me. Stop."

"You need to rest up. Your life is just beginning. Soon you'll be more than you ever could have imagined possible."

Strand stood up and pushed the stool away. "E, please give him something to help him sleep."

The green light flashed.

"Thank you."

E went to the medicine cabinet and loaded a syringe.

"Rest, my friend," Steve whispered. "You have a new life and a new purpose."

E injected the sedative into Vit's IV. Strand watched as

the medicine traveled through a tube and into the vein. But there was no change in Vit's expression. He remained motionless and pale like a corpse. And although he had slipped into unconsciousness, his eyes remained open.

Strand pulled a sheet over Vit's eyes and turned around. Howler was across the room staring at him, saying nothing and everything at the same time.

"Come over here, Howler. Let me take a good look at you."

E signed to Howler, who rolled off the table, down the ramp, and over to Strand. Howler was about thirty-three inches tall when fully erect, but with only half of his body functioning and the other half confined to a wheelchair-type apparatus, he looked a lot smaller.

Strand wheeled a second bed over next to Vit, facing it out over the park.

"Let's see how you're doing, monkey man."

Strand bent over and unhooked Howler from the appliance. His arm and leg fell limp, but he didn't fight or struggle. He simply looked at Strand with unwavering trust and anticipation. Strand gently placed Howler on the bed.

"We owe you our lives. Now let us give you your life back."

Strand took out the pair of translucent devices again and put them on either side of Howler's head. He pulled his hood back and the blue laser started to scan the monkey's skull. He continued the process, rolling Howler's head to the right and to the left and scanning.

E was distracted by all the fascinating parts the robots were organizing nearby.

"E, we need to shave part of Howler's scalp so his cap fits properly."

E was equipped with good shears, as all vets are. She

snapped out of her daze and promptly brought them over. Strand pointed at where the Howler's hair needed to be removed and a few minutes later the deed was done.

Strand spent the time assembling the parts into something familiar with help from the robots. Soon it became obvious what he was building. Howler was going to get his own exoskeleton.

He placed the skullcap on Howler and checked that it fit correctly. He put the translucent devices on each side of his head and scanned it again. When he finished, he put the device away and grabbed the unique exoskeleton from a waiting robot's tray. He fastened it over Howler's left leg and left arm, connecting it at the skullcap and double-checking all the joints. He took one last part from a robot, a single glass lens with a thin metal shaft attached to it. He snapped it onto the skullcap and scanned Howler's head with the translucent devices once again.

"Okay, E, I'm going to activate it now … and here's what'll happen."

Steve paused.

"Nothing, nothing at all. Because nothing can be activated until Howler learns how to use each program. This particular exoskeleton will help him walk and eat, but also a lot more. The lens on top of his skullcap can extend forward and rotate so that it directly covers his eye. When you talk to him, E, it will automatically display graphic images representing whatever you signed. If you're able to teach Howler that the graphic signs are identical to the ones he's using with you, he'll eventually be able to communicate with just about anyone.

"I've also made it so the same is true when he signs." Steve pointed to a raised circular button mounted on the exoskeleton at the hip joint. "When he finishes signing, he presses that button and the audio translator speaks for him."

E was listening silently, in awe.

"I've loaded your database with all of your signs so far, E. If this works, he'll be able to actively participate in our conversations."

Strand bent over and his blue laser shot a single beam directly into a small hexagonal window in the front of Howler's skullcap. The monkey's exoskeleton surged with energy. Luminescent blue light traces shot over the cap and pulsed out from between the joints.

Howler's exoskeleton arm and leg flexed under Strand's control. He extended the lens, rotated it in front of the monkey's eye, and verified that all was functioning correctly. Satisfied, he turned the laser off, and the lens retracted onto the side of the skullcap. The exoskeleton fell limp and motionless.

Howler looked fearful and confused, but he never struggled or tried to get away.

"Howler," Steve said, "you're ready. Now you must learn … and E will teach you."

The lens extended and rotated in front of Howler's eye. The translator was presenting what Strand had said in simple line graphics that looked similar to the signs he learned from E.

Strand waited as the lens retracted against the skullcap and then turned to leave.

"E, the technology is working. Now it's up to you to make history and find a common language we can all understand. This will be more than words, E. No one knows how a monkey thinks. This is all uncharted, undiscovered territory. Think you can do it?"

E didn't really answer. She paused for a moment before looking up at Steve. "This is amazing. I knew you had something in mind. But this is really incredible."

Steve pressed further. "But is this something that can be done?"

"I've learned some things about Howler," E said. "I know he sees life differently; he has rigid beliefs about social behavior and responsibility, which must be from his troop. He perceives all situations in an extremely simple manner, danger or no danger. He senses personality and weakness from body language. He views death differently, but I can't say I understand yet how he sees it. I do know that he's not afraid of it.

"He's not afraid of anything, really. He is pure of heart. That's the best way I can put it." E paused and looked at Strand.

"This is going to work, Steve, I promise you. Howler will talk to us. I mean, he already talks to me."

Strand nodded. He already knew that if it could be done, E would do it.

That matter settled, E's attitude abruptly changed. "What about tonight? The media keeps saying this is it, game over, that there's no escaping the military once you make an appearance anywhere over continental Europe. They say the mystery of Strand will be solved tonight."

Steve smiled. "Do they? Well, don't worry; I have a little surprise in store for them." He winked at E and left the room.

The evening wore on as crowds flocked to London, Paris, Rome, and Madrid in anticipation of Strand's arrival. The crowds were now overflowing buildings, surrounding streets, bridges. The Strand prophecy was being taken seriously by an overwhelming percentage of the public.

Steve put on a full exoskeleton and went down to the first floor. Moonlight streamed through the glass ceiling as Strand walked across the park and upstairs to Vitimani.

"Vit, you need to see something. Are you awake?"

Strand removed the cloth covering his eyes. The green light started to flash.

"I am awake," the synthesized voice answered.

"Vit, your brain will grow and attach itself to the strands. You'll know it's happening when you experience brief moments of profound insight and clarity. It'll be like a light flashing for an instant and then shutting off. That indicates your brain is testing and learning.

"When your brain fully integrates with the strands, you'll be able to exist in multiple places at the same time, all the while thinking a thousand thoughts simultaneously. You can exist physically in one place but mentally in many machines, wherever they are. I can't explain it much better than that, but let me put it this way. It is liberating, Vit, a freedom you could never comprehend unless you experience it for yourself."

Four robots rolled into the room. They stopped and held up large flat screen televisions. E entered the room directly behind them.

"Did you want to see me?"

"Yes, I want you to see this. Come in and sit down."

The four screens were tuned in to different news coverage in each of Strand's possible destination cities.

Strand turned Vitimani's bed away from the window and toward the televisions.

"There are at least a million people at those four locations. The press is covering each event live, and the closer we get to midnight, the bigger the crowds.

"Tonight, in about an hour, I will release a password that will unlock the second chapter to my paper. Billions of people will know the contents just from watching these broadcasts."

He pulled back the hood on his cloak, but left the visor over his eyes.

Another robot carrying equipment rolled into the room. It went to the corner, stopped, and turned to face Strand before going dormant.

E was puzzled. "Steve, how can you be in London at midnight? Isn't it already 10:45 in London?"

"You'll see. Grab a chair. This is going to be quite a show." Strand wasn't looking at her while he talked, his strands deeply involved in something else.

E let him be and leaned back in her chair. She wished she had some popcorn as she monitored events on the four televisions. Before long it was 11:00 overseas.

Time to get this party started, Strand thought.

Reporters were interviewing people on location while airing wide shots of the gathering crowds for their viewing audience. The world waited in anticipation as the minutes ticked away toward midnight.

E watched streaks of blue light dart across Strand's skullcap and exoskeleton. He was clearly expending a great amount of energy. His eyes were becoming a more intense blue. This was going to be quite a show. He wasn't joking.

First, we'll get their attention, Strand thought.

He ignited the engines and fired the boosters on the lone missile cycle hidden at the beach in Normandy. It roared into the night sky and accelerated to 500 miles per hour, flying as close to the water as possible.

Strand knew about the satellite surveillance. He also knew where the media had placed roving cameras hoping to get footage of him flying a missile cycle.

He sent the missile across the English Channel. Just before it reached Dover, he turned on the running lights and accelerated the cycle vertically. He knew both English and French radar would pick up the heat signature now. At 15,000 feet, he changed course and directed the missile toward Paris. It accelerated to supersonic speed with a large sonic boom as it crossed the border of France.

Media outlets broadcast the sonic boom off the coast of France. Every station switched between their reporters to see if anyone had witnessed anything.

When the missile was within twenty-five miles of Paris, Strand slowed it down to subsonic speed, which caused another boom to echo in the sky. The broadcast from Paris showed people ducking at the noise. Reporters broadcast blurred digital video clips of the missile captured by their remote cameras.

The missile circled above the Eiffel Tower. It flew low enough to be visible, but high enough to make it impossible for anyone to see who was riding it. The crowds looked up and pointed, dazzled by the running lights and the loud roar of the jet engine.

The large video screens flanking the stages at each site displayed the arrival of the missile cycle in Paris. Crowds in each city pushed closer to get a better glimpse of the massive images.

Strand fired the rocket booster and the missile headed for Rome, its departure made clear once again by a sonic boom.

The press was going crazy with speculation as to what was happening and why Strand hadn't landed yet.

The missile hit Mach 2 somewhere en route to Italy. It was going too fast for video cameras to capture a clear picture, but slow motion confirmed that it was Strand's cycle.

E sat glued to the television sets, her eyes darting back and forth between the four cities.

The synthetic voice of Vitimani's translator broke the silence.

"I cannot believe what I am seeing."

"Welcome to the tea party, Vit, where every day something amazing happens," E said with a trace of sarcasm, wonderment, and a bit of seriousness.

The president watched the news reports and video clips of the Strand sightings. His daughters were fast asleep on the rug.

"His arrogance will be his downfall. Now there's nowhere for him to run and nowhere for him to hide. It's only a matter of time before we have you, Mr. Strand."

The president's wife sat quietly next to him. They had been married for over twenty years and she was watching him very closely, concerned. She decided to let him continue to vent.

"Can you image the audacity of that man to threaten the president of the United States of America?" His eyes never strayed from the TV screen.

"You're worrying me, honey. It's not like you to say something like that."

The president was in no mood for comments on his behavior. "Not tonight, I don't want to hear about it. Please, just put the girls to bed. I'll be in shortly."

The first lady woke up the children and then hesitated for a moment. She wanted to say something but didn't know how to say it. She finally just turned and left the room, closing the door on her way out.

The phone rang next to the president.

"Yes? Do you have a radar lock on him? Okay. I don't want him to get away with this, do you understand?"

The president waited for a response before slamming the phone down.

"I'm done with you, Mr. Strand," he said out loud. "This is the last night you'll dominate the global media. Whatever your agenda is, tonight, it's over, one way or another."

He sat back in his chair, confident. He had been blinded by the power of his office; he had lost perspective of his duty. He had become lost in his perception of himself.

The missile slowed as it neared Rome with a thunderous sonic boom. The crowd roared as it passed directly above them, but the missile was not alone. Right behind it, four Italian military jets flew by in hot pursuit. The crowd fell silent.

The jets were strafing the missile without firing a shot. The sound of the engines was deafening, and witnesses began running into surrounding buildings and alleys for protection.

The media was covering the chase "live." The running lights and occasional firing of the rockets gave the missile's position away. Jets flew in from all angles like giant fire-breathing beasts moving in for the kill.

Reporters shouted at the top of their lungs to be heard over the jets. Cameras tilted upward at the night sky to bear witness to the modern gladiators dueling above the ancient Colosseum.

E watched the dogfight and then looked at Strand standing motionless only a few feet away. She knew the missile had no rider. It was only the bait.

With the worldwide audience growing bigger by the second, Strand's plan was working perfectly.

The missile cycle circled back over the Colosseum and headed west toward the ocean. Witnesses could see only running lights as the missile flew over the coastline. It fired both rocket boosters and climbed vertically, gaining quickly until only its flames were visible at the Colosseum.

The president was still talking to himself. "That is your final mistake, Mr. Strand. There is no chance of collateral damage over water."

Italian jet pilots targeted the missile, as did eight U.S.

stealth fighters that suddenly appeared right behind them.
The president had another surprise planned for Strand, sixteen U.S. missiles to complement eight the Italians had just launched. The two dozen weapons streaked across the sky, their rocket engines drawing bright lines of fire in the night.

The crowds gathered in each city collectively gasped, yelling and pointing at the huge video monitors displaying a live feed. The world held its breath waiting for a resolution.

The answer came swiftly as all twenty-four missiles converged on Strand's cycle at once and exploded.

The blast was enormous.

All that remained in its wake was a giant, superheated, mushroom-shaped fireball.

The crowds stared in shock. Angry shouts in many languages filled the air as the riot police positioned themselves for the aftermath. It was 11:59.

The president stood up without taking his eyes off the television image of the explosion.

"Good-bye, Mr. Strand, and good riddance."

E stared at the television screens. The broadcast showed streets filled with hundreds of thousands of people; city after city poised on the verge of violence.

They're going to riot, she thought. What is he waiting for? She looked down at her watch just as it struck midnight.

Strand smiled. It was a small smile with a big meaning.

E saw it, and a smile slowly crept over her face, too. She stepped back and sat down again. "Guess it's time for Act Two."

The Password

The crowds that were gathered
in London, Paris, Rome, and Madrid
were on the verge of violence.

CHAPTER 13: The Password

But the riotous din of the crowd was soon drowned out by the simultaneous ringing of a million cell phones. Many answered, without hesitation. Others, fearful, simply stared at the ringing instruments in their hands.

"I am not dead," Strand said in a comforting but stern voice.

Somewhere in London, a young boy shouted, "He's not dead!"

And millions began to cheer.

Strand pulled his hood over his helmet. His face remained in shadow, leaving only his mouth, chin, and piercing blue eyes visible.

The dormant robot came to life, rolled in front of him, and lifted a camera.

The monitors at the stages were still on, and the screens burst to life with color bars. The crowds tucked away their cell phones and turned to face the giant displays. A moment later, Strand appeared on the screens.

The president stood motionless and silent.

"That's impossible, that's impossible!"

He slammed his clenched fist on a desk.

Strand began speaking. "I am not dead, far from it."

The crowds cheered wildly.

"First of all, the password is … protect the innocent."

"Type that in and the file will open for you. As you now know, the missile cycle was unmanned. But two dozen missiles from at least two nations all firing at once demonstrates that many powerful people want me dead."

The crowds were now absolutely silent.

"They need to listen to me carefully.

"I am not the threat. Avoiding the truth is where the real danger lies. We have entered an accelerated evolutionary cycle triggered by radiated particles from our own sun. These radiated particles unlock billions of years of evolution stored in our DNA, making it active.

"We will soon witness an explosion of change in every life form imaginable, as hundreds of variations emerge in each species in a short period of time. Evolution is not a slow process, but a brilliant burst of life which all of us will witness. It will affect us all."

Strand paused for a moment. He had to notify the public that new predators already existed, but at the same time he didn't want to start widespread hysteria. He thought about Anna and how he had tried to protect her. He knew what he had to do.

"New and vicious life forms are emerging, restructuring the food chain while searching for prey. We as humans are the largest source of food for them. We must be vigilant.

Governments worldwide must accept the truth and protect their citizens."

Gasps could be heard in the crowds as mothers held their children close and couples grasped each other's hands tightly.

"We've all been exposed to low doses of this radiation over the past several years. There have been large-scale changes as a result of our exposure, but the blame has been placed elsewhere. We've documented increased obesity, a higher occurrence of multiple childbirths, and a marked increase in irrational violent behavior.

"The radiation is strongest at night when reflected back from our moon for reasons we still do not understand. Nonetheless, included along with the second chapter are specific instructions for weaving cloth laced with metal fibers to protect against those rays. We need to cover our bodies when in direct sunlight or direct moonlight.

"I also ask each of you to observe our environment constantly. Look for physiological changes in the eating habits of lower forms of life like frogs or worms or even simpler creatures, as well as the predatory habits of carnivorous mammals, reptiles, and insects.

"Controlling the rapid mutation of bacteria and viruses will be one of our greatest challenges. An early detection system paired with efficient antidote distribution will be crucial to the survival of the human species."

Strand took a deep breath and continued. "I do believe, however, that with gradual exposure, we will all eventually become what we truly are inside. The active DNA will bring about physical manifestations of our true inner selves. In the simplest terms, good people will become better and evil people will become monsters. This is the beginning of our greatest moment. We must embrace our humanity and face the future with courage and faith."

Strand paused. He wanted everything he said to sink in.

"You'll also find the source code for an e-communication system called StrandsNet. This program will serve as the core for all distribution of information regarding this paper, and a place to report early warnings of dangerous mutations. Anyone with access to the Internet can post sightings.

"I will also post reports, but StrandsNet must be driven by those who desire to participate, provide assistance and ..."

Strand paused for a very long moment.

"... to become something more.

"I am Strand. I am a man and something more. I am only the first of many to follow."

The crowds began to cheer again.

Then, the screens all went black. The crowds, overwhelmed with this new information, slowly and peacefully dispersed.

At the White House, the president stood motionless in stunned silence.

"He played us," he finally managed to say. "All of us. He knew we'd come after him. He let us shoot down his missile on international television. We brought him billions of viewers worldwide on a silver platter."

The president felt more than anger. This time it was his pride that had been hurt. He had been outmaneuvered and outclassed once again.

"A billion people watched him die, then saw him electronically resurrected, and then listened to him preach! This is the most dangerous man of modern times. He must be stopped!"

The robot put the camera down and rolled out of the room. Strand turned to face E and Vit. He pulled back the hood of his robe and retracted his armor and visor.

E was speechless. She didn't know what to say or even what to feel. She was frightened, proud, intimidated, curious, confused, and comforted all at the same time.

Strand smiled a Steve Cutter smile. It was soft and understanding. He looked vulnerable for the first time in weeks. A single tear fell down E's cheek.

"E, I'm still just a man with a lot of hardware, nothing more."

"I almost feel like I'm not good enough to even be here, Steve." She paused and tried to regain her composure. "But I guess there has to be someone around here without wires to make sure you guys don't become cyborgs or something." She was trying to be tough and serious, but soon started to laugh.

Strand began laughing as well. It broke the tension.

Vitimani's synthesized voice broke in. "Will I be able to do that one day?"

"You'll be able to do a lot more than that. That was just a good show, parlor tricks. The first time you experience your own moment of extreme clarity, you'll get a glimpse of what I'm talking about. Your abilities will increase like mine over time. And thanks to some upgrades, your strand integration will happen faster.

"This is only the beginning. You'll still be Dr. Vitimani, but you will be more, much, much more." Strand smiled as his friend responded.

"There is no more Dr. Vitimani. All is lost and all is new simultaneously. I am the embodiment of the process of which I am going through. Do you know how long it will take?"

"Well, it's hard to say, but the best way is to monitor the stages of the strand integration according to the COTAR integration steps. The transfer stage comes when you start integrating with machines. What you become after that process is something you must decide for yourself."

Strand watched the green light flash and waited for the translation.

"You are Steve Cutter ... and you are Strand. I am Vitimani ... and I will be COTAR. My process will define me as your process has defined you."

"As you wish, but I have one request, that your name be followed by the number of years you have your strands. So initially you would be formally called COTAR S1Prime."

Strand leaned over and his voice dropped to a whisper. "COTAR, you and I are only the beginning. There will be many more to follow ... and not all will be human."

E had watched the entire exchange in silence, but now she took charge of the situation. "Okay, robots, put the televisions away. That's enough for tonight. It's time for all good boys to get some sleep.

"Come on robots, let's go!" She clapped her hands to reinforce her intentions.

The robots lowered the televisions and started to roll out of the room.

E turned to Strand. "I know it's you really controlling the robots, but it's way too creepy for me. So from now on, I'm just going to pretend ... that all these robots are individuals able to think for themselves. Is that okay?"

Strand opened his mouth to answer but she cut him off.

"That does not give you permission to bring me a towel when I get out of the shower. Are we clear, Mr. Cutter?"

"Yes, ma'am, perfectly." Under all that technology, Steve smiled.

"Good night, boys," E said. "Time to get some sleep already. This saving the world vicariously stuff is exhausting." E followed the robots and the televisions out of the room.

Strand rolled Vit's bed back to the window facing the park.

"She's right, buddy. We all need some rest. Good night. I'll see you tomorrow." He covered Vit's eyes and left the room.

The next morning, gazing out at the ocean, Steve processed his mixed emotions surrounding the events he had set in motion. There was no turning back; his real identity was now the target of intense scrutiny and speculation. His chief concern was that global focus would shift to him and away from the content of the message. But there was nothing he could do about it now.

The ocean air was fresh on his face, and reminded him what it was like to be human, to be Steve Cutter, if only for a while. With absolutely no technology attached to his body, he again felt what it was like to be a normal, ordinary guy.

Steve put his feet up and took a sip of coffee. He savored the taste in his mouth.

I feel so alive, he thought.

I feel so human.

Steve's darkest fear had always been that he would forget what it was like to be human, that he would surrender his humanity completely to the technology, all because of an obsession to achieve his goals. His blind passion had led to his brother's death. With all his technology and power now at his fingertips, it would be even easier to slip away into obsession.

"Anna," he said aloud.

I haven't even said her name in days.

Steve had long considered Anna the balance in his life, and he realized how alone he felt now without her. He pledged to spend more time with Anna as soon as possible. He closed his eyes and exhaled deeply.

"So, where are we going?" E was standing right behind him.

Steve jumped in his seat. He hadn't heard her approach. Without his hardware he was just a man and nothing more. He had been Strand for so long that he had become accustomed to knowing everything about his environment at all times.

"Wow, E, you caught me off guard. How'd you know I was here?"

"Actually, I didn't. But it was such a beautiful morning,

I felt like getting a cup of coffee and staring at the ocean." She smiled and poured herself a cup.

"We're going to Africa next, following the equator across the Atlantic. By the way, did you know there were up to four species of man that existed at one time?"

E nodded. She had majored in paleontology in college and still tracked scientific journals that focused on the newest discoveries concerning early man.

"It all started in Africa," Steve said, "at least most of it did. And if it's going to happen again, that is the best place to look for it."

E sat down next to Steve. "That was quite a show you put on last night." She sipped her coffee. "You realize now we're the target of anyone who wants to steal this technology … and I suspect that includes just about everyone by now."

Steve looked at E. She was right, but he was unsure where she was going with it.

"Can you protect us, Steve?"

"I'll try my best. In an emergency, we can use a submarine to escape and then self-destruct the ship. At least that's the back-up plan if there's no other option.

"But defend? It depends on the size of the attacking force. If it's the U.S. military or another superpower descending on us, no, we would have to evacuate. But if it were anyone else, we could defend ourselves pretty well. And I think it's just a matter of time before we face that very danger. Now did that answer your question?"

"Yes and no," E replied. "I guess what I'm getting at is you can't do this alone. And you don't know how much time we have. It may be sooner or it may be later. But you're going to need help." She sat up in her chair.

Steve thought E was asking for something. "If you want strands, E, tell me and it's a done deal."

"Me? No, Steve, no thanks. I must resist, I'm the one

that has to make sure you and Vit don't become cyborgs, remember?" She laughed. "Things are different now. With Vit going through the COTAR procedure, you won't be alone. There'll be someone you can trust, someone who's talented, and someone who'll be able to keep up with you for once. You need to get him going as fast as you can to help keep us safe in the future."

E grew more serious. "You know, Anna will be out of school in June. She's planning on meeting up with us; she can't imagine being anywhere else. Really, Steve, can you blame her? This is far more exciting than any internship or summer job could possibly be."

Steve knew E was right. Everything he held dear would be in the same place, under his control but in grave danger. It was a sobering thought, and it brought the harsh reality of recent decisions into perspective. He saw only one solution.

He exhaled and leaned back in his chair.

"What do you think we should do, E?"

"You and I both know there's only one solution. We are now effectively on the run, like fugitives ... and that cannot last."

Steve nodded. "Well, so much for pleasant morning conversation. Why don't we talk about the weather or something that isn't life and death for a while? We could just pretend we're on a cruise ship or something."

Their laughter was tinged with emotion.

"But you're right, you're absolutely right. They could already be on the way." Steve stood up, washed out his coffee cup and put it away.

"I better get back to work."

E wouldn't let him get away just yet. "This is the path you chose, Steve Cutter. There are serious responsibilities and consequences for all of us." She was stating the obvious, but saying it out loud made it seem more real.

A few hours later, Strand and E visited Vit and Howler. They needed to check on Vit's strand implants and COTAR integration.

Howler was having a hard time with his exoskeleton when Strand entered the room. He was on the floor making spasmodic movements, attempting to get his leg and arm to do what he ordered with little success. He was wailing in frustration, and if it wasn't so sad it would have been hysterical.

Strand picked Howler up and put him back on the bed. He scanned over Howler's body and exoskeleton for a long time. He checked and double-checked to make sure Howler's difficulty didn't stem from mechanical failure.

Howler didn't know what was going on, but he knew he trusted Strand. He lay motionless but alert.

Strand shook his head. "There's nothing malfunctioning, Howler."

The small video screen extended and rotated in front of Howler's eyes, translating what Strand had said into the graphic language E had developed.

Howler signed and then pressed the button.

"Why?" the synthesized voice replied

I'm actually talking to Howler, he thought. His mind raced with questions.

Strand turned to E, his face full of wonder.

"Once we get that other arm working, we can expand his vocabulary."

Strand pulled back his hood. He stood quietly for a moment, bent over Howler. His blue laser shot directly into the small hexagon-shaped glass window on the monkey's skullcap. The exoskeleton responded flawlessly, extending and contracting in slow, deliberate movements. Howler looked frightened and confused briefly until he saw his arm and leg being slowly manipulated. As he watched, subtle blue traces from his skullcap illuminated his exoskeleton. Strand slowly pulled away and cut the laser connecting their two skullcaps. "E, I think that did it. We'll know for sure over the next few days. If it worked and he stays with it, he'll be standing and hobbling by the time we get to Africa."

Strand moved on to Vit. His body wasn't showing any signs of rejecting the strand implants. After completing the scan, Strand retracted his visor and skullcap.

"Vit, I can accelerate the COTAR integration, but it may cause you discomfort. If you agree, I'll fit you with a skullcap now. I'll use the connections to send minute electrical charges down your strands. These charges will help your brain recognize the strand implants as they connect with other regions of your brain. It's kind of like a heart defibrillator zapping your brain, if that makes sense."

The green light flashed as Vit coded. "I'm ready, Steve. Nothing is worse than lying here helpless. I'm ready to help now. I may not be enhanced, but I am still who I am and you can't do this alone."

Strand looked at E. It was what she had told him that morning.

She threw up her hands and spoke sarcastically. "Hey, mister only a man and something more, don't look at me. I haven't said anything. Besides, after last night, it's pretty apparent something big has already begun."

Strand looked back at Vit. "Here's the main complication you might experience. There may be times when your brain forges a new connection where things could get a bit scrambled for an hour or so. Don't be alarmed. Your brain is just rebooting itself, so to speak."

The green light flashed again. "I understand. Let's get started. Now."

Amani

It had been several days since Strand
first attached Vit's skullcap and started
the accelerated COTAR development.
The stages were progressing ahead of schedule so far.

CHAPTER 14: Amani

StrandsNet was developing rapidly. A gathering of like minds coalesced over the Internet, cooperating, creating additional software classes, defining programming interfaces, and preparing for the constant integration of new information. Data was culled from field observations, samples, pictures, and anything else relevant. The cumulative results were used to track and identify anomalies or mutations, particularly those that might prove a threat to human life.

The CDC held a press conference acknowledging the release of the second chapter. The spokesman was quick to claim there was a lack of empirical data to support any of the theories mentioned. The CDC's message in brief was don't listen to Strand and everything will be fine.

Strand still worried about what he had started and what was bound to happen. He didn't want to become the center of attention; he just wanted to get his message out. But his efforts with the president had failed. He had tried his best, but what had transpired could never be undone.

His objectives in Africa were simple: find hard evidence that demonstrated active DNA mutation was real, and do so without the CIA or any other foreign governments finding out. He needed to complete the work as Strand, but without a global audience watching his every move.

As *Gaia* approached Africa, Strand launched several flying robot swarms. Each robot was no larger than a small dog, but when deployed as a group, they worked together on reconnaissance. Strand directed the swarms to search the areas surrounding the entrance to the Gabon River, which emptied into the Gulf of Guinea off the African coast. The forests there were too dense to search, but a few places adjacent to the river were clearly visible. Any anomalies could be seen easily from the air.

Small villages dotted the banks of the Gabon, a popular route for commerce and transport. Strand directed the swarm to fly over the smaller rivers feeding the Gabon from deep inside the dense forest. These tributaries were typically well hidden beneath tree canopies and had shorelines thick with vegetation.

The robot swarms were effective above the tree line but vulnerable at lower altitudes. Navigating the smaller rivers proved very difficult, as low branches and strong gusts of wind kept knocking the units into each other. Many crashed to the forest floor.

The size of the swarm diminished quickly, and the few robots that managed to survive ended up over a tributary joining the river on the north side. Strand immediately noticed a drastic change in the height of the water. The levels were extremely low along the entire riverbank and there was evidence that many villages had been abandoned.

The encampments may well have been left behind by nomadic tribes passing through, but Strand had a feeling there was something more to it. There was no carnage and no destruction. He soon realized there were no people around at all. The desertion could be explained in any number of ways, none of them apocalyptic, but it was a strange development.

Strand studied the images captured by the robots. Each time he saw the same thing, which amounted to … nothing. He found nothing exceptional or out of the ordinary other than a frighteningly low water level and a small empty village.

But pictures don't always tell the whole story. He had to be sure it wasn't the proof he needed.

Strand decided to launch an unmanned missile cycle carrying a heat sensitive camera, and plotted its course carefully along the tributary. The missile cycle would fly at night without running lights, making it virtually invisible in the dark.

The fourth floor creaked as the rear wall lowered and a missile gurney locked into place. The missile cycle powered up and launched into the darkness. It accelerated to the edge of the sound barrier. Strand was careful to avoid a sonic boom alerting anyone to its presence.

A forest is a different world after night falls. The law of the jungle is in full effect, where brutality and self-interest reign and only the strong survive. Predator or prey, the drama of life and death played out without fanfare or judgment.

The missile followed its course, hugging the landscape and crown canopies flawlessly. Only the whine of the jet engine was audible as it weaved its way along the river.

Utilizing a heat sensitive night vision camera, the missile documented the terrain and sent back images instantly.

Strand closely examined the video, noticing several creatures hiding in trees and scattered across the jungle floor. So far, nothing appeared out of the ordinary.

The missile finally reached the tributary with the low water level, but the foliage proved too dense for the missile to negotiate. Strand decided to capture a shot of the area from a higher altitude. He cross-referenced the topology with computer imaging to find where the tributary originated, and then directed the missile to fly in a circular pattern, logging the heat signatures in the jungle below.

When he noticed a small body of water along the river, he decreased altitude until the missile was directly over the treetops. Fallen trees blocking water from flowing had gradually formed the lake, and the surrounding forest was thick with life.

After another hour of searching, Strand decided to bring the missile back. It was nearly daybreak and he couldn't risk it being witnessed on its return to *Gaia*. The lake was the only thing out of the ordinary, and Strand decided he would have a look for himself that evening.

That night, Strand arrived at the tributary and leaped off the missile just downstream from the lake. Dropping through the treetops, he landed next to a once-rampaging river now reduced to a mere trickle. As he peered through his visor, he felt humbled by the size and complexity of the jungle.

An especially bright full moon streamed through the trees, illuminating the dried mud on the riverbank. An outline of human footprints appeared to head up the river in the same direction as the lake Strand had come to investigate.

Strand placed the hood over his head and began

strolling confidently to his destination. He felt as though he belonged in the jungle.

Following the footprints along the river's edge, he searched for signs of a recent conflict and kept on the lookout for an ambush. His path was soon blocked by several large trees lying across the river, stopping the flow downstream.

As he went around the trees to the lake on the other side, he expected to finally find where all the locals had ended up. To avoid encountering any potential lookouts, he circled the clearing quietly and stopped behind a tree for a better look.

There was absolutely nothing there; no village, no tents, no fire, nothing except the barren shoreline of a lake. He switched on his heat vision and looked around again. He picked up a lot of life in the trees above, perhaps a tribe of monkeys like the howlers in Brazil.

As he walked along the shoreline, the moonlight illuminated several more footprints clearly, only this time something was different. There appeared to have been some kind of struggle. Additional footprints leaving the area in all directions were accompanied by the tracks of bodies being dragged into the jungle and lake.

Strand bent down and looked around carefully.

It was an ambush, he thought. The fight for water was the fight for life. Perhaps the people coming up the tributary had been trying to find out who had blocked their water.

Strand went over to the center of where the battle had taken place. As he walked he discovered fresh footprints. Not all of them were human.

The toes were webbed.

Suddenly, he detected movement ten yards away with his peripheral vision. He turned to see something sticking out of the mud next to the lake.

Strand calmly walked over to investigate.

It was a young girl buried up to her head, nothing but her face visible above the sand. She was motionless and gagged.

Whatever fate the people walking up the river had met, Strand sensed he would soon know about it. The lasers in his arms glowed blue with readiness, and he could feel adrenaline pumping through his veins. There was about to be a fight and he was ready.

He knelt down to get a closer look. Just as he did, a spear poked through the gag covering the girl's mouth aimed directly at his visor. Strand grabbed the spear before it reached him and snapped it in half.

A dozen assassins buried in the sand surrounding Strand emerged simultaneously.

The girl was not a girl at all; it was just a head in the sand, a decoy for a deadly ambush.

The assassins had pale and nearly transparent skin covered in a layer of slime. Their eyes were larger than those of a normal human and they lacked any noticeable hair on their bodies. Their teeth were pointed, sharp and plentiful like those of a shark, and their hands and feet were webbed.

The strange creatures lunged with their spears and tried to tackle Strand to the ground. He brushed them off with ease and the spears had no effect on his exoskeleton. He merely stood motionless, observing the assassins as they attacked.

More assassins emerged from the soil on the water's edge. They quickly entered the battle but were just as ineffective. Yet they continued viciously attacking him.

Strand remained motionless and stared deep into their eyes. He saw only brutality, insanity, and a lust for killing. More and more assassins emerged from the water and forest to join the fight.

Strand gazed up into the trees. His night vision revealed bodies hanging from ropes. Only a scant few were emitting heat signatures. The rest were dead.

The longer Strand continued to stand motionless and unaffected by the attack, the more creatures emerged from the water and trees. Some wore various body parts of their prey around their neck, celebrating the misfortune of the victims.

It now dawned on Strand what had transpired. These creatures had dammed the river, drawing people from downstream who counted on water from the tributary for survival. The assassins had lured them into the same trap that fooled Strand, using the head of a child before commencing an ambush.

They would drag off those still breathing into the trees and those already dead into the lake. The ones in the trees lived only long enough to be eaten.

These creatures lived underwater. They were human, but radically different and viciously savage.

Strand watched as the creatures' aggression became so intense they would kill each other just to get a chance to kill him.

The four lasers on top of each of his knuckles flashed blue and straight. He lifted his arm up, and a moment later using a swirling circular movement, sliced all creatures within twenty feet of him into pieces.

But as soon as their bodies hit the ground, more creatures emerged to continue the attack.

One of the more wily creatures leapt in the air with a spear, vaulting over the bodies and charging him from on high. Strand twisted his hand to slice the creature in mid-air, and his two halves fell into the lake.

Once again using a swirling movement, Strand cut the remaining assassins into shreds. He continued to destroy them as they emerged from the lake and climbed down from trees. Only those that stood frozen in fear were spared. In a few minutes it was all over, and hundreds of creatures lay dead.

The few that survived remained motionless, watching Strand without moving a muscle, their eyes darting back and forth nervously.

Strand turned to the lake, placed his hands together, and pointed them at the water. The lasers fired into the water with full intensity. Within minutes, steam started to rise from the lake and more creatures suddenly emerged, screaming.

Strand continued firing until the water reached its boiling point. The creatures remaining in the lake were cooked alive. Their corpses soon floated to the surface.

He swung an arm quickly around toward the trees blocking the tributary and fired his lasers. The fallen logs blew up into countless bits and pieces. Water began draining out of the lake as soon as the dam broke.

Strand walked over to one of the petrified creatures waiting for him. As he approached, the creature knelt down on one knee and bowed its head. Strand stopped directly in front of it. A moment later, the creature pulled a spear from behind its back and lunged. Strand fired a quick blast of his laser and the creature crumbled to the ground.

The others watching hadn't seen the spear; they concluded that they had witnessed an execution. Dropping their weapons, they fell to their knees as if asking for mercy.

Strand turned back to face the lake. It was draining quickly and the underwater universe of these creatures was being exposed. Human bones and body parts had been tied together to create an underwater shelter. The stench was unbearably toxic.

Strand grabbed one of the creatures kneeling before him. He drew it close to his glowing blue eyes before pointing to the bodies in the trees. He abruptly threw the creature twenty feet in the air up into the trees while still pointing.

The creature understood and scrambled into the tree. It fetched the nearest body and jumped back to the ground. Strand looked threateningly at the others until they too scaled trees to bring down more bodies.

They brought the corpses over to Strand, placing them at his feet like an offering. Victims still alive were barely hanging on, but the trip down from the treetops was fatal for most. Strand knelt down as each silently died at his feet.

One last creature climbed down from the trees with a body over its shoulder. It looked at Strand and hesitated for a moment, then turned and started to run.

Strand stood up and instantly shot a blue laser to pierce the creature. It stopped, wheeled around, and stared down at the hole in its chest. It staggered momentarily and fell to the ground.

Strand walked over, picked up the creature, and stuffed it in his duffle bag.

He looked at the body the last creature had carried down from the tree expecting to find one more fatality, but instead saw a man in his early twenties struggling to break free of his bonds. Strand quickly cut the ropes and removed the gag.

The man rolled over and started vomiting blood, but he wasn't experiencing death throes. Within a few minutes, he was able to stand with Strand's help.

"Thank you," the man said, "you saved my life." He coughed violently. "Who are you? What are you?"

"I am Strand, a friend. Who are you?"

"My name is Kronos. I am a missionary."

He paused for a moment. "I was a missionary. The tribe I was living with was slaughtered by them." Kronos pointed at the creatures that stood waiting for Strand.

"Our village was downstream when the water stopped flowing. We all came to find out what happened and when we got here…." Kronos stopped. He was doing everything in his power to control his emotions.

Strand put his hand on Kronos's shoulder. "There was no way to know what would happen. Once the attack started, there was nothing you could've done to stop the killing."

"They killed Amani first," Kronos continued quietly, his voice breaking. "The rest of the tribe tried to rescue her … but it was too late." His eyes welled with tears. "She was the most wonderful child, full of life and joy."

He looked up at Strand. "THEY DON'T DESERVE TO LIVE!" His rage dried his eyes as he glowered at the creatures.

"It was an ambush," Kronos said. "They popped out of the sand, came down from the trees and out of the lake." He shook his head in shock and disbelief.

Strand could barely contain his anger and spoke quietly and deliberately. "I'm very sorry, Kronos. There was nothing you could have done. Maybe one day I can do something to ensure Amani did not die in vain," he said. "Please wait here. I will get her remains and take them with me." He walked to the edge of the empty lake. The bodies strewn about the lakebed were a macabre addition to those scattered along the riverbank. A putrid smell permeated the air. Every scavenger within ten miles would arrive shortly.

Strand turned to Kronos. "For now, if you want to live, climb back up the tree and stay as high and out of sight as possible. Do not come down under any circumstances until dawn. Do you understand?"

Kronos nodded, ran to the nearest tree, and started climbing.

The remaining creatures watched Kronos scale the tree. Strand knew if he did nothing, they would continue to hunt humans ... and Kronos would be first on the list.

The creatures remained near the bodies of the villagers they had carried down from the trees. They looked at Strand, waiting for instructions.

He turned his back on them instead and walked over to the child's head in the sand. He dropped to one knee and quietly examined it.

The creatures glanced at each other and without a sound lunged forward, grabbing their spears along the way. Strand heard them approaching, but it didn't matter. They could never hurt him.

All he could think about were Amani's final moments of life, the terror she must have felt, and the mindless savagery of those that used her remains as bait.

The creatures thrust spears into Strand's exoskeleton, but the weapons either slid off or broke in half. They continued circling and stabbing with all their strength.

Strand remained motionless, tears rolling down his face and out the bottom of his faceplate. The creatures upped the intensity of their attack, jumping high in the air with their spears and landing on his shoulders.

These monsters will no longer kill the innocent, Strand thought.

He reached out and grabbed the nearest attacker. Without taking his eyes off Amani's remains, he slowly crushed the creature's rib cage in his metal hand. The sound of crunching bones and air escaping from its lungs meant certain death.

The remaining creatures went into a frenzy, charging Strand. One by one, they met the same fate.

Strand picked up Amani's remains and put them in his cloak. "You did not die in vain, little one. The entire world will hear your story. They will know your name. I promise."

Strand went to his duffle bag and picked it up as the missile cycle came back. Across the clearing, he saw thousands of tiny lizard-like creatures emerge from the foliage. Like a living blanket moving across the ground, they scurried into the lakebed and started devouring the bodies.

Thousands more appeared on all sides of the clearing and began to devour the remains of the creatures Strand had destroyed. They were only interested in carrion and pretty much ignored Strand.

He went over to where they were feeding and watched silently.

These were no ordinary lizards. They had sharp, tearing teeth, devoured their prey like piranha underwater. Strand grabbed a dead lizard from the ground. One of its brothers had taken a lethal bite out of its side. He dropped it in the duffle bag with the other creature. Soon nothing would be left here to bring back except bones.

The missile cycle was almost overhead.

Strand called out to the man in the trees. "Kronos, until we meet again!"

He jumped onto the missile cycle and disappeared into the night sky.

Strand had found the evidence he was looking for, but he had also discovered a new meaning for terror in the death of an innocent. There was nothing he could do to prepare the civilized world for the brutality and mindless killing he had just witnessed.

Human beings had become a fragile species, losing most of their animal instincts over the years. But extinction holds no quarter. Would this weakness be their demise?

Strand felt an overwhelming sense of urgency. StrandsNet was emerging, but it was still in its infancy and not taken seriously yet. It needed to become the global repository for all evolutionary anomalies. There had to be millions of members studying the changing environment and endless data gathered from field testing. It would take time.

When Strand arrived back on *Gaia* just past midnight, E was strolling across the top deck without a cloak to protect her from moonlight. Strand knew what that meant. This wasn't the first time she had walked unprotected; it was just the first time he had witnessed it. He dismounted the missile cycle and landed a hundred feet from E.

E walked over to greet him. "How'd it go? You find anything interesting?"

Strand opened his face plate. His voice came out strained. "Where's your cloak? We're directly over the equator and it's a full moon."

"I was working late in the lab with Howler," E said, "and I was tired. I didn't want to walk all the way to my quarters to get it."

"Do you realize the risk you're taking? Don't you realize what'll happen?" Strand had the fresh memory of the creatures in the jungle.

"Maybe this moonlight will change me and maybe not, but I'm not afraid of becoming more of what I am. We all become more of what we are as we get older." E stopped and tried to gauge Strand's reaction. "Maybe it's the way things are supposed to be for some of us. Have you ever thought of that?"

Strand couldn't believe what he was hearing, especially considering what he'd brought back in the duffle bag for her. It took all of his inner strength to control himself. He turned to walk away.

"Wait, where are you going?" E followed close behind trying to catch up.

Strand stopped and turned. "You don't know what you're talking about, E. You don't know what I've seen. I just don't want anything bad to happen to you. Don't you understand?"

E had not expected that reaction. It was her friend, Steve Cutter, talking, and it caught her off guard. But she would never harm anyone intentionally or unintentionally.

"I know. You're right." E smiled.

"E, you must stay covered at night. Please."

"Okay, okay, Steve, I'm sorry." E quickly changed the subject. "What's in the bag?

"I have a few surprises in here that might be of interest to you. We have to put them on ice soon or they'll start to rot."

After removing his exoskeleton, Steve joined E in the lab morgue. There was a bank of freezers lining the walls and a stainless steel table for performing autopsies. Steve went to the table and emptied out the contents of the duffle bag. The humanoid creature and the lizard flopped out. He took Amani's remains and sealed them in a container.

Strand pointed at the creature. "I'll bet this guy used to be human before changing. Many local tribe members fish at night, and being near water intensifies the effects of the moonlight."

Strand stretched the humanoid out across the table so E could see what he was referring to. "They've adapted to living underwater. All of their hair is gone. Their pigmentation is practically translucent and covered completely with a protective slime. I've seen eels with a similar mucous. It's a very effective way of protecting the skin, or scales, or whatever."

Strand twisted the creature's head to the side. "Look at the hands and feet. There's webbing between the fingers and toes. There are also gills near the neck. These are incredible adaptations, substantial physiological changes in a fairly short period. In fact, if I hadn't dropped in on these folks, they'd be feasting on human flesh tonight."

E reacted with shock. "Cannibals?"

"Well, I'm not sure that's technically accurate. If they're a different species of human, then I don't know if you can call them that. But in the absence of a better term, yes, they're cannibals."

Strand picked up the lizard. "This little fella, well, he's a scavenger, and dines on carrion. They're like a reptile version of a piranha. I saw thousands of them devour a corpse in a matter of minutes."

"That's disgusting," E said.

"Pleasant little catch, no?"

E put on protective gloves and examined the hole in

the creature's chest. The edges of the wound were seared. "This creature was killed by something really hot," she said in mock autopsy tone. "Maybe a laser?" E shot a mischievous glance at Steve.

"What, you're going to pass judgment without all the facts, E?"

E used a flashlight to peer deep into the hole in the creature's chest. "Burned a hole all the way through, didn't ya? It would help our case better alive, you know. Even one of these lizard things would have been good." E never liked to see anything perish, especially something undocumented by science.

She's right, Steve thought. A living creature would have been much more useful than a corpse. He'd have to make special provisions next time if he was going to capture one alive and transport it. He now hoped one of them still survived, when earlier he wished they were all dead. While he had located the lake where the creatures lay in ambush, it certainly didn't mean the lake was the only place they existed. He had to go back.

Steve abruptly turned to leave while E was still examining the corpse.

"If this is a new human species," E said, "isn't killing it … murder, technically?

Steve didn't stop to acknowledge her question. That was a different issue for a different day.

It appeared he was about to spend another night in the jungle.

Strand returned to his sanctuary without checking on Vit or Howler. The adrenaline from his excursion was still pumping through his veins, so there was no use trying to sleep now.

He didn't even check his voice mail. He put on a lighter exoskeleton that he preferred when laying down to work.

He worked through the morning and finally went to bed around noon.

The night came quickly enough, and soon it was time to head back to the jungle. It was certainly the last place on earth Strand thought he would be headed after leaving the carnage behind the night before.

He mounted the missile cycle carrying a modified duffle bag, one that would accommodate a passenger if need be.

Kronos

The missile f inished running internal diagnostics
in preparation for departure above Gaia.
Strand closed his eyes and moments later the rocket
thrusters roared as he rode off into the distance.

CHAPTER 15: Kronos

Even if going back to that jungle didn't sound like much fun, he never tired of riding his favorite toy. He carefully maintained the missile cycle's speed to avoid a sonic boom.

Strand flew directly to where the lake had once been and dismounted immediately. He fired off the shoulder rockets to control his landing.

He was ready for a fight.

But as he looked around, no assassins lay in wait. Strangely, there were no corpses anywhere, either. Not a single bone fragment remained from the conflict the night before. Strand did find two graves marked by rock borders and makeshift headstones over near the tree line.

Walking over to pay last respects, he scanned the forest for what might be lurking or contemplating an attack.

Strand was surprised to see Kronos emerge from the shadows. He opened his mouth to speak, but got cut off.

"Before last night," Kronos began, "I believed ...." His words trailed off for a moment as the man of God tried to find the right words. "I believed that I could turn the other cheek ... but I cannot."

He joined Strand at the mass graves. "Yesterday," Kronos continued, "as I hung helplessly from that tree ... and watched the villagers I have come to know and love ... being slaughtered mercilessly, something changed."

Kronos took a deep breath and exhaled slowly. "They murdered the children, the children of my friends, and used them as bait." Kronos could barely go on, his eyes filled with grief and rage. "This was not killing to eat or to survive. This was something more."

Kronos fixed his gaze on the headstones.

"One grave contains only human bones. The other houses the remains of those godless creatures. But I had to bury them. If I do not honor the dead, then I am no better, I must be something more, even if I do not know what that something is."

Kronos turned to Strand. "Man is more than flesh and bone. We were born to know the difference between right and wrong. We have empathy and compassion, logic and control, but traits like these can also be our undoing."

He paused and looked around the forest for a second. "I have a second chance at life, thanks to you."

Strand started to speak, but Kronos cut him off again.

"There are still more of these monsters, my friend. After you left, a small group of them returned, maybe a scouting party. Once they saw what happened, they turned around and left without a word. They showed no compassion or honor for the dead."

"Monsters, I know," Strand finally managed to blurt out. "You're just lucky they didn't find you, Kronos."

"Thanks to your advice," Kronos said with a smile, "they never saw me up in the trees."

His gaze abruptly turned cold. "But they'll see me now.

I will find them before they kill again."

"Whoa, slow down a minute," Strand said.

"I'll slow down when they're all dead." Kronos was no longer lost in grief or confusion. He looked focused and determined.

Strand decided to trust him. "I will go with you." Deep inside, he feared Kronos would be a liability. The creatures were no match for Strand, but they wouldn't have a problem killing this ordinary man. At the same time, he could never talk Kronos out of the deadly mission, so he would have to do his best to protect him.

"Where were they last, Kronos?"

Kronos walked to the edge of the clearing and motioned. "This way," he said, and plunged into the jungle.

As they walked, Strand accessed the computers on *Gaia*, cross referencing satellite images to locate the nearest body of water. He quickly found a large tributary three miles up stream. The creatures were most likely heading in that direction.

"Wait a second, Kronos." Strand went back near the now-empty lake and used his heat vision to peer into the pile of mud. A moment later, he thrust his hand in and pulled out what was left of a half-cooked creature. It must have gotten buried in mud after Strand blew up the dam and remained hidden from the scavenging lizards.

The creature still had a head, one shoulder, one arm, and a half a torso. Strand opened his duffle bag and threw in the remains. He walked back over to Kronos, who stood at the edge of the clearing looking confused.

Strand held up the duffle bag. "Bait. We need to catch one alive." He left Kronos and headed into the forest.

"Alive? Catch one alive?"

"We each have our own agendas, Kronos, but let us hunt together."

The webbed footprints were easy to follow. Within the hour, Strand and Kronos reached the edge of the large tributary. Strand scanned the trees and water for heat signatures, but there was no sign of the creatures.

They searched the riverbank for footprints leading in either direction, but to no avail. The creatures had walked right into the water, leaving no trace of the direction they were heading.

Strand examined the water flowing down the river closely. "The current is strong, Kronos, too strong to swim upstream. If they were going upstream, they would have walked."

"So they must be headed downstream," Kronos said.

"Riding the current. Come on, this way."

They had been following the river for several hours, with no evidence of the creatures.

Strand stopped. "Where can they be going? If they were hunting in the water, they would watch from the shoreline and pick their prey."

"I don't think they would have traveled much farther than this," Kronos replied.

"Why do you say that?"

"The waters ahead are full of alligators and piranha, not to mention plenty of boat traffic. They prefer to lure their prey away from civilization and then ambush."

Kronos looked around the clearing and upriver. He approached the water's edge and pulled out his knife. He sliced his arm open and let the blood flow into the river.

"I think they can smell blood in the water. Now go hide in the shadows. I will wait here on the shore. I am much better bait than what you have in that bag."

Kronos continued letting blood drip from his arm as he sat down facing the water.

Strand didn't answer as he disappeared into the shadows of the forest.

It isn't going to work, Strand thought. There isn't enough blood and the water is flowing too fast. But he also could not shake the uneasy feeling he had that things were not as they seemed.

Moonlight bathed the clearing as they waited to see what would happen.

Strand had been hiding for over an hour. He sensed he was being stalked. But as he looked around the forest and in the trees with both night and heat vision, he didn't see any creatures. Maybe provoking them would draw them out into the open.

Strand opened the bag and took out the half-creature. He walked over to a nearby tree with several low-hanging branches. He broke one off, leaving a wooden point protruding from the trunk. He lifted up the creature and impaled its remains on the broken branch. It hung like a morbid piece of artwork.

Stepping back, he fired a low-powered laser and slowly cooked the carcass. It sizzled and popped as a thick odor permeated the air. The stench grew stronger and the skin began to burn and char.

Strand stopped and waited. He looked around slowly, but there was nothing but an unnatural silence in the air.

Let's take it up a notch, he thought to himself.

He went over to the carcass still dangling from the tree. The skull was now visible through the melted flesh.

Strand drew back his fist and punched. The skull slammed against the tree and exploded in chunks of flesh, bone, and brain matter. He remained with his back turned to the forest to tempt an assassin to attack from behind.

Why weren't they attacking him?

Strand was about to abandon his ploy of luring the creatures into the open when Kronos suddenly cried out.

A spear hit Strand's exoskeleton and fell to the ground. He wheeled around to see five creatures emerging from the forest running full speed toward Kronos.

Strand had provoked them, all right, but they were attacking Kronos instead. He had to act fast. He wouldn't risk his new friend being killed for the sake of capturing one of these vicious monsters alive.

The creatures leapt in the air with spears in both hands, prepared to drive them through Kronos as he lay on the ground bleeding. A half second later, blue lasers quartered them in mid-air. They fell on top of Kronos in pieces.

Strand ran to his side and cleared slimy body parts of creatures off Kronos's chest. One spear had pierced Kronos's shoulder and he was bleeding heavily.

"I'm sorry, Kronos, this is my fault. I should have been watching you. I have to cauterize this wound. It's going to hurt."

A few quick flashes of the laser and he was finished, but the excruciating pain barely registered on Kronos. He just shook uncontrollably on the ground.

"Kronos, what's happening?"

Kronos struggled to look up before slowly raising his hand. He spread his fingers apart to show Strand. His fingers had become webbed.

"They weren't going to eat all of us," Kronos spit out with animosity, "they were making some of us into them. That's why we were hanging in the trees instead of being killed like the others.

"It's how they multiply. I'm changing, I can feel it.

"Kill me. KILL ME." Kronos said in an impassioned plea. "I cannot become one of those creatures."

"It's the moonlight," Strand said. "It's triggering some kind of genetic change. I am not going to kill you, I am going to help you."

Strand picked up Kronos and walked over to his duffle bag. He opened it and put him in. "I'm going to take you somewhere safe. This will be a bumpy ride, but you'll be fine."

He zipped the bag closed and put it over his back. The strap of the duffle bag ran diagonally across his chest. He picked up what was left of the creatures he'd diced and carefully tied them together along the strap.

The missile cycle soon returned. Getting on would be trickier than usual. He had to make sure he didn't lose his passengers.

But it went off without a hitch. Strand crouched and jumped aboard with all the extra weight.

In a moment, he was speeding away.

The missile cycle hugged the tributaries, staying low to avoid any potential radar detection. But this was the fourth time Strand had flown the same route in two days, and for the locals along the Gabon, his presence was no longer a secret. Many were lined up on the river's edge or crowded in clearings, fires burning in anticipation of his arrival. Some waited in trees hoping to catch a glimpse.

There was no way to avoid them, unless Strand wanted to risk flying higher. The missile was so close to the water that it sent up a rooster tail behind it. The children on the shore ran away in delight from the spraying water. Strand decided to embrace the moment, waving as he passed by on the way out to the gulf.

The missile hugged the river fifty feet above the water at 300 miles per hour as it blasted toward the ocean. Strand quickly checked for aircraft in the vicinity on the radar aboard *Gaia*. He noticed something strange, a shadow in the night, a radar ghost.

Something was out there and it looked like a stealth fighter.

Strand accessed optical systems on the ship to look in the direction of the ghostly radar signature. There onscreen in the green tint of night vision, an unmanned stealth aircraft was heading directly for *Gaia*.

He wouldn't be able to return without being seen. He leaned out from the missile cycle, looked at the forest far behind him, and fired a laser back in that direction.

A large tree burst into flames on the edge of the river. He accelerated the missile to the edge of the sound barrier to put as much distance as possible between him and the burning tree.

He waited to see if the stealth aircraft would turn to investigate. The fighter stayed on course for a moment, then abruptly veered off and accelerated toward the shores of Africa.

Strand slowed his missile cycle. He needed time for the aircraft to get far enough away from *Gaia* so he could land undetected.

He didn't want to take any chances. The massive sliding doors on the ship's deck slid open as if to prepare for a Black Hawk to emerge and take off. But Strand didn't raise the platform that brings them up, leaving open the shaft from the upper deck directly to the second level. He contacted E and told her to meet him at the Black Hawk loading elevator with a gurney.

The floodlights were off in the Black Hawk loading bay as E stood looking up through the open doors at the sky.

Strand slowed the cycle down over the open doors and leapt through them to the floor, landing twenty feet from where E was waiting.

The missile cycle veered away from the ship and dove into the ocean.

The massive sliding doors on the deck closed above them.

Strand stayed crouched for a moment. Kronos was in the duffle bag on his back and the remains of the creatures were still tied to the strap across his chest. In the darkness of the loading bay, Strand's blue eyes and the light oozing from his joints glowed eerily.

As soon as the sliding doors on the deck above closed, floodlights came on. E came running over with a robot pushing a gurney and emergency medical supplies.

Strand put the duffle bag on the floor and stood up straight. He cut the ropes binding the creatures to the straps with lasers and the remains tumbled to the floor.

He bent over and opened the duffle bag. "Kronos, are you okay?"

No answer. Strand checked for a pulse. He was alive but unconscious.

E peeked over Strand's shoulder at Kronos.

Strand opened his faceplate. "Remember the victims in the trees, the ones that were cut down?"

"Yes," E said. "Is this the survivor?"

"Yes, and they weren't going to eat those victims in the trees. They were transforming them."

Strand reached down and grabbed Kronos's hand.

"Look at this, he's getting webbed fingers." Strand spread the fingers apart to show E the webs. "His metamorphosis is not complete and I don't know if it can be stopped. It might still require direct moonlight to activate."

Strand lifted Kronos out of the duffle bag and placed him on the gurney.

"His name is Kronos. He told me he was a missionary. You have to keep him restrained at all times; if he continues to become one of those creatures, he'll kill you without a moment's hesitation. He is very dangerous."

E nodded. Strand looked over at the remains of the creatures that had been tied to the strap across his chest.

"This is what he's turning into, and I didn't have a chance to bring any of the others back alive. They were too busy trying to put holes through Kronos," he said sarcastically.

"So," E asked, "why the dramatic entrance? Were you being followed?"

"No, E, but it was close, too close."

Robo-Beethoven

Strand retracted his visor and faceplate
as he entered his sanctuary. He sat down on the edge
of a table and let the darkness envelop him.
He relaxed in the warmth of glowing blue light
and the hum of the computers.

CHAPTER 16: Robo-Beethoven

He exhaled slowly and deeply. The thought of a stealth drone hovering nearby was disturbing. It brought home the cold reality of being on the run from forces beyond his control. No matter how he tried to rationalize it, the fact remained that everyone still onboard *Gaia* was in danger.

Strand left the sanctuary and took off his exoskeleton. He went to his quarters as Steve Cutter, wig and all. The more time he spent in an exoskeleton, the more it felt too much like home, and the more pieces of Steve Cutter were gradually chipped away. He desperately needed some quality time as the man behind the mask.

But he couldn't sleep. He sat up in bed after a long while and watched through his window as the oranges and yellows of the morning sun crept across *Gaia's* deck.

Steve walked to the bow, propped open the glass door, and started the coffeemaker. The warmth of the sun and the crisp ocean air felt good on his skin. He sat down in the lounge chair, satisfied to simply watch the morning unfold. He leaned back and promptly fell asleep.

E opened her eyes. She was greeted by Howler's hairy face and bad breath only inches away, staring contently at her. Startled, she popped up in bed and rubbed sleep from her eyelashes.

Looking around, E slowly realized she had passed out fully clothed on an empty bed in the lab.

She rose and went over to Kronos to see how he was doing and to check his restraints. He was still alive but comatose, and his appearance was changing gradually. His skin was becoming translucent and his eyes had a white coating over each cornea.

E went to the sink to wash her face. Howler followed close behind.

"Good morning, Howler."

Howler signed and hit the button on his buckle. "A new day."

While Howler had become quite adept at signing and communicating with E, he was not human and didn't perceive the world in the same way. The odd translations from his unique selection of signs were an insight into his mind.

Howler stared at E and then turned to face Kronos. She realized now that Howler had stood guard the entire time she slept.

Howler signed again and hit the button on his buckle. "New born."

E knew the vocabulary available in the translator couldn't translate Howler's thoughts perfectly. But it was also clear this wasn't the first time Howler had witnessed a transformation like the one Kronos was experiencing. None of this seemed new to him, like he possessed a deeper understanding of what was transpiring.

Howler had learned to utilize his exoskeleton fairly well. He walked over to a chair, rolled it over to Kronos, and jumped on top. E joined him at the bedside.

"What is it, Howler?"

Howler leaned over to examine Kronos carefully, and then started to sniff him all over. When he reached the collar area, he suddenly stopped and peeled stained cloth from around the neck. Three red evenly spaced lines running vertically along the skin were visible on both sides of his neck.

"We'll have to keep an eye on that, Howler."

A robot came rolling in. It looked like the ordinary utility bots used on *Gaia*, but this one wore a lab coat, reading glasses, and a pocket protector.

E smiled. "Good Morning, COTAR."

"Good morning, E," the robot replied. "Did you sleep well?"

"I feel good, actually. Thank you for asking." She looked somewhat surprised herself.

"Howler guarded you all night, and he watched the mariner."

E was confused. "Mariner?"

"Yes, Kronos is a mariner. He's developing gills on his neck, a protective coating, and other physical features signifying a humanoid that can live underwater. I've been studying him all night myself."

The robot rolled over and gently rubbed his metal finger along Kronos's head. As he did, the hair on his head wiped off, like so much dust.

"He's continuing to change genetically," COTAR said.

"I've been trying to find out to what extent his behavioral changes resulted from environment factors. I documented his exact condition upon arrival and logged specific changes as they occurred. They're in your computer in a file named Mariner 1-COTAR."

E turned to Howler. "Thank you for protecting me last night."

Howler signed. "Why?"

COTAR answered, "Troop members are expected to protect one another. We're Howler's troop now, so he'll act — and he'll expect us to act — as we would in a troop."

COTAR turned and started to roll away, then spun around quickly. "A human, a monkey, and a robot," he said. "That's a pretty broad definition of family, wouldn't you say?" The robot turned again and wheeled into the next room.

"Cup of coffee?"

Steve opened his eyes to see the COTAR robot, lab coat, a pocket protector, and reading glasses slung around its neck staring down at him.

"Coffee?" He sat up straight and focused. "What's with the lab coat?" He felt like he was dreaming until he remembered something. "Vit, is that you?"

"COTAR, if you please."

"Okay, so what's with the robot? What happened to the exoskeleton?"

COTAR fixed a fresh cup of coffee and brought it over to him. "Well, I thought the coat just … looked good. It goes with my eyes, don't you think?"

"You don't have eyes, you have lenses," Steve replied. "What are you talking about anyway? Something must have gone wrong with the strand implants. You're acting strange." He got up and stretched his back.

"Strange is being a prisoner to a body that will not

move," COTAR said, "but at the same time being free to wander the ship, conduct experiments, to learn and live through these machines. That is strange."

COTAR's voice was crackling with enthusiasm, at least as much enthusiasm as a robot could have. "It's a freedom I never conceived existed. I'm virtually dead physically, but thriving within these machines. I've never been more productive. It's incredible, Steve."

"Be careful not to get ahead of yourself, Vit. You're still in the early stages. This extreme euphoria may be a delayed response to the trauma from your accident."

"Nothing is wrong, Steve. I feel a joy I can't explain. Maybe the injury and all the time I spent trapped in my head have changed me, but…." The robot rolled back, lifted its arms, and started spinning.

"I'm alive, alive in these machines … and it is wondrous!"

Steve stared at the robot in its lab coat and scratched his head. "How many robots can you control at once, Vit, uh, COTAR?"

He waited for a response, but COTAR remained still and silent.

Moments later he heard movement behind him and turned around to face the control tower. Robots were streaming onto the deck in formation. At least a hundred utility robots rolled forward and gathered in the center of the ship. They formed rows like an orchestra awaiting the conductor to signal the start of the concert.

COTAR rolled over to face them and raised his metallic hands like a conductor. Each robot picked up an imaginary instrument and held it ready to play. Violinists had one arm holding an invisible violin and the other ready with an invisible bow. Horn players held their fingers in mid-air. Percussionists held imaginary sticks at the ready.

COTAR looked at Steve, who was impressed that Vit could control that many machines at once.

With the swift motion of an unseen wand, COTAR prompted the violins to begin, and the robot orchestra with invisible instruments began to play a medley of Beethoven's music. The sound of each imaginary instrument came from built-in speakers, as every member of the orchestra played flawlessly and with passion. The robots would weave and bend themselves during certain movements of music. It was a ballet of the machines.

COTAR finally prompted the orchestra to stop. Their last song ended and the robots dropped their arms to their sides, turned around, and wheeled back inside the control tower.

COTAR came over to join Steve. "I can't explain the utter bliss I feel. It's like being reborn. I want to enjoy every second of it."

"What about the exoskeleton?"

"It's not enough. I'm learning it, but in the meantime I've set up a lab in which I'm fully operational. All the tasks I completed for so many years as a scientist are new and exciting again. I'm working on the blood from Howler and the Mariner, I'm isolating genetic material, I'm a part of this team, and I'm producing results. I cannot sit around and wait for pathways to grow in my brain. I must contribute now."

COTAR stopped and waited for a response.

"I understand," Steve finally said. "And I think the lab coat is kinda cool, too. But your pocket protector needs some pens."

COTAR rolled over to Steve and rested its metal arms on his shoulders. It looked him in the eye and said, "I am reborn because of you, and you have my undying gratitude and loyalty. I can and will contribute. You can't do this alone."

COTAR spun around and rolled over to the control tower. "I love these rolling robots. I can really whip around in 'em. Whoo!

"Come on, Steve. Let me show you my lab." COTAR waved his hand.

"Okay, I'll meet you there, but I have something to take care of first. You know, I think I like this version of you better, Vit. By the way, who came up with the name Mariner?"

"I did, Steve. He's growing gills and a second set of eyelids. Come downstairs and see for yourself."

Steve went to his quarters. There were two messages on his voice mail. The first was from Anna. The graduation committee had asked her to see if Steve Cutter would give the commencement speech at her graduation ceremony. The second message was from the office of the president, inviting Cutter to dinner at the White House the day after the graduation ceremony.

Steve's jubilant mood dissolved the moment he heard the president's aide on his machine. He went to his office and the secret room and put on his exoskeleton. He slowly lowered the back of the chair down. Like glowing blue snakes, the conduits surrounding him attached themselves to his skullcap.

There was an explosion of information in his mind. He searched military computers for information on the stealth drone he saw the day before. He soon discovered there were several U.S. warships as well as a number of nuclear submarines within a few hundred miles of their current position.

He found memos about the government conducting naval war games and training exercises on the coast of Africa. The documentation indicated it was a real mission, but he didn't like the sound of it at all. He didn't want any traffic near *Gaia*.

He raised the ship's anchors and made an announcement to prepare all decks for departure.

E called right away. "What's going on? Are they coming after us, Steve? Have we been discovered?"

"I don't think so. I just think it's time for us to move on. Let's see if anyone follows. If they do, then we'll know. I promise to tell you if I think we're being followed, E."

Strand checked StrandsNet to browse what was being reported. Visitors were posting speculative information and useless spam. StrandsNet itself was growing by tens of thousands of members a day, but the information being submitted was unsubstantiated. It took time to sift through it to see if anything posed a real threat.

There were reports off the coast of Mexico about giant herds of reptiles following cruise ships. A photo was posted, but reflections from the water and the shadow of the boat made it hard to see anything.

Well, Steve thought, at least there didn't seem to be anything to be concerned about ... yet.

The offer from the president was disturbing. He didn't know if it meant he was discovered or if it was just a coincidence. In any case, he had a day or two to think about it and didn't need to rush to judgment. Instead, he scanned military databases and studied tens of millions of pieces of information, hoping to find clues to what was going on.

After several hours of searching the NSA, CIA, FBI, and military databases, something caught his eye just as he was about to unplug and take a break.

It was encrypted, but it referenced current military operations in Brazil tracking certain disturbances. Although vague, it was most certainly a clue. If there were government efforts in Brazil to destroy the floating worms and vicious snakes, it would most likely be covert, since the president had never publicly acknowledged their existence.

Strand set a course for *Gaia* to sail to the Brazilian jungle.

The Soul of the Machines

Strand left his sanctuary
to visit Howler, COTAR, Kronos, and E.

CHAPTER 17: The Soul of the Machines

The elevator door opened on the serenity of the quaint town square, but instead of people milling about, robots busily rolled around, like bees in a hive all intent on accomplishing some task unclear to anyone but them.

Strand knew better. None of the robots operated autonomously unless they were completing simple delivery tasks, but these were working toward a common goal. It was a sight to behold, so he stopped and watched for a moment.

He heard a commotion and turned around just in time to see Howler jump from the lab window onto a tree in the middle of the square. He grabbed a branch and flipped around it once before landing upright. The resourceful monkey quickly ambled over to greet Strand.

"Looks like you're getting the hang of that, Howler," Strand said proudly.

Howler signed and hit the button on his belt.

"Where is the little one?" the electronic voice asked.

Strand was perplexed for a moment.

Howler signed again. "Your troop?"

"You mean Anna?

Howler nodded.

"Oh, she's far away right now."

"When will … Anna … rejoin the troop?" Howler's reference was always to the troop and its members, forever watching over them.

"You are more human than most humans," Strand said. "She will not be here for a long time, Howler."

Howler waited as the words were translated into signs on the small video screen in front of his eye. He hung his head and looked pitiful for a moment, then sighed.

Strand started to walk back to the building where Vitimani was staying. Howler brightened up and ran up to follow right at his side.

When they entered the lab on the second floor a few minutes later, E was sitting at a desk studying slides under a microscope.

"Don't forget to tell me if we are being followed," she said sarcastically without taking her eyes away from the specimen. "This molecular reconstruction or reorganization is remarkable. It's fast and aggressive. Kronos will soon be a mariner and there's nothing I can do to stop it or even slow it down." She finally looked up.

Strand let the information sink in as he walked over to Vitimani's bed to check the chart. He leaned over and shined a light in Vit's eyes. They were still wide open but non-responsive.

He checked Vitimani's muscles, respiratory functions,

and strand connections in his skullcap. A small blue laser emitted from Strand's skullcap into a small window in Vitimani's. Strand stood motionless for several minutes while maintaining the laser connection.

The lab-coat wearing COTAR robot rolled in and started speaking for Vitimani in a flood of words.

"What are you fussing about? I'm fine, really. Come with me and let me show you the results of the work I've been doing, some really fascinating stuff. The Mariner symptoms start almost as an infection ... then change into ...." The robot stopped. Strand was obviously not interested in whatever Vit was trying to communicate.

"Vit, you have to start getting used to your exoskeleton. Are you listening to me?" Strand was staring directly into his friend's eyes. "We're headed for dangerous times, and I need you mobile. Your strands have integrated enough for you to advance mentally and learn the exoskeleton at the same time."

Strand paused. "Access StrandsNet, look at what's being posted. Innocents are in danger. We're headed to Brazil now ... to see if anyone's been attacked by the same creatures that did this to you. Listen, buddy, I'm going to need you ready, battle ready if need be. If I die, you're the only one that can carry this forward, the only one with the intellect and understanding to continue. Do you understand that?"

The robot spoke. "Yes, I understand." It took off the lab coat and rolled to the end of the bed, then went dormant.

Strand added something with deadly seriousness. "If something happens to me, you must take care of Anna and E."

The green light flashed. "You have my word."

Strand turned and motioned for Howler to get on the table.

"Jump up, my friend, and let me have a look at you."

He repeated the same procedure of sending the blue laser in his skullcap into a small window in Howler's. Strand stood motionless for a moment.

Wheels could be heard approaching in the hallway, and several robots rolled into the room with arms full of equipment.

"What are you doing to Howler?" E was standing directly behind Strand.

Without answering, Strand began to remove the half exoskeleton Howler had become so proficient with. The monkey stared at him, eyes wide open, not understanding what was happening, but trusting him as always to let him continue without resistance.

Strand felt the muscles in Howler's arm and leg to see if there was any deterioration, and seemed satisfied with what he learned. One of the robots rolled forward with an empty basket in its arms. Strand discarded Howler's half exoskeleton in the basket. The robot rolled away while Howler watched with fascination.

"Just a monkey ... and something more," Strand said. "Much more. Today I fulfill my promise to you."

Howler tried to sign, but when only one arm worked, a look of panic crossed his face. A second robot rolled forward. It carried with it a complete exoskeleton.

The robot stopped behind Strand and held out the brand new contraption. Strand lifted Howler up, cradling him with both hands as he lowered him into the suit. Howler lay back, calmly accepting what was being done without hesitation.

The new exoskeleton fit him like a second layer of skin, enclosing itself around his torso, legs, and arms.

Strand rolled the new skullcap forward, making sure it was properly fastened to Howler's head. The blue laser emitted from his skullcap again. Strand remained motionless while the thin beam continued to shine, slowly raising and lowering each of Howler's arms and legs.

The laser stopped and Strand stood up. "Howler, this exoskeleton makes you much stronger than any other monkey ... or normal human, for that matter." Strand paused to let the video screen extend and translate what he just said.

"You can jump higher and throw farther than you could before."

Howler's excitement was palpable.

"Now, I want you to stand up and jump to that table." Strand pointed to a table on the far side of the room.

Strand lifted Howler up and put him on the floor. The monkey didn't look confused at all anymore. He was methodically moving his arms and legs around as Strand lowered him.

As soon as his feet hit the floor, Howler jumped across the room toward the table using full power. At the top of his arc, he slammed violently into the ceiling. After bouncing off the far wall, he landed on the table and rolled onto the floor.

The exoskeleton protected him from any trauma during the impact and subsequent fall, but Howler still looked dazed as he looked up from the floor.

"You have to understand, Howler, that you are very strong now." Strand stopped to check if Howler was too dazed to hear what he was saying.

Howler slowly looked down at his hands. He raised them with great care until they were directly in front of him. He closed both hands into fists and slowly shut his eyes. As he did, luminous blue streaks raced across his skullcap and exoskeleton. He could feel the power surging as he slowly lowered his head. When his head was tilted forward facing the floor, his eyes shot open.

Bright and intense, he looked at Strand and signed.

"I am new born," the computer voice said.

"Most importantly, you are a member of our troop," Strand said. Howler smiled, a true monkey smile.

E almost started to laugh and turned away. Howler looked cute and fierce and huggable all at the same time. Strand tilted an eyebrow at her and she cleared her throat, regaining her composure.

"You are a part of our troop," E said. "A human troop is called a family." She smiled warmly. Howler waited for the small video screen to translate and stood stoically looking at Strand, waiting for whatever was next.

A robot standing nearby with a basket of parts rolled toward Strand.

"Howler, I have a few things for you. Please come closer."

Howler cautiously moved forward as though walking on eggshells, being careful and deliberate with each step. His recollection of bouncing off the ceiling was obviously still fresh.

Strand reached into the basket and held up a shiny chrome spike that was about two feet long. He twisted the center of it and each end telescoped out until it became a shaft five feet long. He twisted it again and two footrests swiveled down from each side. It was a stainless steel version of the weapon Howler had used in the Brazilian forest.

Strand twisted the end of the spike in the opposite direction and the footrest retracted. Two spikes appeared on either end with electric diodes on the tips. The diodes glowed bright light blue.

He swung the weapon at the basket the robot was holding and it burst into sparks, parts of it melting before hitting the floor.

"Howler, this can kill. Do you understand kill? Only use it to protect the troop, to save Anna or E. Do you understand?"

Howler waited for the translation. The eyepiece retracted.

Strand hadn't seen that look on Howler's face since he was in the jungle about to warn Steve and Anna what was going to happen.

Howler signed. "I will protect until I can protect no more."

"Follow me, Howler." Strand turned to leave the room. "E, I'll be back in a few minutes."

Howler followed Strand down the street and away from the lab.

Gaia was initially designed to be a kind of miniature city and a floating home for Cutter Technologies. Strand recalled, suddenly, the pleasures of the days when he had a full crew onboard. One day … it would be good to see people on these streets again, he thought.

But that time was not now.

Strand stopped at one of the buildings used for testing, opened the front door, and entered. Inside was a large open area the size of an airplane hangar. It was two stories tall with no interior walls.

Howler walked in and looked up. Strand bent down on one knee and reached into his cloak. He pulled out a small bundle of fabric and unfurled it.

"This is your cloak, Howler. You are to wear it at all times. At night, it shields you from the moon … and during the day, it conceals your exoskeleton." He put the cloak on Howler and a hexagon-shaped clasp on the front snapped itself closed.

"Keep your hood up," Strand continued, "except when you're in combat or inside where there's no danger. Do you understand?"

Strand reached around to the side of Howler's skullcap and pressed on it. The visor and faceplate moved into place, covering most of the monkey's face. Strand pulled the hood forward until the only thing visible was the glowing blue of his eyes.

"A monkey ... and something more ... something much more. Have no fear, my friend. Follow me."

Strand crouched and jumped. A second later he was sailing a hundred feet across the room. He landed loudly on an open stairway at the far side.

"Jump, Howler!"

Strand couldn't see Howler's facial expressions, but he saw the blue light under his hood glow with intensity. Howler clenched his fists.

"Feel the power, Howler. Let it surge, become what you are."

Howler crouched and without hesitation or fear hurled himself across the room. His trajectory was way off and he headed toward the ceiling. Strand jumped out and caught him in mid-air. They both landed on the ground safely.

"Again," Strand said. He jumped to another open stairway in the opposite corner of the room.

As soon as he landed, Howler landed next to him. His hood had fallen away from his head during the jump and he looked up with eyes eager for approval.

Strand retracted Howler's visor and faceplate and looked deep into the blackness of his eyes. It was as though they were smiling at him.

Howler turned away and jumped all the way to the steel girders holding up the ceiling. He swung from beam to beam before pushing off and landing on the stairway across the room with grace and ease.

Howler climbed on top of the stair railing and turned

to the wall behind him. He ricocheted off the side of the building and back into the rafters at the far side of the room. Hanging by one arm, he looked down at Strand.

Strand leapt into the rafters and grabbed a beam next to Howler. He took the spiked weapon out of his cloak. "Howler, this is your weapon. You must practice with it. You must protect Anna and E. Do you understand?"

Howler signed. "I will protect until I can protect no more."

Strand handed the spike to him.

On the floor below, several armed training robots rolled into the room.

Strand dropped to the floor below and lunged at one of the large robots, tipping it over and destroying it just as a second machine came at him. It took one punch to smash it to pieces and send it back in the direction from which it came.

The other training robots stopped moving. Tiny robots came into the room to remove the debris.

Howler jumped to the floor from the rafters, weapon in hand.

"Howler," Strand instructed, "here's where you must learn to use your weapon. You must destroy these robots or they will kill you. Do you understand?"

Strand wasn't kidding. The armed training robots automatically swarmed and attacked, reconfiguring tactics and strategies with computer speed and accuracy. All Strand would do was limit their speed until Howler grew more proficient.

The training robots started to move. Howler turned and leapt at the closest one. The point of his weapon pierced the training robot and it exploded in a shower of sparks.

Strand quickly exited the training building. He could

hear the clash of metal behind him as Howler continued his battle. He knew Howler's exoskeleton would protect him against virtually anything the training robots could do. There was a chance that he could get hurt, but Howler seemed to be handling himself well enough for Strand not to worry. At least it sounded like it from all the crunching and crashing that was going on in the building behind him.

He closed the door behind him, and was met in the street by a dozen robots holding Vitimani. He was still lying in his hospital bed still wearing his skull cap, but the bed was propped up at a 45-degree angle facing Strand. Several of the robots held the back of his bed while others made sure that he didn't fall off.

Vitimani looked very much like a corpse, with his white skin, sunken cheeks, and lifeless eyes staring into nothingness.

He was alive on the inside but looked dead on the outside. Robots rolled to both sides and each grabbed hold of an arm. They slowly raised Vitimani's arms as though he was a ventriloquist's dummy.

"Steven, please," the robot said, "this body is broken, but my spirit is strong."

In concert, every robot in the square spoke simultaneously.

"We are COTAR, we are one, and we are many."

They continued speaking, with individual robots in different parts of the group uttering single words to make up a whole sentence.

"I, am, more, than, one, I, am, many, and, I, exist, in, each. I, am, the, soul, of, the, machine, and, the, soul, cannot, be, destroyed, even, if, the, machine, is."

The robots lowered Vitimani's bed until it was flat again. They turned to Strand.

"We are COTAR S1. We are the soul of the machines."

Absolute silence followed, as Strand stared at Vit's broken body on the hospital bed.

Howler suddenly crashed through an upper window behind Strand and landed at his side. He retracted his visor and faceplate and looked at the robots standing next to Vitimani. He jumped next to Vitimani's bed, turned to Strand, and signed.

"Alive and not alive. He is new born," the mechanical voice said.

Howler placed the hood over his head and started walking toward the building he and Vitimani had spent so much time in together. The robots turned with precision, and several picked up Vit's bed on their shoulders and headed down the street. It looked like a New Orleans funeral procession, but this one honored the death of Vitimani and the birth of COTAR.

One of the robots at the rear of the procession turned around and rolled toward Strand. When it reached the base of the step where Strand stood, it looked up as if asking a question without saying a word.

"I respect your decision, COTAR. You are reborn as the soul of the machines."

The robot nodded and rolled backward, spinning around quickly, raising its hand, and bringing it down with a fist to its chest. "Yes!"

The robots began parting as they rolled by E, who now stood in the middle of the street. She walked toward Strand until she was a few feet away.

"I'm glad I didn't wait up there in the lab," she said sarcastically. "I would have missed the parade. Things don't seem to be turning out as you've planned, Steve. Is that going to be a problem?" E's last question was sincere.

Strand didn't answer E. Instead, the luminous blue

lights on Strand's skullcap increased in intensity as he covered his head with his hood.

There was a faint rumble in the deck and E could feel it. She looked around the streets off the square, but could see nothing. As the rumbling grew louder, E ran up the stairs and stood next to Strand.

"Steve," she said, "you're scaring me. What is that sound?"

He said nothing as an army of Strand-like robots marched into the square from all the surrounding streets. They were taller than human men and were cloaked so that only their gleaming blue eyes were visible under their hoods. They assembled in the square facing Strand and E and stopped.

"Yes, E, it's expected. And, no, it will not be a problem, quite the contrary."

The robots pulled their hoods back, exposing their heads and metal faces. They didn't look like Strand. They were clearly robots, but also very intimidating, an army of mechanical soldiers that would never tire and never disobey.

"It is time to place the soul into the machines. Come, will you join me, E?"

"I wouldn't miss it for the world."

Strand marched down to the street in the direction Howler had gone. The soldier bots turned and followed. Strand silently communicated with Howler and COTAR to stop and wait for him, which they did instantly. Howler could sense the vibration of the deck and leapt from the front of the procession to the rear to see what was going on.

E was almost running to keep up with Strand as he took off again. The soldier bots walked in unison and she was feeling uneasy at the presence of a mechanical army directly behind her. She kept looking back as she tried to keep pace. "Um, they don't look too friendly, could you slow down a little please?" Strand continued his march and she continued her trot to barely keep up.

Strand turned the corner where COTAR's robots waited. A minute later, Howler caught his first sight of a mechanical army marching in perfect unison behind Strand.

He walked up to Howler and without word or motion, the doors of the building they were standing in front of opened. "E, Howler, please follow me."

Strand turned and walked toward the open doors. He took control of the robots carrying Vit's body, and they too turned and walked toward the open doors.

"This is a special place that I have constructed for COTAR," Strand said. The robots carrying Vit's body carried him into the building. The inside was mainly dark except for a single spotlight shining on the floor in the middle of the room. The robots placed the hospital bed under the spotlight and disappeared into the darkness.

The ceiling of the room was a sea of wires and conduits all glowing an eerie shade of blue. They flowed from all corners of the room to the center, where they were attached to a smooth egg-shaped device hanging from the ceiling.

Machinery whirred as the device began descending to the floor. As it got close to the bed, it tilted downward like a ramp, exposing a flat tabletop. Recessed in its top was the outline of a man. In the cavities of the recesses were technologies that glowed blue, awaiting the man that would take position within them.

Strand walked over to Vit, disconnected and removed his skullcap. He scooped his friend's limp body from the hospital bed. Vit lay draped in his arms, disconnected from the world he had come to love, eyes wide open and

233

helpless. Strand gently carried him over and lowered him into the recessed area in the flat surface.

He fit perfectly. As Strand lowered Vit's head, the table came to life and glowed with energy.

"COTAR, you are reborn as many, you are the soul of the machines."

Strand stepped back. The conduits and wires surged and rumbled as COTAR started to access the equipment, sensors, and cameras of the soldier bots. The egg-shaped object slowly began to rise until it was about ten feet off the floor and tilted toward the entrance to the building.

"COTAR," Strand said.

"Yes, I am here," a deep booming voice echoed in the building. Out of the darkness walked a new robot. It was clearly different than the others, the sleek metal face resembled a gladiator's helmet, with the distinction of metal eyebrows. Cloaked like the other robots, with glowing blue eyes, it stepped forward into the light. It came to a stop and its eyes faded to black.

"This is your primary. COTAR, please access and activate COTAR Prime."

The robot jerked slightly and its eyes regained their glow. It looked around and slowly raised its arms and hands, examining the front and back of its new body. COTAR flexed his arms and made fists with his hands, the blue traces shooting across its skullcap.

COTAR Prime stepped forward and walked to the entrance of the building. He opened the doors, went outside, and turned all the soldier bots to face him.

The soldier bots spoke in unison. "We are COTAR."

"We are one," COTAR Prime said.

"We are many," they all said together.

"Okay, I'm impressed," E said.

Strand chuckled under his visor and faceplate. The

soldier bots raised their hoods to cover their heads, leaving only the glowing blue light of their eyes visible. They turned to walk back down the street.

COTAR Prime stepped forward and stood with Strand, E, and Howler.

Strand retracted his visor and faceplate and looked around at his team, his family.

"We have a problem. The president wants to see Steve Cutter and I don't know if it's a trap, but I'm going to California and then to Washington to find out." He paused.

"We are also sailing to Brazil. I've discovered there's some kind of military operation going on there. I think it has to do with the creatures in the forest we encountered, but I don't know. We have to find out if the president has authorized covert operations, because he certainly has not admitted to anything publicly.

"You all know that StrandsNet is operating and there are anomalies being reported, but they are all unconfirmed. Frankly, we don't know what's real, since what's being reported is mostly written by people with active imaginations and nothing more. StrandsNet must evolve into a reliable source of information, and we need to find a way to do that.

"I don't know if we'll live through this, but there's no turning back now. I do know that we have enemies in high places. I tried my best to handle this in the politically correct way by going to speak to the president directly, but I failed and put us all in danger. For that I am sorry." Strand looked at his family intently for a moment before turning to walk away.

Without looking back, he spoke over his shoulder with a hint of light sarcasm. "That's enough fun and games for one night, I think. Good night, everybody. Get some rest; you're going to need it!"

Evidence

"Rose, Trib, look at this!" Anna was furious.
"They're turning StrandsNet into a joke."

Rose and Trib walked over to the computer
where Anna was sitting in her dorm.

CHAPTER 18: Evidence

ook at these postings," Anna read on. "A man-eating guinea pig in Chicago, dogs the size of eighteen-wheelers in Texas. They're making a mockery of this."

She slammed her mouse down on the table. "Nobody believes it's real. Well, they weren't there in the jungle; they don't know what those things can do to a person."

She caught herself talking about Brazil and stopped. Steve had made her promise she would keep quiet about what she'd seen, especially the floating jellyfish worms, the eyeless snakes and the howlers. But it ended up being too big a secret to keep from her best friends, the identical twins Rose and Trib.

Rose and Trib weren't included in most social groups and were always referred to as "the twins" instead of individuals, but it was fine by them. They always had each other and now they had Anna.

237

Anna didn't fit into social groups, either. She was different and she knew it; and so did everyone else. She was friendly yet reserved, cordial but not approachable. Anna always seemed to have an itinerary, an objective, a higher calling. She couldn't be just another college student even if she wanted to be. Rose and Trib saw that, accepted her for what she was, and considered her their sister. They were the only people Anna had told about Brazil, and both had sworn to keep it a secret.

When Strand released the second chapter, all three stayed up that night to read it and compare notes. When StrandsNet was established, they immediately signed up and actively looked at the information posted everyday. The girls had a world map on the wall and would use push pins to mark the location of any story that seemed even remotely possible.

During several of the White House and military press conferences, sarcastic remarks had been made about StrandsNet and the quality of its information. Officials compared it to a sensationalistic newsstand tabloid, and they were right. It wasn't a place for real information, at least not yet.

"Anna," Rose asked, "have you heard from your uncle? Is he going to speak at the commencement ceremony?"

"Yes, he is. He said he would fly in the night before commencement so we could spend some time together. I really miss him."

"Have you told him you're not going back to *Gaia*? Does he know your plans?" Trib was skimming the postings on StrandsNet and didn't even look up when she asked the question.

"No, I haven't even talked to him on the phone for days. I talk to his voice mail and he talks to mine and that's how we communicate. It would be funny if it was funny, you know what I mean?"

Anna turned to look at Rose and Trib. "Well, looks like I'm going to tell him at the dinner, which is probably the safest place to talk about it anyway." She started pacing. "I don't think he's going to be happy about it, but I can't stand by and do nothing. I was there and I know it's real, and I won't stand by and do nothing."

"Calm down, Anna," said Rose. "If your uncle is half as cool as you say, he'll be fine with you putting off going back to the ship for a while."

"Are you kidding? He doesn't want me to put myself in danger. He doesn't want me to get hurt. If we're really going to find out if any of these reports on StrandsNet are real, we're putting ourselves in serious danger. Believe me when I tell you, he will not be happy." Anna frowned.

"We won't be gone very long," Rose said. "All we need is video or some piece of solid evidence we can bring to the press, and then the president will have to take StrandsNet seriously."

"That's right," Trib said, "listen to what Rose is saying, Anna. Now, unless you're having second thoughts, let's get back to it and see if there's anything on here that seems real."

Trib was all business. "Who's in?" she asked and held her fist out in front of her.

Rose got up and walked over. "I'm in." She put her fist next to her sister's.

Anna jumped up, "Of course I'm in." She put her fist next to the others.

"Let's go find some monsters and kick their butts," Trib said. The girls exploded into laughter.

The Mariner

Gaia had been sailing for about a week.
For the last several days,
Strand had observed a submarine,
silently trailing them.

CHAPTER 19: The Mariner

Strand figured the submarine's sole objective was to observe and follow, like police tailing a suspect. If the sub planned on sinking the ship, he reasoned, it would have done so when they were in the middle of the ocean, with no possible witnesses or evidence. Strand's second trip to Africa had proven costly. *Gaia* was now in jeopardy, with the CIA and NSA watching its every move. The government was investigating strong leads on the true identity of Strand, and the submarine was part of its plan.

Strand had countermeasures in place that would keep them safe in the event of an attack, but it was unsettling nevertheless to have a nuclear sub swimming so close behind.

One morning as the ship was nearing the edge of international waters, a thick fog rolled in that cut visibility to less than five feet. Strand took advantage and launched several swarms of flying robots. The dense mist would not be an issue for them since they were guided by GPS and were small enough to go unnoticed on radar. Best of all, they were disposable. Strand could send a self-destruct command at any time.

He launched twelve swarms of thirty-six robots, all flying in formation similar to flocks of birds. By daybreak, the swarms had been airborne for three hours and were nowhere to be seen.

Strand was in his sanctuary controlling the swarms and watching their video feeds. He carefully plotted courses to avoid undesirable wind and weather conditions.

Later that day, just as *Gaia* was about to cross from international to Brazilian waters, the submarine surfaced. Strand monitored the surveillance cameras as it rose out of the ocean not more than a thousand yards off *Gaia's* stern. It was the USS *Ohio*, a Trident class nuclear sub, one of the largest in the U.S. Navy fleet and one of the most deadly warships afloat. At 560 feet long, *Ohio* was a little more than half as long as *Gaia*.

They were being hailed by the surfacing vessel. "This is the USS *Ohio*. Please state your purpose."

"We are private research vessel *Gaia*," Strand answered.

"What is your purpose in these waters?"

"We are conducting tests on marine anomalies along the equator."

"You are hereby instructed to change course. You are entering a military training area. Do you copy?"

"Yes, *Ohio*. When will the exercise be over?"

"That information is classified, sir. Please alter your course due northward immediately. We will escort you to safe waters."

"We will comply. It will take approximately fifteen nautical miles to complete the turn." Strand knew that in fifteen nautical miles they'd be in Brazilian waters. The sub had hailed them too late.

There was a long silence from the sub. Then the radio crackled.

"You will reverse your engines and complete your course change while traveling in reverse."

"We cannot comply," Strand said. "It will take twenty nautical miles to bring our vessel to a halt before we can start traveling in reverse. We will immediately change our course due north at that point."

Strand waited patiently. This was a serious game of chicken with a submersible battleship. The rudders on *Gaia* started to turn her north, and Strand slowed her speed to five knots. At that speed, the fifteen-mile turn would take hours, just the time he needed.

"Understood, *Gaia*, we will escort you to safe waters."

"Thank you." Strand exhaled.

On the video feeds from the swarms, Strand saw several U.S. Marine vessels in the water ahead, as well as Harriers and helicopters in the sky. It didn't look like a training exercise; it looked like a military engagement.

Whatever was happening, the government was intent on keeping it secret. Strand directed one of the swarms to fly to a higher altitude for a broader perspective of the military action. As the coast of Brazil came into view from above, Strand saw massive burning holes in the forest. Some areas were now devoid of any trees or foliage at all. There was nothing to be seen but smoldering ground, as smoke rose into the early evening air. Harrier jets were still hovering in the distance, firing missiles into the jungle below.

The explosions were enormous. Anything alive on the jungle floor before the rockets hit would be incinerated instantly. This was extermination on a massive scale.

More Harriers screamed past the swarms as dusk settled in. Bright light from the fires was visible in all directions.

Had some mutations already caused so much destruction that this level of military response was necessary, or was this just an extra dose of insurance? Strand couldn't be sure.

Just as the swarms passed over the jungle, a Harrier shot several missiles at a target below. The explosions, heat, and fire instantly destroyed most of the swarm, but not before a few frames of video were sent back to Strand.

He looked at the footage closely. There was something alive down there, but it wasn't clear what it was, or even if it was human. The beings were nothing more than a small heat signature and a blur.

They're shooting at anything that moves, Strand thought.

Better safe than sorry, huh, Mr. President?

Gaia had completed her turn and was heading due north. The USS *Ohio* stayed behind for several more hours and then simply disappeared underwater.

Strand checked the sonar closely. He released a swarm of fish-like machines that would encircle *Gaia* and swim along with her. Each machine was the size of a large sea bass. It swam by moving its body and could generate

244

bioelectricity from seawater.

The school of fish was equipped with sonar, heat sensors, and microphones. If the *Ohio* were still following, Strand would know it immediately.

As the hours passed, Strand felt more and more secure that the *Ohio* wasn't behind them. The only thing he saw that was out of the ordinary was the distinct lack of sea life. *Gaia* continued north along the coast of South America toward the United States.

Anna's commencement was two days away.

Strand left his sanctuary to become Steve Cutter once again. Without his technology, exoskeleton, and communications, he felt so naked.

What if they know who I am? Steve wondered.

The president's invitation was too coincidental, and Steve was wary about leaving *Gaia*. But Anna would be one of the youngest college graduates in the United States, and as much as he didn't want to speak at the commencement, he wouldn't miss the ceremony for the world.

Steve went below deck one last time before departing to see how everyone was doing. Howler was practicing with the training bots. COTAR Prime had resumed his scientific research in the lab, and E was completely consumed with her study of Kronos's transformation.

Steve walked into the lab and was greeted once again by a robot with a lab coat, pocket protector, and reading glasses hanging around its neck.

"We have discovered what we believe to be the reason for the Mariner's aggressive behavior," the robot said.

"A robot with a lab coat, haven't we been through this?"

The robot put the clipboard at his side. COTAR Prime walked up behind Steve.

"We are COTAR," they said in unison.

"I am Number Two," said the robot in the lab coat.

"Steve, this helps me organize my thinking. I have created individual characters, so to speak, to complete a particular set of objectives. Ideally, each robot would be specialized to increase efficiency. I'm compiling a list of design parameters that I will submit to you."

Steve stood still for a minute and looked at Number Two. It actually seemed like a good idea.

"Lab coat, pocket protector, and reading glasses," Steve said. "Do they increase efficiency?"

"No, they increase my humanity, and I don't like dull robots. I like robots with personality. Are we done now? Can we get to the issue at hand?" Number Two was doing the robot equivalent of tapping its foot by rolling backward and forward slightly.

E approached them. "Steve, come take a look at this blood panel. The Mariner has a testosterone level a hundred times that of a normal human male."

"That explains the aggressive behavior," Steve said.

"I've created an antidote — a serum that will lower his testosterone to a manageable level, but he'll have to take it everyday. If he stops, the levels will rebound within forty-eight hours and he'll become a killing machine."

E looked up at Steve. She was happy she'd found a way to keep the Mariner alive, but at the same time she was worried.

COTAR Prime spoke: "The Mariner has completed his transformation, and he is currently sedated. I've relocated him to another room that's more secure. He has twenty times the strength of a normal human.

"He can breathe underwater by bringing water into his mouth and out of the gills in his neck. A second set of eyelids protect his sockets from saltwater. His pupils can expand to absorb as much light as possible in the deep darkness. His nose is equipped with internal flaps that block water from entering when he's submerged.

"Wide bumps above his ears act as sonar, capable of producing a low frequency tone he can hear when it bounces off objects. His hands and feet are completely webbed and are longer and flatter for faster swimming. He also excretes a protective coating that covers his body and protects his skin from the water."

"He's an amazing creature," E chimed in, "humanoid for sure, but completely adapted to water. It's really incredible."

"One more thing," COTAR Prime said. "We believe the Mariner will experience a severely reduced lifespan. His body will essentially burn itself out at least twice as fast as a normal human's."

Steve called out for Howler to join them in the lab, and seconds later, the monkey landed on the windowsill.

"He doesn't use the stairs," E said, "now that he's super monkey. We just leave the window open for him."

Howler held out his stainless steel weapon, which was scratched and had lost much of its sheen. It had obviously gotten a lot of use.

"Is Kronos sedated and have you administered the antidote?" Strand asked.

"Yes, we have," E answered.

"COTAR Prime, please come with me. Howler, please guard E." Strand stopped and looked at Number Two. "Your pocket protector is crooked."

COTAR Prime followed Steve into the room where Kronos was secured. Kronos was unconscious, yet still formidable, his arms and legs bulging with muscle.

"COTAR Prime, please stand by the door."

Steve scanned Kronos from head to toe. The restraining

straps holding the Mariner clicked open simultaneously. Strand rolled Kronos over to examine his gills and muscle structure. He finally put him back in the restraints and motioned to COTAR Prime that it was time to leave the room.

When they closed the door behind them and left the room, E was waiting outside with Howler.

"Wake him up," Steve said. "I need to talk to him, and he needs to be 100 percent lucid." It was easy to hear the stress in his voice. He was dead serious and no one dared ask why.

Steve headed for the door. "Call me when he's ready, thank you," he said, as the door swung shut behind him.

Steve went back to his sanctuary and became Strand again. He hadn't responded to the president's offer, but there was a message on his voice mail that presumed otherwise. It was from the White House confirming his meeting with the president.

Someone must have figured me out, he thought.

Why else would the president just assume he could order Steve Cutter to a meeting at his discretion?

He felt no need to respond to the president's invitation. He sat back in the chair, the conduits connecting to his skullcap like so many glowing blue snakes. There was a lot left to do before he left for California.

Several hours later, E phoned Strand. Kronos had woken up.

Strand emerged from his sanctuary with a heavy heart. There was only one way to handle Kronos, and he didn't like it.

COTAR Prime and Howler met him in the lab. When they arrived, E looked apprehensive, but said nothing. She could feel his intensity and knew she was helpless to stop whatever he intended to do.

"Howler, COTAR Prime ... hoods, please ... and come with me. COTAR Prime, Number Two does not provide enough protection for E. Please bring additional soldier bots to ensure her safety."

E sat down in a chair as Number Two rolled over and stopped at her side.

Strand, COTAR Prime, and Howler put their hoods up until only the blue glow of their eyes was visible underneath. Strand looked at Howler and reached out an open hand. Howler understood, took the weapon off his back, and gave it to Strand.

They walked forward and opened the door into Kronos's room.

Kronos was awake, sweat pouring across his massive arm muscles.

"Why didn't you kill me? I TOLD YOU TO KILL ME." Kronos was livid. Strand lifted the table holding the Mariner and leaned it upright against the wall. Kronos still was restrained, but could look them directly in the eyes.

Kronos became silent when he saw the three hoods with nothing visible but glowing blue eyes. Strand extended Howler's weapon, exposing the sharpen tips before leaning it against the wall next to Kronos and stepped back. Without a word, the latches securing Kronos simultaneously clicked open and he was free.

Kronos stepped forward and looked down at his body. It rippled with muscle. He flexed his arms with clenched fists. He felt his newly bald scalp with his webbed fingers and blinked with a second set of eyelids. He open and closed the gills on the sides of his neck and listened to the low humming of *Gaia's* engines.

Kronos looked over at the weapon and understood what was happening. "I have no need for that weapon. I am not going to attack. I stand here now as something more than I was before." He paused for a moment, as though listening to another voice talking to him that no one else could hear.

He looked again at his arms and hands, flexed his gills and gritted his teeth.

"I AM THE HUNTER of those that would prey on the innocent." Kronos stared straight ahead.

Strand, COTAR Prime, and Howler remained motionless. The silence was unbearable.

"Will you slay me now?" Kronos asked.

"You are a living virus," Strand explained. "Your aggression is in check only because of an antidote created specifically for that reason."

"You're the same as the mariners we saw in the jungle, Kronos. You are what you seek to destroy."

Kronos looked at the weapon again, only this time he saw it not as a weapon to kill Strand, but a weapon to kill himself.

He picked up the weapon, his massive forearms gripping the dull silver shaft and stared at the three cloaked figures. Kronos pointed the tip of the weapon at his bare chest. He placed his other hand on the dull silver shaft and extended his arms, preparing to thrust the shaft through his heart.

All emotion left his face. He thrust the shaft into his chest with all his might. His death would be the death of the mariners, and repayment for those in the jungle the mariners had butchered, especially the children. *Especially Amani.*

But the shaft didn't penetrate him. In fact, as strong as he was, it didn't budge at all. Kronos looked up and saw a metal hand holding it back. Strand had stopped him from killing himself.

"I didn't know if the good man you were at one time was still inside," Strand said. He took the weapon, retracted it, and gave it back to Howler.

"I have one other option, but it comes with a catch. I'll tell you what it is, and then you can decide your fate." Strand stopped and waited for a reply.

Kronos was silent. He had just returned from the edge of death, so the possibility of a better option was almost more than he could comprehend. He simply nodded and waited to hear what Strand had to say.

Strand, Howler, and COTAR Prime removed their hoods and pulled back their cloaks. Kronos stared as the three metal-clad beings revealed themselves.

Strand silently directed COTAR to escort E into the room. They waited as she entered, then continued.

"What I'm going to tell you," Strand said, "you must accept without question. If you decide to join us, you will learn more at that time. If not, it won't matter anyway."

Kronos nodded again, still in a state of disbelief.

"You'll have to wear a skullcap, not unlike the ones we're wearing. You'll also have to wear an exoskeleton, which will automatically administer your antidote daily and carries a three-month supply. But there's a catch. I will always know where you are at all times as well as your exact physical condition. If at any time I feel as though the monster residing within you is escaping, I possess the power to send you into deep hibernation ... or even kill you ... with a thought. And I will not hesitate."

Kronos finally spoke. "What about my blood? What if I'm killed or wounded and I start bleeding?"

"Your exoskeleton will protect you from most injuries, but if you're killed, it will incinerate you instantly. As for bleeding, the initial mariner virus takes quite a bit of plasma to get a foothold in the body. Back in the jungle, the converts were pumped full of mariner blood and unconscious for at least twenty-four hours prior to the virus fully taking hold. That's why you vomited when I cut your bonds. Your body was trying to reject the virus. The mariner transformation normally takes at least a week. And during that time, they can be destroyed easily."

Strand locked his gaze on Kronos. "Your mission, like ours, is to protect the innocent. That may mean educating the public about mariners, or it may entail hunting down reported anomalies. Wherever your mission brings you and whatever you're asked to do, your life is now dedicated to protecting others."

Kronos was excited and overwhelmed.

"One more thing, Kronos. If I die, you die. For as long as we both walk this earth, we're tied together as one."

Strand let the last part sink in. "Would you like us to wait outside to give you some time to think?"

Kronos didn't need any time. "I would gladly and without a moment's hesitation accept that mission." His voice was steady and in control.

Strand's visor covered his eyes and his faceplate enclosed his visage. "Get down on one knee please and tilt your head to the floor."

Kronos knelt down and lowered his head.

Strand placed his hands on both sides of Kronos's skull and started to scan.

"Please lift your arms up high, Kronos, until they're outstretched parallel with your body."

Kronos lifted his massive arms as Strand walked behind him and reached for an exoskeleton, which was hidden in the shadows of the room. He lowered the spine onto Kronos's back and it extended around his chest. Strand held the arms of the exoskeleton up like wings until he was sure they were attached before he let go and stepped back.

It was not a solid exoskeleton. It was flexible ribbons that mimicked Kronos's muscular structure. As they lowered onto his arms they flattened and wrapped his skin like so many bandages.

Strand broke the silence as the arms lowered down over Kronos's shoulders. "Kronos, you are a mariner ... and something more."

The exoskeleton arms went around his biceps.

"With these strands and your exoskeleton, you have exceptional abilities."

The metal closed over Kronos's forearms and locked.

Strand walked to Kronos and knelt on one knee. Kronos raised his head and the laser from Strand's skullcap shot into the small window in the mariner's. There was a long, drawn-out silence, as though no one dared move a muscle.

The laser stopped and the hexagon symbol glowed a brilliant blue before going dark.

Strand got on his feet again. "Please stand, Kronos."

Kronos stood and as he did, the leg portions of the exoskeleton wrapped themselves around his thighs and calves.

"You now have an additional sense of magnetic north. You'll always know which way you're heading. In addition, your exoskeleton will feed you the depth and temperature of the water while submerged, although it may take some time for you to process the full amount of information coming through your strands.

"Your legs can deliver bursts of exceptional power, giving you the ability to jump a great distance if you're on land, and swim at an incredible speed if underwater."

Strand paused as the suit finished making final adjustments. The hexagon symbol on the skullcap once again shined a brilliant blue, but this time remained on.

Kronos moved his arms, stretching them forward and off to the sides. He smiled as he saw how the exoskeleton fit his massive upper torso. "I can't even feel it," he said. "It's light as a feather."

"There's something else," Strand said. "Please flex your shoulders back. Can you feel a strange buzzing in the back of your head?"

Kronos flexed his shoulders back as far as he could. E saw him wince for a moment. Strand noticed the discomfort as well.

"Stay there for one moment, please," he said and reached around Kronos's back. E couldn't see what was going on, but she saw a sign of relief cross Kronos's face.

"Your back has a water jet of sorts. Extend it as you've just done and it will open. While it's working, bring your shoulders forward, and it'll force water through a small opening at the base of your spine. Your upper body strength acts like a thruster on a jet." Kronos turned around enough for E to see an oblong funnel protruding.

"This is fully extended," Strand explained. "Now move your shoulders back again until you feel the same strange feeling."

Kronos pulled his shoulders as far back as he could and the water jet on his back folded into itself, like paper in a pop-up book.

A robot rolled forward with mesh cloth. Strand took it out of the basket and unfolded it. It was a set of long dorsal-type fins that were made of a rubberized material.

"When you're underwater," he said, "these will act as fins. They also double as an antenna and will generate electricity from seawater." Strand clipped the cloak over Kronos's shoulders and down his back.

"This is how your cloak operates out of water," Strand said, and the cloak unfurled. The ridged fins transformed into a flowing cape.

"Please place the hood over your head," Strand said as he did likewise. Strand stopped talking and tried to use Kronos's strands to communicate with him.

"There's more, Kronos. We can communicate with each other without speaking. Please picture me in your mind for a minute, and then try to send a thought."

Kronos looked confused but closed his eyes and strained.

"What's happening, Number Two?" E whispered.

"He's learning ..." the robot started to answer, but stopped, suddenly aware that Howler was shooting them a fierce stare. It was clear they were not to be talking.

"If you can hear me, Kronos, please shake your head up and down."

Kronos moved his head as Strand directed. He turned to see Howler, Number Two, COTAR Prime, and the other robots shaking their heads.

"We're all in constant communication with each other. It may take time to learn, but you will, eventually. Remember, we'll be in endless contact with each other for the foreseeable future."

Kronos heard Strand in his head. It was a bit startling, because it wasn't Strand's voice but a number of voices speaking at the same time.

"Now for your first mission, Kronos," Strand said.

Kronos looked surprised and excited at the same time.

"We've been tracking reports of a large herd of reptiles following cruise ships traveling from South America to Florida. We're currently shadowing the same route as the ships allegedly in danger, but we have yet to identify anything even close to fitting the description.

"We have noticed a frightening lack of sea life, as though a giant net scooped all the fish up and took them away. You must discover the truth of this matter. The cruise ships purportedly being followed are due in Florida in two days. A Black Hawk is ready to take you directly to the vessels."

Strand left the room. COTAR Prime, Howler, and Kronos followed close behind. E was running to keep up. The soldier bots brought up the rear.

They soon emerged on the upper deck of *Gaia*. The spray of ocean mist in the wind was overpowering for Kronos. His body was pumping adrenaline and his senses were exploding with new awareness.

He knew he must travel north and he knew which way it was without thinking. His body started to excrete protective film and he blinked his second set of eyelids as he walked to the ship's railing. The gills on the side of his neck pulsed as he stared out at the ocean.

Strand knew what was happening inside Kronos because he could feel it himself. He knew Kronos had an urgent need to jump in the water, and with his natural strength enhanced by the exoskeleton and his water jet, it wouldn't take him long to catch up to the cruise ship. The Black Hawk was unnecessary.

Strand joined Kronos at the railing overlooking the ocean. E, Howler, and COTAR Prime waited behind with the soldier bots, their cloaks flowing in the wind. Nothing could be heard but the sound of waves crashing against the ship.

"Kronos, you are a mariner and something more."

Strand paused for a moment. "You must decide if what you've agreed to is a gift or a prison. You have your mission. Now go, Kronos, the sea calls."

Before he had finished his sentence, Kronos leaped high in the air and over the railing, diving straight into the water.

E, Howler, and COTAR Prime ran to the railing next to where Strand stood. They peered at the small splash some ten stories below them where Kronos had entered the ocean

At that moment, something pierced the surface of the water directly below. Like a missile launched from a submarine, Kronos shot straight out of the ocean and along the ship's hull until he was floating in mid-air, directly across from Strand.

"A GIFT, STRAND, NOT A PRISON! A WONDROUS GIFT!" Kronos shouted as he descended again.

"I WILL NOT FAIL YOU!" was the last thing audible before Kronos disappeared under the waves. He left nothing but a trail of bubbles as he swam away at full speed.

"That was impressive," E said.

Strand turned and scowled at E. He shook his head and started walking back to the control tower.

E ran to keep pace with Strand. "What? It was. It was impressive, really."

E stopped as a modified Black Hawk suddenly rose to the deck, and a flurry of robots started working on it as soon as it stopped. When she turned back around, Strand was gone. He had jumped to the third level of the control tower and disappeared inside.

"Where did he go?"

Number Two pointed up at the tower.

E sighed and called Strand on the phone. "Can I see you before you leave?"

"Meet me in my office in ten minutes," Strand said and hung up.

Nobody aboard *Gaia* had noticed the rocky shoreline a few thousand yards away littered with thousands of empty reptile eggs. The massive nursery had served its purpose and its occupants had abandoned it recently for waters rich with prey.

E arrived in Strand's office and was surprised to see Steve Cutter in street clothes and wig, looking as ordinary as the next guy. He was busy stuffing his briefcase with papers.

"Steve, what's going on? Why don't you just ignore the president's invitation? You don't have to go, you know."

"Maybe I shouldn't, but … I have to find out if he knows who I am. If it's me he's after, I'll lead him away from here and from Anna. I'll deal with him on my own terms. If I lose, then only I die. If he doesn't know who I am, then there's nothing lost by going there."

E was frustrated. "Steve, if he was going to sink us, he would've done it when we were in the middle of the Atlantic. We would've been gone in a flash and there was no one within a hundred miles to witness it. It doesn't make sense that he'd know."

Steve finished packing his briefcase with papers, closed it, and headed for the door. "Maybe you're right, maybe you're wrong, but I can't risk it."

E smiled. "I know. By the way, what you did for Kronos was a good thing. I know you had reservations about it, but I think he's a good man … err … mariner."

Steve smiled as well. It was good to hear her being so positive. "Thank you, E. I hope we're both right." He turned and gazed out the window. "There's a possibility I won't make it back."

E interrupted. "Steve, this is not the end. It is only the beginning of something new. And while it may be tough for a while, we'll survive. I have no doubt. Now go see

Anna and give your speech. Maybe it will be so good that the president will change his mind about the meeting."

What E could not know was that Steve already had decided that even if he did survive this trip, Steve Cutter would not. This was the end for Steve Cutter.

Hoods

The modified Black Hawk
was awaiting Steve on deck.
It was fast,
but certainly no missile cycle.

CHAPTER 20: Hoods

COTAR Prime and Howler were waiting near the helicopter when Steve walked up, wearing a cloak with wireless communication technology, but no exoskeleton. Steve would have access to all of the software and information aboard *Gaia*, but he was otherwise human, and physically vulnerable.

COTAR Prime could tell how uncomfortable Steve was. "Don't you worry about a thing. I have everything here under control."

Steve brushed past them without a glance and climbed into the Black Hawk. He was clearly agitated. "You must be battle ready, COTAR, which means you must train and learn how to fully utilize the soldier bots. Do you understand?"

Steve looked down at Howler. The primate's cloak was billowing from the helicopter rotors, exposing his exoskeleton.

Howler looked pretty fierce, especially for a monkey, Steve thought. But he did a double take when he noticed the intense focus in Howler's eyes.

Howler signed to Steve, "Danger," and suddenly leapt into the Black Hawk and sat next to Steve. The monkey didn't even glance at Steve; he just looked out the window as if to say, "Why haven't we left yet?"

Steve's first instinct was to tell Howler to get out and wait on *Gaia*. But on second thought, he kind of liked the idea of Howler tagging along. Besides, Howler was determined to go. Of course, Howler would have to stay with the Black Hawk at all times.

The doors closed and the helicopter started to lift off. Next stop: California.

Steve glanced at his watch. It was going to be a long flight.

They landed adjacent to Cutter Technologies at Mojave Airport. Steve instructed Howler to remain inside the Black Hawk except at night when no one could see him.

It felt like a lifetime since Steve had been at Cutter Technologies. Most of the staff had relocated here from *Gaia* a few short months ago, but it had been an eternity in Steve's life.

It was early evening now and most of the employees had left for the day. Steve jumped out of the Black Hawk and took in the scenery, savoring the warm desert breeze against his face.

A limousine was parked in front of Steve's office ready to take him to meet Anna for dinner. During the long drive, Steve used the time to communicate with Howler, and with COTAR back on the ship.

He also checked StrandsNet for any additional information concerning the reptiles off the coast of Florida. When he was finished, he closed his eyes and fell fast asleep.

It was dark by the time the car came to an abrupt stop in front of Southern California University near Pasadena. Steve woke up with a start and stared bleary-eyed out the window.

Small college towns always seemed so quaint to him, and SCU was no different. There was something scholarly about all the well-kept, Craftsman-style homes visible from the limousine. The driver turned a corner and immediately hit a snarl of cars and trucks, and a cacophony of horns.

"Sorry sir, something's happening in front of the Cloak and Dagger … it looks like several cars are blocking traffic," the driver said.

The Cloak and Dagger. That's the restaurant where Steve was supposed to meet Anna. It suddenly occurred to him that those cars could be the NSA or the CIA … and Anna was alone inside.

He opened the door while the limousine remained stopped in traffic. He thanked the driver and briskly walked down the sidewalk.

Don't worry so much, Steve thought to himself. She's fine, and this is nothing more than a coincidence.

Steve pulled the hood over his head to protect himself from the moonlight and strolled off. As he looked around, he noticed few people covering their heads. The handful that did have hoods all appeared to be students.

As Steve neared the Cloak and Dagger, he saw three drivers in black suits standing next to three cars stopped in front. Several other men dressed in suits had just gone inside.

Steve started to run. He was flashing back to the night

in the Brazilian forest when they barely escaped with their lives. A feeling of helplessness washed over him as he remembered the promise he made to himself never to put Anna in danger again.

Steve sprinted as fast as he could, but he was human and nothing more. No matter how hard he ran, it was merely a fraction of what Strand could do. He reached the entrance to Cloak and Dagger, pulled the big double doors open, and bolted inside.

The men in suits had surrounded Anna in the lobby.

As far as Steve could see, they hadn't pulled any weapons, which was good because he didn't have any weapons. If this was going to be a firefight, he was completely unarmed. As he got close, he realized she wasn't alone. Identical twin girls stood next to her.

It was Trib and Rose ... and everyone was smiling.

Steve stopped and practically tripped over his own feet as he reached the girls. Everyone turned to greet him.

"Uncle Steve," Anna said, "this is Robert Greenback, president of the university."

A gray-haired, pencil-thin man in his fifties, Greenback held out his hand. "Pleasure to meet you, Mr. Cutter. May I introduce some of the board members?"

Steve didn't hear a word Greenback said. He went over to hoist Anna in his arms in a big hug. The board members didn't mind. Most were older and all had children, so they understood the power of family.

"I'm sorry, gentlemen," Steve said. "I don't mean to be rude. It's nice to meet you all."

Greenback forged ahead. "Mr. Cutter, I cannot thank you enough for the generous donation you've made to our university. We would be honored if you would join us for dinner. We have a special table in the back room waiting for us."

Steve shrugged at Anna. So much for spending any time together before the commencement tomorrow, he thought.

Anna knew tonight was not the night to tell her uncle about her plans after graduation. She looked at him and nodded.

"We would be honored, Mr. Greenback," Steve said.

"Wonderful. Please follow me. Anna, can your friends join us?"

"No, they were just leaving," Anna said and secretly gave Trib the "get out of here" face.

As everyone turned to walk to the back of the restaurant, Steve noticed that Anna, Trib, and Rose wore hooded cloaks and Greenback did not. He caught two of the board members taking a quick glance at his cloak.

One of them, a middle-aged woman, spoke up as they sat down at a large table in a private room. "I see you're wearing a cloak. Does that make you a hood? Do you support all these end-of-the-world predictions?"

"A hood?" Steve was dumbfounded. It seemed like everyone there knew what a "hood" was but him. It also appeared that being a "hood" was not looked upon as a good thing.

Steve glanced at Anna, desperate for an explanation.

The woman continued, "If you follow the Strand Prophecy, you wear a cloak and a hood. The common slang term for those who do is a hood." Her lips curled in a sneer. "We academicians frown on unsubstantiated claims … especially when they come from masked men." Several in the group chuckled.

Anna glanced at the president and board members and turned to Steve. "Tell them, Uncle Steve, that this is real. Tell them there's real danger. Go ahead; tell them, maybe they'll listen to you."

Anna had broken the festive mood of the dinner party. But the president of SCU wasn't interested in starting a debate at the table and instead proposed a toast.

"Please raise your glasses and join me," Greenback said, "in toasting our guest of honor and keynote speaker at tomorrow's commencement ceremony, Steve Cutter." Greenback raised his glass and everyone at the table toasted.

Anna kept staring at her uncle, her eyes asking him why he remained silent. While Steve knew the truth better than anyone, he wasn't sure of the dynamic of those in the room. He didn't want to say anything that could have a negative impact on Anna at the university. And as much as he wanted to put these people in their place, he would hold his tongue until after the graduation ceremony.

Just before dinner ended, Greenback leaned over and whispered to Steve. "This is certainly not the forum for debate, but I'm surprised that you would wear a hood. There's no empirical evidence for any of the claims in that Strand paper. Frankly, Mr. Cutter, without solid evidence, we cannot condone anyone following what it says. We're an institution of higher learning, not prone to rash decisions."

Steve simply nodded and went on eating his dinner. Anna was fuming. She couldn't understand why he kept silent, but decided she would play along anyway.

Busboys started clearing the table when Greenback leaned over once again to Steve. He took a deep breath and then quickly said, "I must ask you to please not wear the cloak and hood at tomorrow's ceremony. It would send the wrong message to the students. I hope you understand."

Greenback gave Steve a nervous grin, which exposed something green lodged between his teeth. *Lettuce, or the string beans?* Steve wondered.

Mr. Greenback was clearly nervous. After all, Steve Cutter had donated a large sum of money to the university and pledged even more gifts in the coming years, all of which were discretionary.

"I see, Mr. Greenback. You want me to compromise my beliefs to support yours."

Greenback was getting frustrated "Well, I'm acting in the best interest of the students, I'm sure you understand that."

"What I understand is that you're imposing your own personal beliefs on them instead of promoting independent thinking and accepting their freedom of choice."

"Of course we recognize freedom of choice, Mr. Cutter, but this is a university and we must set an example." Greenback stopped when he heard how his words sounded.

Steve looked at him as he fidgeted. "There's always a 'good reason' to take away freedom, always. Isn't that what history teaches us, Mr. Greenback? People need protection, protection from themselves by those who know better.

"Yes," Steve continued, "you're setting a fine example by masking intolerance with rhetoric, when in fact it's nothing more than pompous arrogance and an inflated perception of your own value. I will not compromise my beliefs to support your agenda with the student body."

Steve smiled and took the last bite of chicken on his plate. He recalled how much he disliked politics, and this conversation reminded him of his failures at the White House.

Greenback was clearly shaken by Steve's remarks. He didn't know if he'd lost his main benefactor or his speaker for the graduation ceremony or both.

Steve looked over at Anna and winked. Although she didn't know what had just transpired, she could tell it must have been good, because Greenback's face was pale.

Steve stood up and announced, "Thank you all for a wonderful dinner. However, Anna and I must leave now. It was a pleasure meeting everyone in person." He smiled and motioned for Anna to get up.

They left the table together, leaving Greenback and the directors sitting in stunned silence. As they crossed through the restaurant, Steve received a communication from Howler. There was trouble, in the form of men with weapons, back at the Black Hawk.

Anna had other things on her mind. "Uncle Steve," she blurted, "I'm not going to *Gaia* when I graduate. I'm going to work on leads from StrandsNet with Trib and Rose for a few months. That should be enough time to find proof of what we saw in Brazil and to show the press and make everyone believe."

Steve was stunned. He stopped and turned when they reached the lobby of the restaurant. "Anna, you know more than anyone else how dangerous this situation is. We need to talk about this."

Anna exploded. "This school, this graduation ceremony, these people, they're all so full of themselves! I should've never asked you to come. After tonight, I don't think I'm even going to the ceremony. I have my diploma already, so there's nothing they can do to me."

Steve stopped in his tracks. "You have your diploma? I thought you got it tomorrow."

"Technically, I graduated in December. I just hung around to the end to be with Trib and Rose. My diploma came in the mail months ago." Anna smiled and waited for a reaction.

But Steve had just received another Mayday call from Howler. Men in suits were surrounding the aircraft with guns and about to make a move. He checked systems on the Black Hawk, confirmed that the doors were locked, and started the engines. He didn't have much time to get the Black Hawk off the ground and out of weapons range. The limousine was waiting in the front of the restaurant as they emerged.

Steve put his hands on Anna's shoulders. "The CIA or the NSA just made a move on the Black Hawk at Cutter Technologies. If anything happens, you know how to contact me. Are you wearing the necklace?" He opened the limousine door and got in.

Anna pulled the amulet from under her blouse and showed it to her uncle.

"This conversation is not over, by the way," Steve warned through the window. "I'll call you in a few hours. For now, make yourself scarce until I can find out what's going on."

Anna didn't move.

"Go. Now! I'll contact you shortly." Anna took off running without saying a word. She knew her uncle. If he said it was real, she believed him. Steve slammed the rear window of the limousine as it peeled away from the curb.

So much for an uneventful trip, he thought. Things are heating up and I haven't even been here for a day.

The Death of Steve Cutter

The limo headed north out of town and threaded its way
east along the streets in the surrounding foothills.
Steve spied a large open field by a dirt road
and instructed the driver to turn.

CHAPTER 21:
The Death of Steve Cutter

They were on the dusty path for a few minutes when
Steve told the driver to stop by a large tree, where he
got out.

"Drive directly to San Francisco and wait there for
instructions," Steve told the driver.

The driver was confused but nodded. He turned the
car around and disappeared down the dirt road.

Steve walked over to the tree and sat down. The Black
Hawk would be there within fifteen minutes. "I guess the
president was expecting an answer to his invitation," he

said sarcastically. "An armed escort, how flattering."

He called Anna on the cell phone he'd given her. "Get out of town tonight, princess. Catch a flight somewhere and take Trib and Rose if you can. It looks like there'll be no ceremony for you tomorrow."

It was a short conversation. He just wanted to make sure she was far away from him until he could settle matters once and for all.

"With pleasure!" Anna said, "This place pi--umm, ticks me off. I'll call you from wherever I am when I get there." She hung up.

Steve had done as much as he could for the time being. He leaned against the trunk of the tree and waited.

Soon, he heard the Black Hawk circling overhead. As it descended, the door opened and Howler jumped out. He landed near Steve as the Black Hawk dropped a large rectangular crate and several small crates to the ground.

The helicopter didn't land, but immediately headed west along the foothills, staying below radar.

Howler gave Steve a long and piercing stare. He looked down at his dust-covered suit and mud-caked shoes. He didn't look much like an executive at a major company, and he didn't look like Strand. He looked like what he was, a man on the run and nothing more.

Howler signed. "You are hunted now. A human weak and easy to kill."

Steve walked over to the crate containing his exoskeleton and pried it open.

Howler came over and stood next to the crate. "You are reborn," he signed. "It is time for you to live … and it is time for you to die."

Howler was right. It was time for Steve Cutter to die.

It didn't matter what his reasons were in the past for not telling Anna, or that she still didn't know the truth.

Steve had rationalized his behavior for far too long.

Howler saw matters much more clearly. There was no more Steve Cutter. The whole charade had become too dangerous.

Once the exoskeleton and cloak were on this time, Steve Cutter ceased to exist.

Strand pulled the hood over his head. The familiar glowing blue eyes were easy to see on such a dark night.

"No more running," he told Howler. "It's everything or nothing."

He checked on the status of the Black Hawk. It was flying seriously low between the foothills several miles away.

"If they want a target," Strand said, "let's give them Steve Cutter. Shall we, Howler?"

The Black Hawk veered away from the foothills and headed across the beach to the ocean. It was flying over the water at about three hundred feet when proximity sensors went off.

Strand saw the trail of a small shoulder-held missile streak through the sky. An instant later, the Black Hawk exploded in a fireball, and its burning debris disappeared into the blackness of the Pacific.

Strand opened the rectangular crate, which contained the missile cycle. He lifted it out and carried it behind the tree, hiding it in some leaves and vegetation. He broke the crates into pieces to conceal any evidence that might give their position away.

The government had deduced the true identity of Strand. But with Steve Cutter dead, Strand was dead in their minds, too, and that's how he wanted it. It was better for the president and any other enemies, wherever they were, to think they'd accomplished their goal.

Strand and Howler would remain by the tree through

the night to leave Anna plenty of time to reach safety.

He burned his symbol into the tree trunk. He was done running.

The local news channels had started running news alerts regarding the explosion of an unidentified aircraft that had just occurred offshore. Strand saw the lights of Coast Guard helicopters circling and inspecting the crash site, and searching for survivors.

Within a few hours, a portion of the Black Hawk's tail was recovered. The media confirmed it shortly thereafter. Steve Cutter's helicopter exploded over the ocean with no reported survivors.

Howler was perched as high in the tree as he could climb without being seen, standing guard. Strand accessed surveillance cameras at Cutter Technologies. No one was in the parking lot and the landing pad for the Black Hawk was empty. That was a good sign. They obviously weren't expecting me back from the grave, he thought.

Strand called E and COTAR to let them know he and Howler were fine. He told them Kronos was on his way to *Gaia* and asked them to have Kronos contact him immediately upon his return.

Strand read all the postings on StrandsNet while he waited for the morning sun. He knew Anna would be traveling all night and that made him feel better. By daybreak, she would be safe and out of sight and he could make his next move.

Reading entries and viewing photographs taken from the back of the cruise ship, he became concerned about the reptiles. The pictures were clear enough to show the ocean underneath the cruise ship teeming with life.

Strand wondered why so many reptiles would follow a cruise ship. After a quick Internet search, he read that cruise ships dump an average of seven tons of ground garbage daily, a good portion of which is uneaten food. The waste from the ship was feeding the reptiles and attracting fish as well for the reptiles to feast on. As long as the reptiles followed the ship, they had easy access to food.

The reptiles were real, Strand thought.

His heart began to race as he went over all possible scenarios.

Anna, Trib, and Rose landed in Florida without a hitch. They too had followed the information about the reptiles. Their own research determined the trajectory of the herd would lead to Fort Lauderdale. Walking through the airport, Anna glanced up at a newscast repeating the top story of the day: Steve Cutter's helicopter was involved in an accident with no known survivors.

Anna stopped in her tracks and stared at the screen in disbelief.

Trib turned around. "Anna, what's the matter?"

Rose tapped her sister on the shoulder and pointed up at the television.

"Oh. Oh, no." Trib put her hand over her mouth.

Anna's eyes welled up. "They killed him. They killed him because he knows they're covering up the truth." She stood motionless, too stunned to move.

She reached for her necklace and pressed down on the jewel in the middle of the setting. Tears rolled down her cheeks as she held the jewel down desperately.

"Please, please, please be there. You can't be dead." Anna lowered her arms and felt weak in the knees. Trib and Rose were already at her side holding on. They were at a loss for words and didn't know what else to do except be there for her.

Rose finally spoke up. "Anna, something's ringing in your backpack."

"Anna, Anna," Trib said loudly, "do you have a phone in your backpack?"

Anna looked around in a fog. "No, no, I don't have a — wait a minute — I do have a phone in my backpack."

She dropped the backpack to the floor, flipped it open and tore into its contents looking for the phone Steve had given her on *Gaia*. She found it and answered.

"Uncle Steve!"

"Are you all right?"

"You're not dead?"

"No, not at all, ignore the reports. I'm fine, don't worry."

She turned to Rose and Trib. "He's not dead! Uncle Steve, I thought you were — I thought for sure you were dead. They're showing the crash site." Anna was crying tears of joy now.

"Anna, I'm fine. Someone wants me dead, that's all. They shot down the Black Hawk with a missile, but I wasn't in it. They don't know that; they think I'm dead." Strand paused. "Is anyone looking at you right now?"

Anna looked around. Several people had their eyes glued on her as her drama unfolded in the airport terminal. "Yeah, I thought you were dead. I kind of lost it."

"Stand up," Strand told her, "and get out of there as fast as you can. I don't think they're looking for you. They assume I'm gone, so you should be safe for now. Where are you?"

"We're in Fort Lauderdale. Those reptiles are headed right for us. When they get here, we'll take pictures and make sure the media sees what's happening. The president will finally have to acknowledge it, and we won't have to be on the run anymore."

Anna motioned for Rose and Trib to leave the airport

with her.

"Anna," Strand said, "I'm trying to keep you out of danger and you're walking right into it. These reptiles are extremely dangerous and it looks like there might be thousands of them."

"This has to stop once and for all, Uncle Steve. I mean, they tried to kill you! We're getting the evidence to expose the truth."

The girls were outside the terminal now and Anna was practically screaming into the phone. "I'm not going to let them get away with it, Uncle Steve. I have to do this!"

"Promise me you will stay away from the beach for the time being. A lot of people could get hurt and I don't want one of them to be you." Strand was getting the feeling that no matter what he said, Anna wasn't going to listen. She would apologize later if she had to, but she had made up her mind.

"Okay, Uncle Steve, I'll be careful. What are you going to do?"

"I'm coming to Florida as fast as possible. I'll call you when I have more details, but until then, promise me you'll stay away from all bodies of water except swimming pools, you got it? Promise me."

"Okay, I will. I'm just so happy you're alive. Don't let anyone else try to hurt you. I don't want to lose you," Anna's voice was cracking with emotion.

"I promise you, they will never get me, and I'll be in Florida soon."

"Okay, call me soon."

"I promise."

Anna hung up.

Strand felt the same helplessness as when he was escaping Brazil. Anna was in danger and not equipped to handle it, only this time he wasn't with her. He had spent so much time trying to save the world that he hadn't taken the time to protect his own flesh and blood.

Strand stared in the direction where the Black Hawk was obliterated from the sky. "That was your last move, Mr. President," he said to himself. "It's time for you to step down permanently."

He paused momentarily. "Howler, shall we let them know we're still alive?" Howler jumped down from the tree and landed beside him. Strand always had an intensity in his voice when something big was about to happen and Howler sensed it.

Just then, E contacted him from *Gaia*.

"Kronos is back," she said, "and it looks like something tried to eat him. His cloak is shredded and there are scratches and teeth marks on his exoskeleton. He's bruised and bleeding." E sounded upset.

Another voice broke the silence. "Strand, this is Kronos. The reptile herd is real. I've never seen anything like it before. There are maybe 10,000 trailing the cruise ship. They're eating every living thing along the way. Passengers on the ship are throwing leftover food overboard and watching it get devoured for fun." Kronos was out of breath.

"Were you attacked?"

"Yes, they're very aggressive and very hungry. They're similar to crocodiles or alligators, but they've changed. They've all taken different shapes. Some have long necks and flippers; others have large rear legs and small front legs. The one that attacked me had the body of a croc and a head like a T-rex. And let me tell you, they are mean and vicious. Anyone near wherever that cruise ship is headed will be devoured.

"If these things hit a populated beach, things will get ugly very quick." Kronos sighed, exhausted.

"The ship is headed to Fort Lauderdale," Strand said. "Can you get ahead of them and try to warn everyone near the beach?" Strand knew Kronos was a frightening sight to behold and simply emerging from the ocean would send most people running for shelter.

"I don't know, Strand, those T-rex crocs are smart and quick. But I'll try. Here's E again."

"E, you're in danger," Strand warned. "Everyone onboard is in danger. I don't know if they're planning on sinking *Gaia* or boarding her to steal the technology, but they have some sort of plan and it's not looking good."

Strand's voice was getting strained. "COTAR is preparing all of the hovercraft for departure should it become necessary. If anyone tries to board *Gaia*, you must find a way to get off immediately. I will sink her myself before I allow our technology to fall into the wrong hands. Do you understand me, E? I'll be in contact soon. Good-bye."

E was trying to process what Strand told her and what it meant for her future. Not only might *Gaia* be destroyed, but there was nowhere left to run and hide. E remembered the submarine that simply disappeared under the ocean with all its firepower. It could be following them from a distance and surprise them with a torpedo at any moment.

E turned around and saw only a robot. "Where did Kronos go?"

COTAR Prime answered. "He was here for a few minutes but he dove overboard again."

E was dazed. "He's gone already?"

COTAR tried to reassure her. "Don't worry, the hovercraft are almost ready. We can get out of here in a matter of minutes if need be. I know exactly what to do. Everything will be fine, E."

"They know who we are and where we are. We can't

outrun the entire U.S. Navy, that's for sure. I don't know what to do."

E slowly tried to regain her composure. She knew keeping busy would help, and decided to gather her research and samples in case they were forced to evacuate. She started out the door, before stopping abruptly and spinning around. "COTAR, what about you? Can you get off *Gaia*? What will happen to you?"

"I've lived through something worse than death, so I am no longer afraid to die. I will protect you with my life for as long as I am alive." COTAR Prime's electronic voice lacked the subtle inflections of the human voice, but E had no doubt he would protect her to the death.

She turned and ran to her lab.

Strand lifted the missile cycle up and put it on its base, its nose facing the morning sky. He began the prelaunch diagnostic routine.

"Are you ready, Howler?"

Howler gave his patented intense stare that told Strand the whole story. This monkey was ready for just about anything.

I wonder if you're ready for Mach 3, Strand wondered.

"You are one tough monkey, you know that, Howler?"

Strand hopped on the missile cycle and motioned for Howler to get on as well. Howler sat in front of Strand. Strand leaned over and covered him with his body while grabbing hold of the control levers on both sides of the missile.

"No more running," Strand said, "it's time to ride." He fired the rocket booster on the back of the missile. It roared to life and within seconds they were airborne. They shot almost straight up to gain as much altitude as quickly as possible.

The level of power and thrust involved made the

ride rough but exhilarating. A few clicks later, the rocket boosters fell away and the jet engines took over. Strand and Howler were traveling almost 200 miles per hour and climbing. He double-checked the systems on the missile cycle. It was going to be a breakneck, dangerous trip from California to Florida.

As they shot through the sky, Strand reflected on how he'd been on the run since the beginning, since that day in front of the White House.

Today he was done running.

No matter what the outcome, he was done with it. As long as he was being hunted, Anna, E, and anyone else he cared about were in danger. It was time to bring it to an end one way or another.

Strand veered the missile cycle toward the university. The dinner conversation was still fresh in his head, as was Greenback's pompous arrogance. He wasn't going to let the students think something was wrong with wearing a cloak and protecting themselves from the moonlight.

Strand monitored the radar on *Gaia* to see if any ships were in the vicinity. Then he checked the fish swarms for any submarine activity. There was nothing above or below the water. All was quiet.

COTAR Prime prepared the Black Hawks on the lower deck and loaded them with soldier bots. They were ready to depart at a moment's notice.

E was in her lab backing up and copying her work. While the possibility of leaving the ship had always been there, she never thought it would ever get this close.

The research on Kronos, the effects of the strand implants, the progress with Howler, it was all so valuable, but it was more than that. *Gaia* had become her home. The thought of everything she'd come to love being destroyed was too much to contemplate. E fought back tears as she prepared to leave.

The hovercraft were ready. But they were empty so far. If *Gaia* were to be sunk, she would take the technology with her.

COTAR Prime entered the lab where E was frantically trying to organize her data before leaving. "E, you know, if we got boarded now or caught on the one of the hovercraft, they'd take all of that research. It must be destroyed."

E stopped dead in her tracks and spun around. "What are you saying?"

She had a dazed look in her eyes. She suddenly understood.

"Give everything to me that you want to save," COTAR Prime said, "and I'll have it scanned and transferred to Cutter Technologies computers in the Mojave."

E held her collected research tight against her lab coat, clutching it like a newborn baby. She walked over to COTAR Prime and handed it over. She was visibly upset. Even though she knew COTAR Prime was right, she didn't want to let it go. It was more than the research. It was one more step toward leaving and the end of *Gaia*.

"There you go," E said painfully. "Please do whatever you have to do quickly. That information is valuable to me."

COTAR Prime took the files from her. "You've been wearing your gloves a lot lately. Is everything okay?

"What's that? Oh, gloves. Yes, I'm fine, my hands are sensitive, that's all."

"Okay, I'll go take care of this. Call me if you need anything at all." COTAR Prime turned and left the lab.

Strand spotted the university on the horizon. Local TV stations were reporting missile cycle sightings and the military had scrambled fighters to intercept him. Soon the whole world would know.

The chase was on, just as he had planned. He was going to give them a show they would never forget, a cross-country chase that would take hours and would be played out to a global audience live, on television.

The cycle reached supersonic speed and a sonic boom rumbled above the university, rattling windows and sending flocks of birds into the air. Within seconds, students were pouring out of dorms to see what made the noise. Strand whipped the missile cycle around and slowed it; once again, a sonic boom rocked the campus. More and more students emptied out of the dorms and witnessed the missile cycle approaching.

Suddenly every student's cell phone began to ring. Most had witnessed the televised events in London, Paris, Madrid, and Rome. They answered their phones knowing it was Strand.

"I am Strand, I am the harbinger. I have important information. Bring your laptops and meet me at the statue in front of the library. Hurry, I don't have much time."

Hundreds of students darted across campus.

When Strand reached the statue, he grabbed Howler and leapt from the missile. They landed in a crouched position to help absorb the impact of the jump. The friction of supersonic travel had heated their cloaks, and steam rose from the black cloth into the crisp morning air.

Strand and Howler stood up and greeted the welcoming faces of the students surrounding them. They had very little time. Strand had confirmed the military had already scrambled jets and helicopters to the area.

He immediately accessed the surrounding laptops remotely and began downloading video of the mariners he had taken in Africa. Taken from Strand's perspective, it showed him walking up to Amani's decapitated head in the mud, the ensuing attack from below, and the savagery of the outcome.

The students watched in horror as the video streamed onto their laptops.

The missile cycle was on its way back to pick them up as fighters approached in the distance.

"I am Strand, I am the harbinger. The video is real. I was there and saw it with my own eyes. Wear your cloaks outside. Protect yourselves from the moonlight."

Everyone stared at the laptops and at Strand and then with amazement at Howler. The monkey pulled back his hood and opened his faceplate. He stared intensely at the students surrounding them. He was looking for someone. He walked into the crowd and up to a young woman still in her bathrobe.

Howler signed. "Mayuta." He looked at Strand and repeated the name. "Mayuta."

He grabbed her by the hand and brought her to Strand. She did not resist.

"Mayuta," Howler repeated.

Strand looked at the woman carefully. She was blind, but that wasn't what Howler was referring to. She seemed to have a faint glow about her.

Howler signed again. "Mayuta, Kronos, newborn."

She was changing, she was evolving, and Howler knew it even if no one else did.

Strand retracted his faceplate. "What is your name?"

"My name's Rebecca," the pretty girl said quietly.

"If we survive this day, you are welcome to join us at any time."

"Thank you."

The missile cycle was close. Strand and Howler closed their faceplates and stepped back. They crouched and jumped simultaneously. Moments later they were accelerating to the speed of sound.

As Strand looked back, he could see the students dispersing. Their phones started to ring again, but this time, he said only one word: "StrandsNet."

Strand accelerated past supersonic speed and rattled the windows of SCU with a parting sonic boom. He could see jet fighters on the horizon.

The cable news channels and the local television stations were interrupting programming to report that Strand was supersonic over California.

The chase was on. Strand smiled under his faceplate and went to Mach 3. Few planes could catch him at that speed.

The fighters behind him fired missiles, as did additional fighters that suddenly appeared on the horizon. They were trying to catch him in the crossfire.

The news media broadcast glimpses of fighters and missiles from handheld camcorders and digital cameras. Within minutes, the dogfight was being shown internationally.

Strand slowed the missile cycle and sat upright. He watched the missiles streaking toward them and raised his metal arm. Bright blue lasers shot across the sky as every missile exploded in mid-air.

He accelerated and overtook one of the jets. As he passed over the cockpit, he flipped the missile cycle over. The pilot looked up in surprise. Strand wagged his finger at him like a schoolteacher scolding a student, and shot straight up and away from the fighter. The pilot changed course to give chase just as Strand expected. Soon more fighters would join them.

Strand suddenly became aware of motion in the water beneath *Gaia*. The fish swarms were detecting four large submerged vessels approaching from behind.

Strand called COTAR, but before he could say anything, COTAR spoke.

"I know about the submarines approaching us on all sides. We're ready to go. The hovercraft will act as an initial diversion, and the Black Hawks are being raised as we speak.

Strand watched the video feeds as they streamed into his head from the ship's cameras. The ocean surrounding her was relatively quiet, but it was only the calm before the storm and he knew it.

"COTAR, they're positioning themselves around *Gaia*. As soon as the boats are in the water, send them off in different directions. Get off the ship now and head for Fort Lauderdale. I'll meet you there shortly."

As a few Black Hawks took to the air, the submarines emerged from underwater. COTAR launched the hovercraft, navigating them away from *Gaia*. Although Strand knew the they wouldn't distract the subs for long, it would force them to slow or risk a collision.

There were many hidden areas on *Gaia* behind large locked doors. They were Strand's own laboratories. He could invent and research and operate machinery at the same time. He had developed a passion for building robots, from small utility bots to soldier bots, but none of them had weapons that could kill.

Robot construction was one of his most closely guarded secrets, one too dangerous to be made commercial through Cutter Technologies. He battled for years with the idea of developing a robot with full-power lasers, but it disturbed him to have machines able to kill. The technology might fall into the hands of a subversive well-funded government that could create a mechanical army.

As usual, it was Anna that had provided him the guiding light. If she ever was in danger, they would have to exist, so nothing else mattered.

So he had built the Full Power Laser (FPL) bots and stored them in compartments no one had seen since *Gaia* was rebuilt, and the doors were sealed after her christening.

Now more than ever, Strand was grateful that he had made that decision, and now was the time to break them out. A hidden door in the Black Hawk hangar bay swung open. Three dozen FPL bots burst through, running at full speed toward the elevator platform that raised the Black Hawks for takeoff. They jumped through the opening onto the top deck.

The FPL bots' lasers glowed with the same intensity as Strand's. Their cloaks covered small rocket boosters on their shoulders and made their upper torsos appear massive. They had large internal power supplies, causing their arms to bow slightly away from their bodies as they walked.

Strand opened the back of the fourth level on *Gaia*, and commenced a preflight check on the thirty-six missile cycles.

COTAR Prime gazed at the FPL bots as he heard the missile cycles firing. He looked above the control tower at the missiles climbing into the bright sky. They were launching in sets of three. Just as soon as three more cleared the tower, another three were launched.

The missile cycles circled back around. COTAR Prime looked carefully at the three dozen bots. Their eyes were an intense red under their hoods and their cloaks billowed in the wind.

The FPL bots stood motionless as the first set of three missile cycles crossed overhead. The front three jumped straight up and mounted the missiles perfectly. These bots would make it to Fort Lauderdale before the Black Hawks.

COTAR Prime understood exactly what was happening. The reptiles must be close to the beach. He turned and raced to the last Black Hawk preparing to lift off and jumped onboard.

As he took off in the Black Hawk, he watched the ship get smaller as they climbed. All the Black Hawks were in the air now, and each had six soldier bots onboard. They flew in a massive V-formation toward the coast of Florida.

COTAR Prime monitored the submarines surrounding *Gaia*. There was one in front, one in back, and one on each side. Someone wanted the secrets badly to put that much military hardware in one location. The Trident class submarines were almost half as long as *Gaia*.

The last trio of FPL bots mounted their missile cycles and all thirty-six came around the back of the control tower. It was an incredible sight as they flew in perfect formation and accelerated in unison. From his vantage point in the Black Hawk, COTAR Prime saw the flare of the rockets and heard the whine of the jet engines all around. The entire flock blasted by the Black Hawks as if the helicopters were only hovering. Sonic booms started crackling in the atmosphere like popcorn. One by one, the missile cycles streaked into the distance with a thunderous roar.

COTAR Prime peered back at *Gaia* and wondered if he would ever see her again. She was his home, his haven, and the place of his rebirth. He never wanted to believe she would be destroyed. They were tied together in every aspect.

He felt like Dr. Vitimani again for a moment, as if recent events were only a dream and he was still a normal and healthy man.

Then he caught a glimpse of his metal hand.

He was the same scientist who lost everything before being reborn as something more. Living on *Gaia* had sheltered him from reality. Although Steve had tried to warn him, he had become completely consumed with being born again. But the seriousness of their current predicament finally overshadowed the wonderment at his rebirth as COTAR. What he did now was all that mattered.

He pulled the hood over his head and sat back. He double-checked all sensors and systems to recalibrate each soldier in preparation for what lay ahead.

Strand observed the Black Hawks and missile cycles as they pulled away from *Gaia*. She was surrounded by nuclear submarines that she couldn't outrun or avoid. He wouldn't sink her, not unless he had to, and he hadn't even begun to fight yet.

Gaia had several defensive measures in place short of destroying the attacker. Warfare at sea required a keen sense of your opponent's weaknesses. The submarines surrounding the ship had propellers and computers, and that was all Strand needed to stop them without destroying them.

The fish swarms underneath *Gaia* regrouped into four separate schools. They immediately separated and headed for each submarine. Each fish-like robot was armed with a small explosive charge; while each fish was not very effective on an attacker by itself, hundreds of them collectively could cause serious damage.

The schools headed directly for the propellers on the submarines and detonated simultaneously. The explosions damaged the blades on all four sets of propellers and sent them careening out of balance. The subs still had propulsion but at a severely limited speed, virtually eliminating the option of submerging.

Strand then deployed *Gaia's* electromagnetic pulse bomb.

After an EMP is detonated, all objects within a certain radius are rendered inoperative. The pulse was a combination of varying wavelengths, magnetic particles, and accelerated electrons.

The computers, radar, and weapons systems all failed simultaneously in each submarine. The EMP disrupted all communications and corrupted any data not already written to the hard drives onboard. The weapon wasn't designed to sink or to kill, it was designed to paralyze.

It worked magically. The four submarines floated listlessly off course and slowed to a dead stop on the surface of the ocean.

Gaia had shut all systems down prior to releasing the EMP. When the effects of the pulse dissipated, Strand turned everything back on. The ship steamed by the Trident class submarines at full speed.

A Trident class submarine is the deadliest weapons platform to be launched in history. Every vessel stores 154 Tomahawk cruise missiles, which can be launched in a matter of minutes. Thirty of the cruise missiles are equipped with 250-kiloton nuclear warheads, ten times more powerful than the ones used at Hiroshima and Nagasaki.

For the Pentagon to simultaneously lose communication with four submarines carrying such a payload was catastrophic.

The matter was immediately brought to the attention of General Asmore at the Pentagon. He discussed it feverishly with officials in the White House situation room.

"Lost communications? How can you lose four at the same time? Is there any missile activity in that area? Get me recon! What the hell is going on?"

The general was livid. He had opposed bringing that much firepower together in one place without additional precautionary measures in place. Now his worst fears were being realized.

A naval officer spoke up. "Sir, there are reports of multiple Tomahawks in the air as we speak … as many as three dozen headed directly for the U.S."

The general was stunned. "I don't believe it." He knew that if these Tomahawks contained nuclear warheads, they could destroy everything from Florida to Texas.

Everyone in the situation room was thinking the same thing. They all turned to face Asmore. The general picked up a phone that connected directly to the Oval Office, used only in emergencies.

"Hello?" The president was in a cabinet meeting. Everyone knew the phone rang only during a crisis, so the room became thick with tension.

"Mr. President, this is General Asmore. We've somehow lost communication with four nuclear submarines near the Gulf of Mexico. At the same time, we have reports of thirty-six inbound Tomahawk missiles. We estimate they will reach U.S. soil in less than thirty minutes. And we have to presume they're carrying nuclear warheads."

The president decided quickly. "You have my full authority to use any available means to stop those missiles."

Everyone in the Oval Office stood up. The president's face told the story that something disastrous was happening.

"I want an update every five minutes. Do whatever it takes to stop those nukes."

The president hung up and looked around at the anxious faces turned to him.

"We're under attack. Thirty-six Tomahawks with nuclear warheads are headed for U.S. soil. We have less than thirty minutes until they hit.

"It appears we've also lost four nuclear submarines. Mr. Strand is alive and well. He's waging a war, and he's using our own weapons against us. I knew he was dangerous, but never in my wildest imagination did I think he'd try to destroy us." The president glared with anger.

Within minutes, every military base and aircraft carrier from the Gulf of Mexico to the Atlantic launched fighters.

The general knew that even if planes could get there in time to stop some of the missiles, they could not stop them all. And while no one said it out loud, everyone in the White House had drawn the same conclusion. Millions of people were going to die and there was nothing they could do about it.

Strand was flying the missile cycle at nearly Mach 2 across Texas. He was monitoring military communications and knew a massive number of aircraft were in the air. He expected additional aircraft to join the chase, but he never expected this many.

Strand checked the video feeds on *Gaia*. The submarines were adrift in the surrounding waters. The pulse had worked beautifully. Even if it only bought him a few hours, that was plenty for now.

He checked the location of the cruise ship heading into Fort Lauderdale. It was close enough to be visible from the port and he knew he wasn't going to make it in time, nor were any of the missile cycles.

If the reptiles went onto the beach, the bloodshed would be catastrophic. Maybe a phone call to the president could persuade him to take action. It was a long shot, but there was no other option.

The phone ringing in the Oval Office broke the uncomfortable silence, but it was the regular line this time. An aide answered it and slowly turned to the president.

"It's him, it's Mr. Strand on the phone," the young man said sheepishly.

The president went over and grabbed the phone. "This is the president speaking."

"Mr. President, many innocent people are going to die within the next thirty minutes. It may be too late to stop it, but if there's any hope to even minimize the death toll, only you can do it."

"And what would you have me do, Mr. Strand?"

"Clear every beach and waterway from Miami to Fort Lauderdale. Get everyone in those areas to shelter before there is massive bloodshed."

"And what makes you think only those on the beach are at risk? Surely you know the risk extends beyond the shoreline?"

Strand thought it sounded like the president was already aware of the reptiles.

"They will surely come on land, but through channels and over beaches first. You'll need the military to patrol the area and prevent them from attacking. These creatures are hungry and aggressive, sir. I'll get there as soon as I can."

"What are you talking about, Mr. Strand?"

"I am talking about the reptiles about to attack Fort Lauderdale."

"Is that why you've sunk four nuclear submarines and launched thirty-six Tomahawk missiles? Is that your rationalization for destroying Southern Florida with nuclear weapons?" The president was trying to contain his anger.

It took Strand only a moment to realize what had happened. "Mr. President, your submarines have not been destroyed. They will contact you in the next twenty minutes. The missiles you speak of are bringing fighting robots to the beach in Fort Lauderdale to try to stop the reptiles from murdering tourists."

Strand knew as soon the sentence was out of his mouth, it was no use. The president would never believe him. Strand quickly thought of an alternate way to use the call. Since the president wouldn't save the people on the beach, the world would know without question that their blood was on his hands.

A moment later he turned the phone call into a streaming audio broadcast.

"Mr. President, you're making a terrible mistake. Hundreds, maybe thousands will be killed within the next thirty minutes, and you're the only one who can do something about it.

"You've lost your focus. Don't fall victim to your own perceptions of the importance of your office. Don't let them die because of your hatred for me and my abilities."

The president still wasn't listening. He took a cold and stoic tone. "Why don't we just talk about it, Mr. Strand, and you call off the missile attack? I'll send a special envoy to that area to assess the threat."

Strand knew the president was trying to placate him. "Innocent people are going to be ripped apart by these reptiles, the likes of which the earth hasn't seen since the Jurassic period. I'm trying to save lives and you, sir, are still playing games. I'm flying at almost

Mach 2 on my way to Fort Lauderdale because I know what's coming up the coast. They're more dangerous than any of the creatures in Brazil. You covered that up, but this time the world will witness it firsthand and you will forfeit your office."

"We have the Brazilian threat well in hand, I assure you, Mr. Strand."

"Are you listening to me, sir? Ignoring this will be the last mistake of your political career."

Every television and radio station on the planet was broadcasting the exchange. Billions were listening, but no one was sure if it was a hoax.

"This is the last day of your presidency," Strand said.

"Do you expect me to believe you have robots flying missiles to rescue these people? Really, Mr. Strand, I'm not that naïve. Now why don't you recall these missiles?"

Strand lowered his altitude to 200 feet and the pursuing fighters followed suit.

"I'm about to pass over Baton Rouge, with a squad of jet fighters about to shoot me down. I don't believe you're naïve, Mr. President, I believe you've forgotten why you were elected."

Residents of Baton Rouge ran outside and looked in the sky. A lone missile cycle screamed across the afternoon sky. Moments later, twenty jets followed in hot pursuit. The roar of their engines rattled windows.

Within minutes, footage of the chase was being broadcast live worldwide. There was no mistaking the truth this time.

Strand was on a roll. "You could have been remembered as one of the greatest presidents in history, but instead you'll be remembered as the one blinded by his ego and self-righteousness that let thousands of people die." Strand wanted to stoke the president's anger so he lost control before becoming aware the conversation was being broadcast.

"I brought you the second chapter before I released it to the public. I let you review it and hoped you would validate it, but you tricked me into thinking you're sincere. You're a fraud, Mr. President. Your intentions aren't to protect the people, but to protect your bruised ego."

"Mr. Strand, I assure you that isn't true." The president was just barely containing his anger.

Strand knew the president would be alerted any minute. There was only one thing left to talk about. "Dr. Vitimani was there in the Brazilian forest and he was paralyzed by the toxin."

That was it. The president lost control. "Dr. Vitimani was killed in a HELICOPTER CRASH and he's very much DEAD, Mr. Strand!"

"He was brought back from Brazil very much alive, but paralyzed, and you authorized exploratory brain surgery to study the effects of the toxin. Then, you moved him to a military base and the CDC announced he was dead. Even his wife mourned. But I assure you, he is very much alive."

"That's ridiculous. Nothing of the sort happened, and like I've said before, nothing happened in Brazil."

"You have covert operations in Brazil hunting and killing those same creatures in order to cover up the truth. But I know the truth, Mr. President. You, sir, are a liar, and unfit to hold the office of president."

The president exploded. "How dare you insult this office and the people that it serves! There's nothing going on in Brazil. Your delusions have gotten so dangerous that you can now rationalize a missile attack."

"Those missiles aren't attacking. Those are my missile riders bringing reinforcements to Fort Lauderdale to fight off the imminent reptile attack you're ignoring, the one in which thousands are about to die, the one you've not even attempted to check on. If they were actually missiles, why would they all be attacking the same city? If they were explosive or nuclear, why send thirty-six when one would do? Why would I do that, Mr. President? You're making a grievous error, one that will cost lives and your career."

"CALL OFF THE MISSILES NOW, MR. STRAND, YOUR ATTACK IS AN ACT OF WAR AND OUR MILITARY HAS FULL AUTHORITY TO SHOOT YOU DOWN." The president was screaming, his face red with anger.

"I DEMAND AS THE PRESIDENT OF THE UNITED STATES OF AMERICA THAT YOU IMMEDIATELY CEASE AND DESIST YOUR ATTACK."

"I'm going to Florida as fast as I can to save as many people as possible." Strand had what he wanted. The president had lost control and his words would echo across history.

An aide burst into the president's office. "Your call is being broadcast, Mr. President. Everyone everywhere can hear what you're saying."

"Good-bye, Mr. President. The blood of the people killed today is on your hands. I only hope your vice president doesn't make the same mistakes as you when he takes office." Strand terminated the call.

The president looked around the oval office. The expression on everyone's face told the story. He had lost his temper, and he had lost control. If Strand was right, he had just committed political suicide live for the world to hear.

"THIS MAN IS A LUNATIC AND MUST BE STOPPED, DO YOU HEAR ME? HE MUST BE STOPPED! SHOOT HIM DOWN, FIRE AT WILL." The president barked orders to the generals, who did nothing in the situation room. The cabinet members excused themselves from the Oval Office.

The president was too angry to hear what Strand was saying, but the military was not.

"Why would he send thirty-six missiles to destroy an area when one would do it?" Asmore sat back in his chair and barked at his assistant. "What's going on in Brazil? Get me the information now!" Things weren't adding up in the general's mind, and he knew from experience that meant something was wrong.

An officer approached with a document. It was the order to fire at will and shoot down Strand.

"Strand is flying over heavily populated areas. What is the president thinking? What's he asking us to do?"

He picked up the phone. "This is General Asmore. Do not, I repeat, *do not* fire without my direct order. Inform me when you have a firing solution. Is that understood?"

Another aide ran into the situation room carrying a file. "Sir, the Brazilian operation is real."

The general shook his head and grabbed the file. "What about this reptile thing, what is this about?"

"StrandsNet, sir, StrandsNet."

"Get me everything on it now!"

Asmore sat down, opened the file, and started to review its contents. He pulled out a photo out of an enormous dead snake as tall as the soldiers in front of it.

He slammed his fist on the conference table. "You mean this is REAL?"

T-Rex Crocodiles

Anna's ears were still ringing with her uncle's words.
She'd promised to stay away from the beach
and technically she was,
since the beach was still across the boulevard.

CHAPTER 22: T–Rex Crocodiles

She knew she was playing games with her promise, and she knew they weren't equipped to fight off the reptiles or anything even close. They had no weapons, only the sabers from their fencing class.

She looked over at Rose and Trib. They couldn't possibly understand the danger they might be facing since they never saw what went on in the Brazilian jungle in person. Soon the cruise ship would be here, and Anna hoped they could just take pictures and bring them to the press.

But when she saw the vessel appear in the distance, her heart sank. She'd forgotten the brutality of the creatures in the forest until that moment. She suddenly became terrified. She looked at Rose and Trib and knew they were now in mortal danger because of her.

Rose saw it, too. "That's it, that's the ship!"

"I know," Anna replied in a low voice.

Trib noticed a change in her friend. "What's wrong, Anna?"

"You two shouldn't be here. Promise me you'll stay put and let me get the pictures. Please promise me." Anna was pleading.

"Anna, we haven't come this far to back out," Rose said. "We'll go together and everything will be okay. Don't worry about it." She put her hand on Anna's shoulder.

"If this gets too dangerous, promise me you'll stay here and not go over to the beach. Promise me."

"Not a chance," Trib said

"Not a chance," Rose repeated.

"Listen to me, I have a whip with a 100,000-volt charge on the tip, and you have sabers from fencing class with the plastic tip removed and the ends sharpened. You won't have a chance."

Anna turned to find the cruise ship halfway down the beach and heading for the docks.

"Anna, look," Rose said, "the ship has almost passed already. Let's not get too dramatic."

It was true. The ship seemed to be passing without incident.

"Come on, let's go," Trib said. "I didn't come this far not to at least cross the street and take a picture." She started across the boulevard. Rose followed her and Anna came running to catch up.

They reached the boardwalk on the ocean side of the beach. Suddenly music from the next block could be heard. A few hundred yards down was the back of an outdoor stage.

Anna pointed. "What's that?"

"Video Music Television's Summer at Fort Lauderdale

Festival," Trib answered.

"How do you know?"

Trib pointed at the back of the bus stop bench. A billboard sponsored by VMT announced the details of the event. "Because they're advertising it, that's how."

As soon as the girls stepped onto the sand, something shot out of the ocean directly to their left. The sound and motion startled the girls. They quickly turned to see what looked like a human flying fifty feet in the air and descending to the beach. It landed in a crouched position no more than twenty feet from where the girls were standing.

The strange being had a bulbous back which, when flexed, folded into itself and against his body. He had torn and tattered fins extending down each shoulder to his feet, which were clearly not organic. He had a massive upper body, muscular arms, and wore some kind of advanced exoskeleton technology. As he stood, the girls saw its face and stepped backward to put more distance between them. It was human and something more, and it was bleeding.

Anna barked orders at Rose and Trib. "Stay here and get pictures."

She pulled her whip out and charged over the sand. She got to within eight feet of the creature and assumed a fighting stance. It was one that Uncle Steve had taught her, where anything within range could be stunned or killed in an instant.

The creature spoke. "Would you kill me then? Kill the harbinger?"

Anna knew those words. Those were the words of Strand. "Harbinger of what?"

Rose and Trib were running to join Anna with their sabers drawn.

"Girls, I am not what you fear. My name is Kronos and

my duty is to protect the innocent. What you fear is still in the water ... but they will arrive in a matter of minutes. We must warn everyone on the beach." Kronos spied the back of the stage at the music festival and sighed. "We better start there."

Anna was still poised and ready to attack. "Who sent you?"

"Strand, COTAR Prime, E, and Howler." Kronos began to sprint to the stage a block over.

Anna was speechless. She couldn't believe what she was hearing. She ran after him with Rose and Trib right behind her.

Kronos looked back. "The reptile herd is large, maybe 10,000 animals. At the front are crocodiles with T-rex heads. They're fast and strong. Behind them, the herd fans out with every variation of croc you can fathom. Some have long necks, others have fins and no legs, and a few have legs but no fins.

"They all have teeth ... and they're all hungry. The herd extends from the back of that cruise ship to that stage over there. Hurry."

Anna was running as fast as she could, but failing to keep up with Kronos. Still confused, she yelled out another question. "Where do you come from, and who sent you again?" But it was too late.

Kronos had crouched and jumped high in the air, covering a city block in a single leap and landing within yards of the festival stage.

The reptiles had observed their prey from the water. Far from being mindless killing machines, they were pack hunters, and sizing up their prey was almost a ritual. They remained far enough from shore to remain undetected, but close enough to hear the humans party and dance, oblivious to the danger lurking in the water.

Pack hunters instinctively know to divide the herd they're about to prey on and then set traps. With infinite patience, they look to each other for signals and subtleties that guide the strategy of an attack.

The T-rex crocs were the undisputed leaders. All of the other types of crocodiles remained behind them. Any reptile that swam too close ran the risk of being mauled and devoured mercilessly.

The hunters sensed that most of their prey was crowded around the stage. The reptiles clustered into four groups. Without a sound, they started to swim for shore.

They moved forward slowly and methodically, barely disrupting the water as they swam. Reaching the surf zone, between the breakers and the wave uprush, the T-rex crocs stopped. The rest of the herd knew an attack was imminent and instinctively sensed it was feeding time, but remained quiet and motionless.

Tens of thousands of hungry reptile eyes poking just above the surface of the ocean peered at their prey on the beach. They remained patiently behind the four columns of T-rex crocs waiting to spring their trap.

A few minutes later, two college girls covered in spilled drinks walked into the surf to wash the stickiness off. They were giggling as each pointed out stains on each other's yellow bikini.

The T-rex crocs in front of the reptile columns watched the girls wade deeper and deeper into the ocean. Two at the front of the pack submerged silently and headed directly for the girls.

In the crowd at the festival, nothing seemed out of the ordinary. They were enjoying a band named Catherine Wheel, playing a song called "Black Metallic."

"It's the color of your skin ... your skin is black metallic ...."

The revelers danced blissfully away, unaware of the grave danger lurking less than thirty yards away.

Even those looking out at the ocean failed to witness the sudden disappearance of the two girls, who in a series of violent tugs, were pulled underwater.

The blood in the water signaled a start to the imminent feeding frenzy. The reptiles could no longer remain lurking in the water.

The four T-rex crocs at the head of the columns ferociously lunged forward, emerging from the surf and running quickly over the sand.

Screaming and terrified by the sight of the storming herd, the crowd ran wildly in all directions, tripping in the sand and over each other. They froze in fear as the columns of T-rex crocs ran past them, snapping but not attacking.

The reptiles maintained their rapid march up the beach as they divided the fleeing crowd into three separate groups. Taking advantage of the complete chaos, they encircled the crowd. In less than a minute, the crowd was caught in their trap. Unable to escape down the beach in either direction, there was only one place left for the crowd to run: the ocean.

Without a sound, the T-rex crocs stood up on their hind legs. In that position, they were even more intimidating, ranging in height from eight to fifteen feet tall. They snapped and lunged at the crowd of ensnared people, sending them running into the surf.

A billion years of genetic pack-hunting expertise worked flawlessly. As the separated crowd backed into the surf transfixed on the T-rex crocs, they were completely unaware of the thousands of reptiles waiting a few yards behind them.

The T-rex crocs broke ranks and attacked from the

front and sides. Simultaneously, the rest of the herd ambushed from the rear. There was no escape, nowhere to hide, and most victims were too stunned to think clearly. They simply froze in fear, seconds before being overrun by the rampaging reptiles. They were nothing more than meat to feed a Jurassic appetite.

Anna reached the backstage area of the festival just as satellite news crews raced in the direction of Kronos. The music had just been replaced by screams and Anna knew it was too late.

The fastest route for Strand to reach Fort Lauderdale was to cross the Gulf of Mexico. As he raced across, he was convinced the fighters would try to shoot him down over water since there was no risk of any collateral damage.

Asmore picked up the phone in the situation room.

"We have a firing solution, sir," a voice said. "Do we have authorization to proceed?"

Asmore studied the papers spread out on the conference table. A television in the corner tuned to CNN broke in with reports of a massacre in Fort Lauderdale.

"Do not fire," the general ordered. "Maintain firing solution as long as possible."

Strand crossed the remainder of the Gulf of Mexico at Mach 3. More jet fighters joined the chase, bringing the total to more than forty.

Strand prepared to take evasive maneuvers. Stopping missiles from that many fighters would take time. He fired a booster to put as much distance between himself and the fighters as possible.

He braced for the expected attack. The fighters remained in a an aggressive formation, but they were holding back. That could only mean someone at the Pentagon was beginning to believe him.

Anna rounded the corner of the stage and was almost

stampeded by a crowd of panicked concertgoers running from the beach. She could hear the sounds of animals chomping and grunting, and the screams of their prey.

Further down the beach, T-rex crocodiles had been crawling about on all fours. Anna stared in disbelief as they stood up on two feet and started to charge the people running from them.

The victims were no match for the creatures' speed. A T-rex croc took one bite out of a person with its massive jaws and discarded the body over its shoulders, hurling it back toward the surf. Young T-rex crocs waited at the water's edge to feast on the remains.

Behind the young crocs, the water bubbled furiously. A moment later, thousands of reptiles came out of the surf as far down the beach as Anna could see.

It wasn't an attack; it was an invasion.

Trib and Rose finally caught up to their friend. "Anna, we have to get out of here … now."

"Anna, let's go," Rose added. "Or we'll all die." She tried to grab Anna's arm to pull her away from the inevitable.

But Anna wasn't leaving. She turned and charged toward the nearest reptile.

She hadn't gone far when something stopped her cold. It was Kronos, who had jumped on the back of a huge T-rex croc and was riding it like a horse. The Mariner reached over the beast's head, grabbing hold of its top jaw and pulling.

The snout finally burst apart, snapping the reptile's head in half. Kronos landed back on the beach with one jaw clenched in each fist.

Holding the jaws at the base and without a moment's hesitation, he attacked the nearest reptile, swinging the jaws and using their sharp teeth as weapons.

Kronos swung the jaws and ripped through several

attacking crocs, knocking them back toward the ocean. The reptiles were frenzied at the smell of blood. Even the scent of another croc's blood was a signal to attack.

Kronos' messy weapons were effective. As long as he wounded the animal, the others would finish it off.

A T-rex croc stood on its hind legs behind Anna and lunged. With a quick turn and flick of her wrist, the chest of the croc exploded from the tip of her whip. The gash was fatal, and the T-rex croc fell backward in a heap.

Before it even hit the ground, other T-rex crocs began devouring it and dragging it back to the sea.

Kronos was doing the same thing. He would wound an animal and let the smaller members of the herd devour it. The reptiles instantly switched their focus to devouring their own dead; they didn't seem to care what was on the menu, as long as they were eating warm meat.

Anna stopped in shock as she saw a T-rex croc bite into a man, carrying him in its mouth back to the water. The distraction was costly, as another reptile lunged at her.

Kronos saw what was happening out of the corner of his eye. He raced over just in time and struck the head of the reptile with one of the jaws he was using for weapons.

The force of the blow split the jaw in half, leaving half of it embedded in the skull of the creature. The reptile fell dead on top of Anna. She was pinned under a portion of the 2,400-pound animal and couldn't get up. Kronos continued on, immediately engaging in another battle.

Rose and Trib saw what happened and ran over to help, but the dead animal proved too heavy to move. More reptiles were advancing up the beach. Smaller alligator-type reptiles were approaching Rose and Trib, who stood guarding Anna with their sabers at the ready.

Thousands more reptiles emerged from the ocean, some small, some large, some T-rex crocs, others just crocs.

A large croc approached Rose and Trib. When it got to within ten feet, the girls separated, waited for the perfect opportunity, and drove their sabers deep into the creature's skull on either side. It roared in pain, thrashing back and forth with the sabers still embedded in its head.

The croc opened its mouth in a final fight for life. Its mangled jaw swung at Rose and Trib and knocked them over. The sharp teeth cut their shoulders as the croc fell dead to the ground.

With more reptiles on their heels, Rose and Trib ran over to the dead creature to pull out their sabers. They slashed any croc that approached until the bleeding and wounded animals became prey for the healthy ones. Soon they were drawing more and more reptiles to them instead of driving them away. They stood back-to-back, their clothing stained with blood, fighting off anything that got near Anna.

The pile of dead animals surrounding them was stacking up. They looked down the beach at hundreds more still emerging from the surf.

Trib lunged forward to fend off the next attacking croc. As she did, a smaller one grabbed her foot and ankle in its mouth and dragged her to her knees.

Rose jumped to her sister's aid and pierced the croc's eye with her saber. She failed to see another croc crouched next to her. An instant later, the beast grabbed Rose's arm in its jaw and clamped down.

Trib tried to stand up and help Rose, but couldn't move fast enough. She threw her saber like a javelin and pierced the reptile in the back of its head. Rose pulled her arm away and fell on the ground next to her sister.

They both lay panting, exhausted, and bleeding.

Rose looked at her friend trapped under the T-rex

croc. "Anna? Anna, can you hear me? There's too many, Anna, we can't hold them back anymore!"

Rose tried reaching under the body of the T-rex croc to get a response from Anna. "Trib, she's not moving, I think she's dead. Oh, Anna!"

Tears streamed down her cheeks, but Trib realized they didn't have time to mourn. "Rose, we're on the menu next! Get up now, we're surrounded. Get up now!"

Four enormous T-rex crocs circled the girls. They stood up at the same time and leaned their heads forward, slowly opening their mouths and exposing rows and rows of sharp teeth.

A Lie Revealed

The sky crackled with a sonic boom
that startled the T-rex crocs for a moment,
distracting them from the twins.

CHAPTER 23: A Lie Revealed

Strand had arrived in Fort Lauderdale and slowed to subsonic speed. He scanned the beach searching for Anna, but could only find Kronos fighting reptiles a quarter mile from the stage.

He didn't have much time, as the sky rumbled with the sonic booms of the forty jet fighters arriving.

He flew by the thousands of reptiles emerging from the surf. They were devouring anything in their path and dragging the remains back into the water.

The sky thundered again with the arrival of the FPL bots. They immediately headed for the beach, firing lasers from atop their missile cycles. When they reached the shore, the bots leaped from the missiles and continued to fire as they dropped to the beach. Electric blue lasers shot in every direction, slicing reptiles into pieces quickly and easily. Shooting the reptiles and avoiding the survivors running in all directions was a daunting task.

A wave of reptiles reached the row of satellite news trucks parked near the beach and went into a feeding frenzy. Reporters, camera operators, and crew members were decimated quickly in the rampage. Only a few fleeting frames of video captured the terror of their final moments.

Those few frames showing the press being violently devoured were broadcast across the planet within minutes.

The president stared at the television in the Oval Office with shock and disbelief. He fell backward into his chair. The cabinet members present knew it was time for them to leave the room again.

The leader of the free world was inconsolable. "What have I done?"

The first lady walked over and put her hands on his shoulders gently as they silently watched endless clips of men, women, and children being mauled by the reptiles, their bodies hurled down the beach into waiting mouths.

"What have I done?"

Howler found what they were looking for first and leapt from the missile without warning. Strand looked down and saw four T-rex crocs standing on their hind legs about to attack Rose and Trib.

Howler rode his weapon down as he had in the Brazilian forest and impaled one of the T-rex crocs, killing it instantly. The other three lunged at Rose and Trib, but a moment later a flash of blue lasers cut them into bits. The pieces landed on top of the girls in a pile, pinning them with their dead weight.

Strand distributed the FPL bots along the beach. They stopped the reptiles from advancing and were driving them back into the ocean.

Hoods were appearing from everywhere and darting onto the beach looking for survivors. They'd been following the postings on StrandsNet, watching video on the Internet obtained from student laptops at SCU, and monitoring news broadcasts for the last several hours.

Asmore watched in the situation room as everything Strand had predicted unfolded before his eyes.

He picked up the phone. "Do not — repeat — *do not* fire on Strand." He watched as the FPL bots continued driving the reptiles back into the ocean.

"Let's finish what Mr. Strand has started here," Asmore said and picked up the phone again. "Use whatever ordnance is available on those fighters to destroy those crocs in the water."

The fighters circled back to the beach and started firing missiles just off shore. The ocean exploded with each hit, sending plumes of water filled with pieces of the reptiles high in the air.

Strand watched the jets relentlessly pummel the rampaging reptiles along the beach. He knew he was no longer their target, but he still had to find Anna. He leapt off the missile and landed near Howler. He immediately saw Rose and Trib pinned under the remains of the T-rex crocs.

Strand lifted off the fragments and threw them into the ocean. The twins scrambled to their feet. They were bloodstained and dirty, but they were alive.

"Where's Anna?" Strand voice was strained. The girls were still in shock.

Strand repeated the question, emphatically. "WHERE IS ANNA?"

The twins turned to face the corpse of a T-rex croc nearby, pointing in unison. Strand lifted the body of the croc with one hand and discarded it to the side. He leaned over and scooped up Anna. She was barely alive. Her breathing was distressed from the broken bones and internal bleeding.

Rose was crying. "We tried to protect her, Strand."

Trib was weeping as well. "There were too many of them, just too many."

The fighter jets were working to eliminate reptiles further up the beach. In the distance, Strand saw his Black Hawks approaching.

Strand leaped onto the deserted festival stage still carrying Anna and carefully laid her down. The laser on his helmet flickered as he scanned her body to see how badly she was hurt. The weight of the T-rex croc had broken several of her ribs, and her lungs were filling with fluid. Anna was slipping away slowly in his arms.

She didn't have much time.

Howler and Kronos jumped onstage. They knelt down to offer help, but there was nothing they could do.

A Black Hawk approached and hovered over the stage. Strand saw COTAR Prime holding E in his arms inside.

The robot jumped from the helicopter and landed on the stage next to them. He gently set E down on her feet. She ran over to Strand as he retracted his faceplate and visor.

"Anna's … dying. Her lungs are filling with fluid." Strand's voice was cracking with emotion and tears were streaming down his face. "I was too late. I couldn't save her."

E opened her backpack and looked inside, but there was nothing in there that could turn back time. "I don't think I can either. I …."

All she had ever wanted to do since she was a little girl was help others and make them feel better. Now she collapsed helplessly to her knees weeping, while she watched the girl she loved like a daughter disappearing before her eyes.

E felt sick to her stomach, and then she felt something else ... something wonderful. Energy was surging through her insides, and she could feel it increasing rapidly as an incredible calm took over.

"Steve, please let me hold Anna. I think I can help."

E said it with such serenity and confidence that Strand nodded his head in agreement and prepared to hand Anna over without knowing exactly why.

E took off her gloves and Strand finally saw what she'd been hiding.

The moonlight walks had changed her. The pads of her finger tips rotated and opened like an iris on a camera. Rows of small barbs rose vertically. She was something more than human.

Strand remembered what E had confessed; she wasn't afraid of becoming what she truly was, and now neither was Strand.

E sat cross-legged on the stage floor and held out her arms.

Anna was gasping for air. Strand placed her limp body on E's lap.

E put her hand on Anna's heart. She closed her eyes and remained motionless.

Strand scanned her from a few feet away. E's fingertips contained a thousand barbs through which she injected a cocktail into Anna containing powerful antibodies, white blood cells, and an antigen that began to heal the wounds.

E was slowly repairing Anna's body.

COTAR Prime, Howler, Kronos, Rose, Trib, and Strand stood in silence as Hoods and the media horde gradually encircled the stage.

Strand scanned Anna again. "She stopped the bleeding."

E opened her eyes and repositioned Anna face down. A moment later, Anna began coughing up the fluid that had filled her lungs.

A SWAT team had hit the beach, scrambling out of their vehicles to surround Strand. They lined up in front of him on the sand and behind him in the wings of the stage. They pointed their guns at him.

Strand gazed at the thousands of dead reptiles along the shoreline. At least a hundred soldier bots were scouring the beach for survivors. The FPL bots were leaving the beach and sprinting to the stage. Hoods were monitoring the ocean and helping family members search for lost loved ones amid the carnage.

Emergency medical teams littered the boulevard and ambulance sirens wailed. Local police were setting up barriers and cordoning off the beach area. Crowds of people from the suburbs had arrived to witness the drama for themselves.

More satellite news trucks arrived. Camera operators and reporters with wireless microphones speaking every language conceivable hopped out and ran to the stage.

E handed Anna back to Strand. She was breathing normally again.

Anna slowly opened her eyes and the first thing she saw was her uncle's face peering out from inside Strand's helmet.

"I knew it was you, somehow I always knew," she whispered.

"I wanted to tell you. If I had, this wouldn't have happened. I'm so sorry, Anna." There were tears in his eyes. He couldn't bear the thought she'd almost died again.

"And I'm sorry I didn't stay off the beach like I

promised."

"You're grounded, young lady. No missile cycle riding for you."

Anna looked confused.

Strand smiled. "Well, at least until you're healed."

Howler turned around and knelt next to Anna. He pulled his hood back, and his visor and faceplate retracted. He looked relieved and serious at the same time.

He signed. "You're safe now. We will protect you," the electronic voice translated.

Anna's jaw dropped. "Howler? This is Howler? *My* Howler?"

Howler waited for the translation and signed. "Your Howler, always your Howler."

"And he talks?"

Howler pulled his hood over his head, closed his faceplate and visor, gripped his weapon, and turned around to face the SWAT team.

Rose and Trib were teary-eyed and exhausted. They were leaning on each other as though one was holding up the other, but they were smiling. Their friend was alive.

It wasn't over, though. The fighter planes had retreated, but the SWAT team still stood awaiting orders. Most were shifting their weight uncomfortably as they gripped their weapons.

Strand knew any orders had to come from the president, and he also knew the media would document whatever happened. Strand took comfort in the fact that someone at the Pentagon had prevented the fighters from shooting at him over the Gulf. He knew that the longer he waited, the more reporters would show up, and the more cameras would be present to show the entire world the truth.

The media lined up behind the SWAT team. They

could easily capture footage of Howler, Kronos, COTAR Prime, Rose, and Trib. Some were holding cameras high over their heads trying to get footage of Strand and Anna.

Strand hugged Anna and looked at E. "Thank you. There are no words to thank you, E. You saved her life. You were right, you've become what you are, something wonderful … and more than I imagined was possible."

E smiled and Strand thought he saw a slight glow under her skin. He closed his visor and looked at her again.

She was illuminated from the inside.

No one could see it but Strand. He knew E was still changing and evolving, and that one day everybody would see her the way he did.

Strand verified that all FPL bots were in position, so if necessary the SWAT team could be disarmed in milliseconds.

He stood up and walked to the front of the stage. Howler, E, COTAR Prime, Kronos, Rose, and Trib flanked him on either side. The Hoods formed a semi-circle behind them, and the SWAT team trained their weapons on Strand.

The reporters turned around as Strand approached the front of the stage.

The president watched the television in the Oval Office as the monitor on the stage behind Strand flickered to life.

There was an image shot outside Air Force One that zoomed in on a window where the president could be seen talking on the telephone.

It was the voice of Strand that was first heard.

"All I know is that at this very moment, you have the opportunity to lead this great nation into the future or to just ignore what's happening … bringing about only death and destruction."

The president spoke next.

"That is nonsense and you know it. Listen, Strand, I don't know what your agenda really is, but I have lost my patience. ALL I KNOW is that there is not enough scientific evidence to support your radical conclusions."

"Are you aware, Mr. President, of the new predatory life form in Brazil that floats in the air, paralyzes its victims with a toxic gas ,and then eats them alive? Are you also aware that those creatures could float into any city in the U.S., bringing untold suffering? I have samples of their tissue that you could have analyzed if you still don't believe me."

"I am not interested in your claims of Armageddon. You need hard evidence. You have utilized this office for as much as I will allow you to, Mr. Strand. In fact, unless you release the communications on this plane now, I'm going to consider this an act of war or treason."

"I cannot release your communications and continue this conversation."

"Then this conversation is concluded, Mr. Strand."

"This choice will be your downfall, Mr. President. Innocent men, women, and children will die as a direct result of your decision. You are compromising the safety of those who elected you.

"History will remember you as the president who failed his country, but I will not stand by and let the innocent be slaughtered.

Good-bye, Mr. President."

The screen flickered off and on. Once again, Strand's voice was heard speaking with the president, but now the footage that his robot swarms had taken over the Brazilian forest came onscreen. It showed U.S. helicopters and Harrier jets firing missiles into the jungle and the smoldering fires in the aftermath.

"Nothing happened in Brazil."

"You have covert operations in Brazil hunting and killing those same creatures in order to cover up the truth. But I know the truth, Mr. President. You, sir, are a liar, and unfit to hold the office of president of the United States."

"How dare you insult this office and the people that it serves! There's nothing going on in Brazil. Your delusions are getting so dangerous now that you're rationalizing a missile attack."

"Those missiles aren't attacking. Those are my missile riders bringing reinforcements to Fort Lauderdale to fight off the imminent reptile attack you're ignoring, the one where thousands are about to die, the one you've not even attempted to check on. If they were actually missiles, why would every one attack the same city? If they were explosive or nuclear, why send thirty-six when one would do? Why would I do that, Mr. President? You're making a grievous error, one that will cost lives and your career."

"CALL OFF THE MISSILES NOW, MR. STRAND, YOUR ATTACK IS AN ACT OF WAR AND OUR MILITARY HAS FULL AUTHORITY TO SHOOT YOU DOWN.

"I DEMAND AS THE PRESIDENT OF THE UNITED STATES OF AMERICA THAT YOU IMMEDIATELY CEASE AND DESIST YOUR ATTACK."

The video on the massive screen changed to show the devastation on the beach and the wailing of those who lost loved ones.

"Your call is being broadcast, Mr. President. Everyone everywhere can hear what you're saying.

"Good-bye, Mr. President. The blood of the people killed today is on your hands. I hope your vice president doesn't make the same mistakes as you."

The video changed again, this time showing Strand punching a hole in the wall at the military base where

Vitimani was being kept. The picture followed him through the darkness of the room to a single bed in the middle surrounded by plastic curtains. The curtains parted and Vitimani could be seen on the bed with his head bandaged. The video froze on this last frame, but Strand's conversation with the president was heard again.

"Dr. Vitimani was killed in a HELICOPTER CRASH and he's very much DEAD, Mr. Strand!"

"He was brought back from Brazil very much alive, but paralyzed, and you authorized exploratory surgery on his brain to study the effects of the toxin. You moved him to a military base and the CDC announced he was dead. Even his wife mourned."

"That's ridiculous. Nothing of the sort happened, and like I've said before, nothing happened in Brazil."

COTAR Prime stepped forward and pulled back his hood. All cameras were immediately trained on him. He retracted his faceplate and visor revealing the face of Ned Vitimani for all to see. And although his face remained frozen from his paralysis, his computer voice spoke.

"I am Dr. Vitimani. Everything Strand has said is true." He paused. "The president knew of my condition and ordered an exploratory operation. When the operation revealed nothing, I was taken to a remote military base and the world was told I died in a helicopter crash. But I'm not dead, far from it.

"Strand rescued me and gave me a new life. My body is still paralyzed, but I'm here walking and talking as you can plainly see. I am Vitimani and I am something more. I am COTAR." COTAR closed his visor and faceplate and stepped back, covering his head with his hood as he did.

The president jumped up in disbelief, staring at the television set in the Oval Office. The first lady reached her hands out to comfort him, but he shook her off.

The vice president walked in and closed the door behind

him. He stood motionless, waiting for the inevitable.

The president looked down at his desk. He slowly sat down and wrote the letter he never believed he would ever write.

Once complete he stood up, the vice president met him behind his desk and he handed him his resignation.

The vice president opened it and read the letter inside. "I accept, Mr. President."

"It's time for me to go." The president reached in his pocket and pulled out a brand new mirror similar to the one that broke. "My wife just gave this to me … and now I'm giving it to you. You're going to need this" He paused for a moment, looking at his former vice president before adding, "Mr. President."

The ex-president walked to the French doors with his wife on his arm. He stopped to look around one last time before heading out to an Air Force helicopter waiting on the lawn to carry him away.

The SWAT team had gradually disarmed, some even taking off their helmets. They joined the police, fire, and emergency personnel at the stage where Strand was standing holding Anna in his arms.

It was a silent acknowledgement, a wordless memorial, a vigil that echoed across the planet. There was no cheering and no applause, only the cold, hard realization of the dead on the beach and the wailing of the mourners.

Strand jumped down from the stage, still holding Anna in his arms. The crowd parted to let him through. Kronos, COTAR, E, Howler, Rose, and Trib followed Strand as he walked toward the blood-stained beach. Small plumes of black smoke rose from the flesh of the burnt reptiles.

The shoreline was now piled with the remains of reptiles that the jet fighters had bombed out of the ocean. More corpses continued to hit the sand with the waves of the rising tide.

Strand stopped to survey and record all that he saw.

We will remember this day, he thought to himself. We will remember those who needlessly died.

I will make sure of it.

E and COTAR stepped over to Strand. He gently placed Anna in the robot's metal arms. E stood next to him holding her hand.

Anna grasped E's hand tightly and whispered, "Thank you."

Kronos, Rose, and Trib stepped up behind them.

"We'll take her back on a Black Hawk," COTAR said.

It arrived and hovered just inches above the sand, the beach too littered with death and destruction for it to safely land.

COTAR carried Anna to the helicopter and lifted her inside. E jumped in with Trib, Rose, and Kronos. The Black Hawk lifted off and headed back to *Gaia*.

The missiles were circling back. The FPL bots formed rows of three and jumped to their rides as they passed overhead.

Howler walked over to join Strand.

"It is time for us to leave," Strand said to the reporters and the crowd. "While this day may be done, it is only the beginning.

"We now enter an age of rapid change. Each of us will become more of what we truly are, and each of us will one day look in the mirror and decide if we have chosen wisely."

Two missiles passed overhead, pausing as Strand and Howler jumped on and took off into the twilight.

The sky rumbled with multiple sonic booms as the silhouetted missile riders flew into the sunset.

It was over.

And it had just begun....

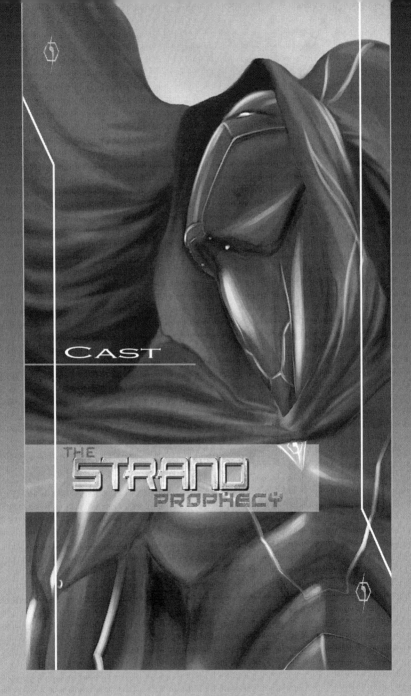

CAST

THE STRAND PROPHECY

STEVE CUTTER

STRAND

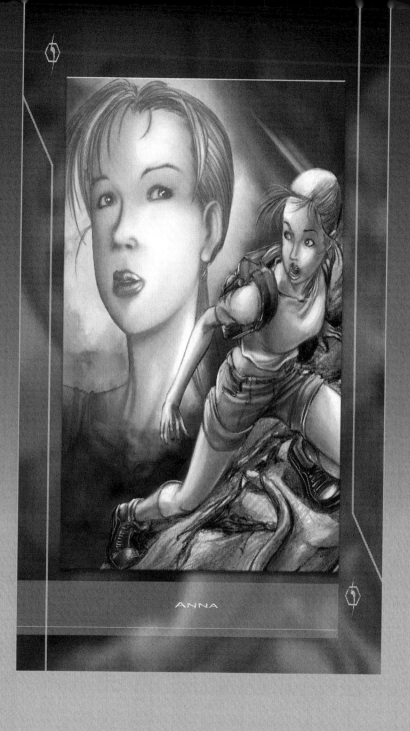

ANNA

DR.E

HOWLER

#2

COTAR

KRONOS

TRIB & ROSE

TECHNOLOGIES

THE STRAND PROPHECY

DOWNTOWN GAIA

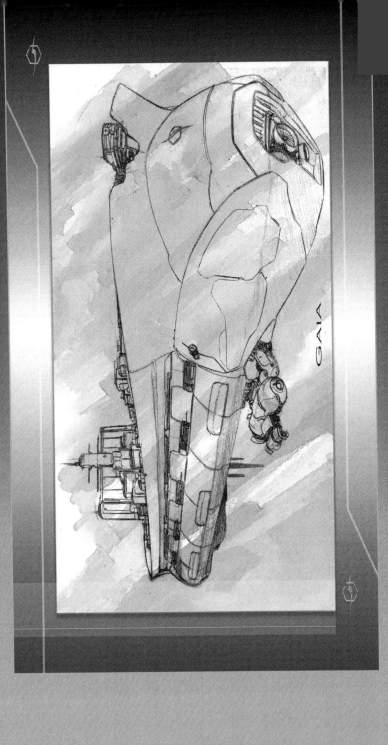

GAIA

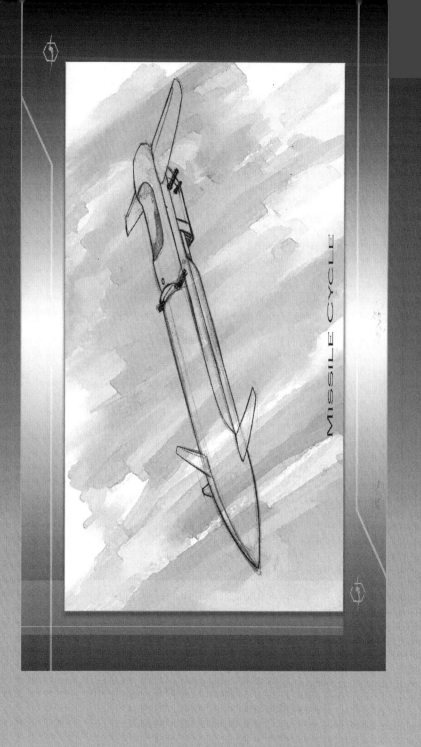

MISSILE CYCLE

STRAND SANCTUARY

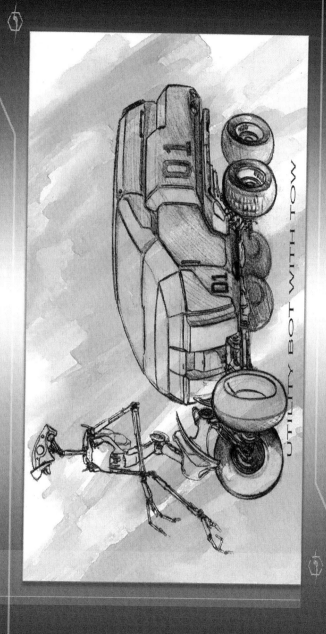

UTILITY BOT WITH TOW

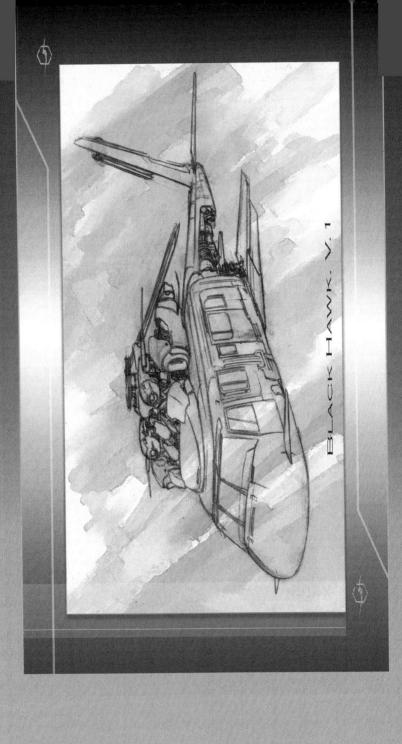

BLACK HAWK. V.1

FPL Bot

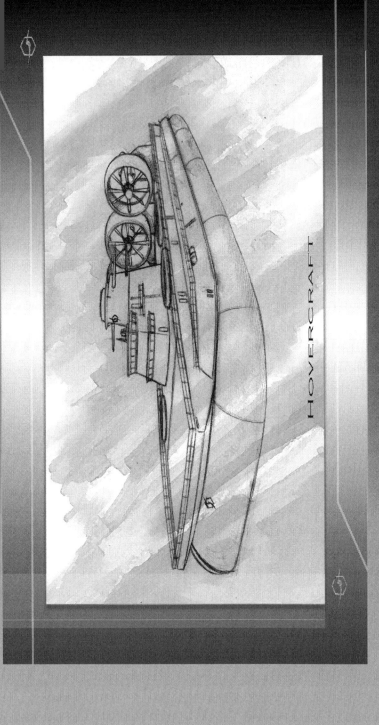

HOVERCRAFT

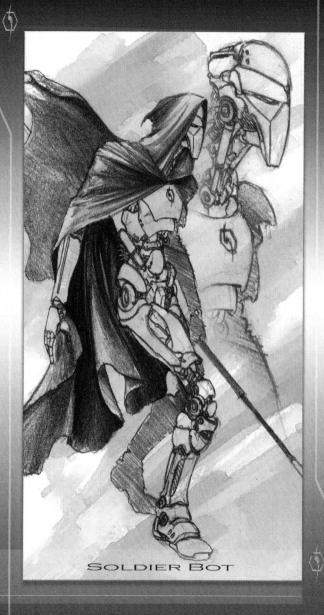

SOLDIER BOT

STRANDSNET CENTRAL

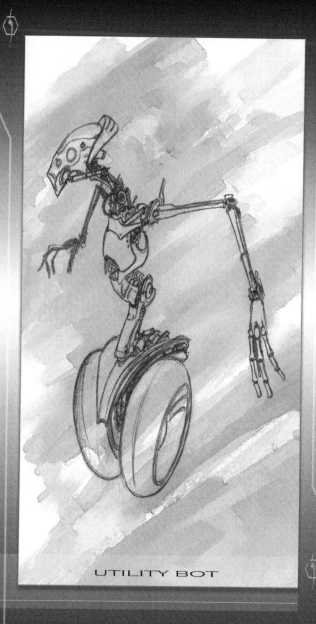

UTILITY BOT

CREATURES

THE STRAND PROPHECY

GIANT TOAD

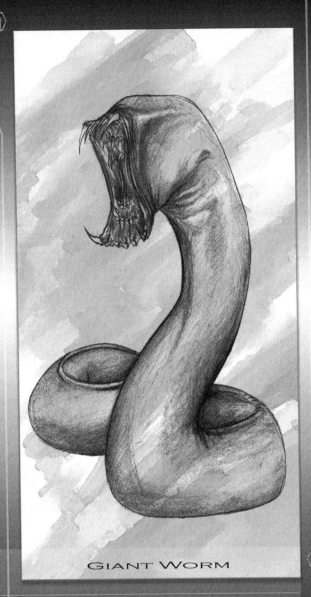

GIANT WORM

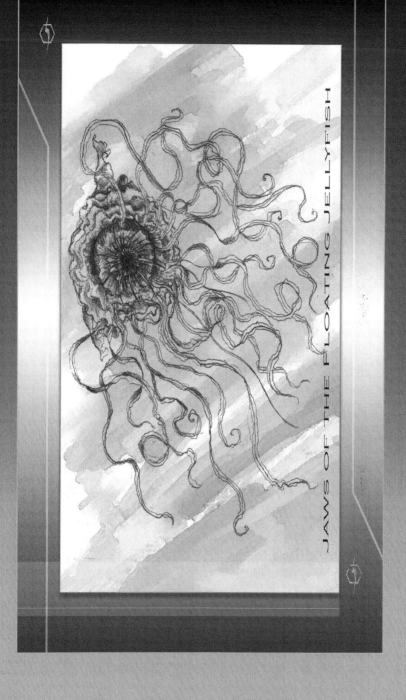

JAWS OF THE FLOATING JELLYFISH

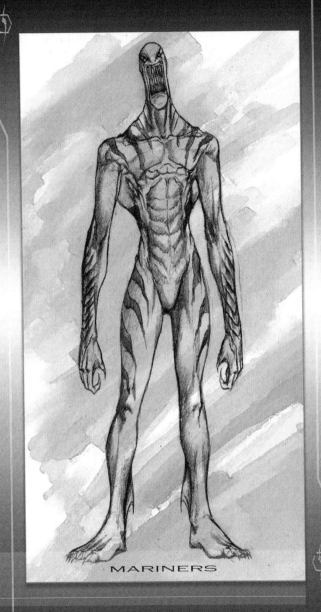

MARINERS

T-REX CROCODILE

BOOK II

EXTINCTIONS
EMBRACE

THE STRAND
PROPHECY

ANNA

DART FEM

DART MALE

HIERO

HOOD

PORTMANTEAU

SENPAI

UTILITY BOT WITH HOODS

TRIB AND ROSE

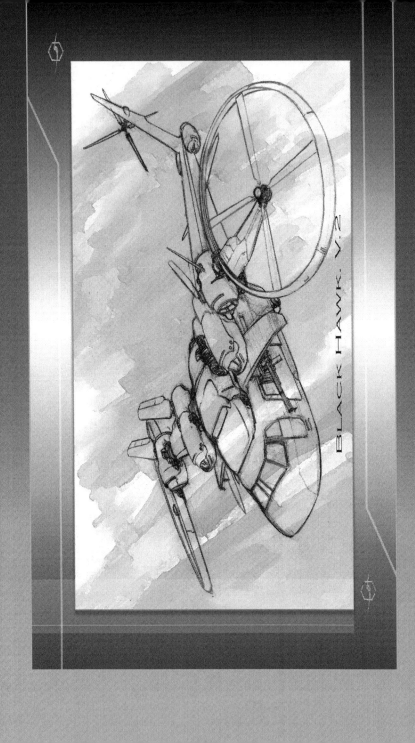

BLACK HAWK. V.2

CAPSULE

FEATHERED DINOSAUR

MISSILE SLED

46823011R00208

Made in the USA
Middletown, DE
01 June 2019